# "You don't want to come in?" Jake sounded disappointed.

Ethan looked across the front seat at Jake then toward the front of the Venettis' house. "I'd better not." Even though there was nothing Ethan would have liked better. But...Laura had had him to dinner. She'd blushed a couple of times. Once, their fingers had brushed when she passed him a dish, and she'd stopped talking midsentence and gone very still, a hint of yearning in her eyes.

Or so he'd convinced himself.

No, he wasn't going to push it.

And...he'd better think long and hard before he spent any more time with Laura. He had a hard time picturing her having casual affairs. Anything else—well, they had some major strikes against them. It really might be smarter not to start anything.

But he waited until Jake let himself in the front door, only then acknowledging how disappointed he was not to catch a glimpse of Laura.

And admitting how much he wanted to see her again.

Dear Reader,

Writing this book made me think about being a mother, and how fierce that love is. My daughters are adults now, and yet I still feel protective of them. One is involved in international development work—she's been to Africa as a Peace Corps volunteer and was in Nepal with a small nonprofit—while my older daughter has a high-stress job in the film industry. It's not the same as when they were little and I agonized after a friend snubbed one of them, or watched as each headed off solo in a car, newly minted driver's license in her wallet, but I still worry.

My quintessential, and most ridiculous, moment as a mother came years ago when we were camping with my parents. We were about to head into a limestone cavern in Montana when I discovered I was absolutely terrified of going underground. I mean knee-knocking, gasping panic attack. I knew I was afraid of heights, but this took me by surprise. Of course I could have slunk back down the trail to wait for my family to emerge from the caverns. In a burst of courage, I realized that if my kids were going to die in there, I would be there to die with them. So I took a deep breath and plunged in, overcoming my fear.

Ridiculous, right? But there was truth in that moment. I channel it when I'm writing a heroine like Laura Venetti, whose life has been all about her son since something terrible happened to him. But what is sexier than a man prepared to take on this boy and love him just as fiercely?

I hope you fall in love with Ethan, just as I did!

*Janice Kay Johnson*

USA TODAY Bestselling Author

# JANICE KAY JOHNSON

—

## To Love a Cop

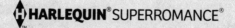
HARLEQUIN® SUPERROMANCE®

Recycling programs
for this product may
not exist in your area.

ISBN-13: 978-0-373-60904-8

To Love a Cop

Copyright © 2015 by Janice Kay Johnson

This edition published by arrangement with Harlequin Books S.A.

For questions and comments about the quality of this book, please contact us at CustomerService@Harlequin.com.

Printed in U.S.A.

An author of more than eighty books for children and adults, *USA TODAY* bestselling author **Janice Kay Johnson** is especially well-known for her Harlequin Superromance novels about love and family—about the way generations connect and the power our earliest experiences have on us throughout life. Her 2007 novel *Snowbound* won a RITA® Award from Romance Writers of America for Best Contemporary Series Romance. A former librarian, Janice raised two daughters in a small rural town north of Seattle, Washington. She loves to read and is an active volunteer and board member for Purrfect Pals, a no-kill cat shelter. Visit her online at janicekayjohnson.com.

### Books by Janice Kay Johnson

#### HARLEQUIN SUPERROMANCE

*The Baby Agenda*
*Bone Deep*
*Finding Her Dad*
*All That Remains*
*Making Her Way Home*
*No Matter What*
*A Hometown Boy*
*Anything for Her*
*Where It May Lead*
*From This Day On*
*One Frosty Night*
*More Than Neighbors*

#### *The Mysteries of Angel Butte*

*Bringing Maddie Home*
*Everywhere She Goes*
*All a Man Is*
*Cop by Her Side*
*This Good Man*

#### *A Brother's Word*

*Between Love and Duty*
*From Father to Son*
*The Call of Bravery*

Visit the Author Profile page at Harlequin.com for more titles.

# CHAPTER ONE

"WILL YOU LOOK at this," a complete stranger said reverently.

Only a few feet away, among the crowd in the aisle between vendor tables at this opening day of the gun show, Ethan Winter couldn't resist taking that look, even if the guy hadn't been talking to him.

The price tag caught his eye first. $12,500. He had to shake his head, even if it was a Perazzi MX3 ORO twelve-gauge shotgun with original case lying there. Engraving, gold inlays, damn near mint condition.

Still nothing that would tempt him. After a moment, Ethan wandered on, leaving a cluster of men staring covetously at the shotgun and listening to the vendor expound on its virtues. His gaze continued to rove the exhibit hall, and he half listened to the buzz of conversation around him, picking out snippets here and there.

He wasn't a collector, and wasn't in the market for a new weapon. Like many in law enforcement, he carried a fourth-generation Glock .40 caliber and was accustomed to its feel at the range and on his hip. He had friends who liked to upgrade more often than he replaced his vehicles, and, sure, there were some nice handguns out there. Once in a while at the range, he'd try out something new and always handed it back without any inclination to whip out his credit card. His Glock had saved his life, and that was good enough for him.

He was here today to keep an eye on the crowd, not the merchandise. It was something of a personal mission he'd taken on the past few years, after watching and reading coverage of too many mass shootings, the weapons purchased at gun shows like this. He hadn't told anyone else what he was doing. Odds were against him ever witnessing anything significant. Big as this exhibition hall at the Portland Expo Center was, a deranged individual could be buying an armory worth of weapons right this minute two aisles away without him seeing a thing.

Still…there hadn't been anything special he'd wanted to do today. And you never knew.

To avoid standing out, he needed to look at something besides faces, though. He actually enjoyed studying some of the antique guns. In fact, a minute later he was contemplating a Confederate revolver imported from England into New Orleans in 1861. He knew the A.B. Griswold revolver was often carried by Confederate officers. This one was in good enough condition to have a price tag of $9,500. He winced again.

"Man, that is so cool."

He turned slowly, his attention caught by how youthful this voice sounded.

And, yeah, it was a kid standing at the next vendor, looking down at a semiautomatic rifle. Ethan carried a similar one in his police vehicle. The one for sale was equipped with a fixed sight. It looked, and was, lethal, manufactured for the tactical professional. The kid's expression was eager enough to bother Ethan.

"You don't look old enough to be shopping for anything like this," the vendor said easily, and to his credit. Plenty of people brought their kids to gun shows, but Ethan didn't see a parent nearby.

"Huh?" The boy lifted his head. "Oh, my dad's around. I was just getting bored."

"Ah." The vendor, a middle-aged, balding man, started talking about the DDLE duty rifle's effectiveness and versatility. The kid seemed to be drinking up every detail.

Ethan drifted on, but not far. He wondered a little about the boy, who, at a guess, might be thirteen, fourteen at the oldest. Hard to tell, when some boys shot up way younger, and others lagged. This one was skinny, five foot seven or eight, with dark hair and eyes. Seemed early for him to be out of school, but middle schools and high schools did let out pretty early in the afternoon. Still, Ethan didn't see any other kids yet. Today was Friday, and the show had opened at noon. Right now it was—he checked his watch—barely two thirty. Most of the business would come on Saturday and Sunday, although the crowd so far was respectable and he'd seen a few sales taking place already.

The boy moved on, too. He appeared uninterested in the antique weapons, although he paused briefly to study a World War II "Liberator" .45 pistol, a strange looking, stubby weapon made by General Motors to be air-dropped to Resistance fighters in Europe. Maintaining a little distance between himself and the boy, Ethan paused to look at that one, too.

Mostly, the kid was fixated on semiautomatic handguns. The Heckler & Koch VP9, a new Beretta, the oversize Desert Eagle, an HK polymer-frame pistol with a barrel threaded to accept a suppressor.

And *fixated* was the word. He looked at every one of those damn guns with a hunger that disturbed Ethan. This kid could care less about .22 rifles, hunting rifles, BB guns. Nope, he was fascinated by handguns designed for the sole purpose of killing human beings.

And Dad was nowhere to be seen.

Nothing and no one else caught Ethan's attention so he kept wandering at roughly the same speed the boy did. Finally, curiosity overcame him and he stopped right next to the boy, who was currently studying a FNH FNP-40, another polymer handgun

"I've fired that one," Ethan said with a nod. "Nicely balanced."

The kid looked at him eagerly. "Really? At the range?"

"Yeah, friend of mine has one. He says it felt like his best friend the first time he shot it." Ethan was careful to keep his posture relaxed to avoid any hint of threat. He was a big man, towering over the kid.

The boy's gaze slid to his holstered weapon. "That's a Glock, isn't it?" He was hungry still, but there was an extra hint of heat in those dark eyes taking in the butt of the Glock. It was as if he was looking at a favorite food that had made him sick the last time he'd eaten it.

*Or maybe I'm imagining things*, Ethan thought. "It's a Glock 22," he agreed.

"Are you a cop? Lots of cops carry those, don't they?"

"They do, and I am." Ethan held out his hand. "Detective Ethan Winter, Portland Police Bureau."

They shook hands.

"So you don't wear a uniform anymore? Or is this your day off?"

"It is my day off, but I don't wear a uniform on the job, either, except for special occasions."

"Do you work homicide?"

Ethan shook his head. "I may request a transfer here someday, but I'm currently part of the unit that investigates assaults and bias crimes."

"What are you talking about, bias crimes?"

"We're plugging up the works here." Ethan nodded. "Let's get out of the way so we're not blocking the table."

The vendor nodded his appreciation. "Can't interest you in this FNP, Detective? Since you liked the feel?"

"I'm happy with what I carry. Familiarity is important."

The man smiled and shrugged both. "Can't argue with that."

"What do you mean, familiarity?" the boy demanded as they stepped out of the way of traffic. They'd been close to the end of an aisle, and weren't far from an exit.

"We don't draw often except at the range," Ethan explained. "You don't want to fumble or hesitate when the moment comes you need to. The more you've used a particular weapon, the less you have to think about it, which allows you to focus on the situation."

"Oh." He frowned. "So how come you're here, if you don't want a new gun?"

Ethan gave his standard response. "I like to keep up on what's out there."

"'Cuz cops aren't the only ones with guns."

Feeling the rueful twist to his mouth, Ethan scanned the ever-growing crowd filling a hall that had to be sixty thousand square feet or more, packed with weaponry and shoppers. "You could say that."

"Have you ever been shot?"

Ethan shook his head. Shot *at*, yes. Which wasn't the same thing. "Hasn't happened yet. I try not to make myself a target." He raised an eyebrow. "You have a name?"

Alarm flickered in the boy's eyes. "Oh. Um, yeah, but…my dad says I shouldn't tell strangers my name. You know." He started shuffling backward. "I should go find Dad now anyway. He might worry. I'll, um, maybe see 'ya."

The clear subtext was, *But not if I see you first.*

He awkwardly flipped a hand and melted into the crowd. Only he didn't wander slowly and browse this time. He walked fast, casting a couple of looks back over his shoulder.

Ethan went down the next aisle, keeping pace. If the kid thought he'd lost him—

But one of those darted glances back spotted Ethan, who cursed his height, and not for the first time.

Alarm segued into panic, and the boy began pushing through the crowd, his eye fixed on the doors that led outside. He was quick, and small enough to squeeze between people where Ethan had to bull his way, so he reached the exit first.

So much for the fiction of a father elsewhere in the exhibition hall.

Ethan stepped out and momentarily failed to see

.. More people were streaming in, either from the parking lot or the covered walkway that led—

Oh, yeah, there he was, and running now.

Ethan broke into a run, too, unsure why he was so determined to get his hands on this kid, but set on it anyway. The boy couldn't possibly be old enough to drive, which meant a bus or the light-rail.

Sure enough, he was headed for the light-rail station. Ethan didn't see a train, but knew they ran often between the expo center and downtown, something like every fifteen minutes.

Eight or ten people waited beneath a shelter. No restroom to disappear into. The boy tucked himself behind a family group as if he thought Ethan would assume he belonged.

When he saw Ethan's jog settle to a purposeful stride, he took a few steps back, his head turning in panic, but, with the rails behind him, there was nowhere to go.

"Excuse me," Ethan murmured as he sliced through the cluster of people.

"I don't know this man!" the boy cried. "He's been following me." He shuffled his feet, edging behind a beefy guy whose gaze first dropped to the holstered gun on Ethan's belt, then rose to meet his eyes in challenge.

Ethan dipped a hand in his pocket and held up his badge. "The boy knows why I want to talk to him."

The kid's shoulders slumped. "I didn't do anything wrong!"

They all heard the train coming. Ethan latched a hand around the boy's skinny upper arm.

"I didn't say you did. But we need to talk."

"Can't I just go home?" he begged. "All I wanted was to look."

"I'll be glad to take you home," Ethan agreed.

The white bullet-like light-rail train glided to a stop and disgorged a whole lot of people. Everyone waiting climbed aboard. Ethan turned his young captive back the way they'd come.

He deliberately dawdled so they fell behind the eager beavers headed for the expo center. He had the time now to assess the boy, who was good-looking and dressed in blue jeans, long-sleeved T-shirt and expensive, gleaming white athletic shoes. Common for his age, his feet looked too big to go with the rest of him. This was no homeless kid—somebody bought him nice clothes, kept them clean, trimmed his hair regularly. At first sight, Ethan would have guessed Hispanic, but wasn't so sure now despite the near-black hair and brown eyes.

"Why didn't you want to tell me your name?" he asked.

The boy shot him a defiant look. "Why should I?"

"Because I'm a police officer, and I asked. Because I suspect you cut school to come to the gun show."

Ethan felt like a jerk when the kid's lower lip trembled.

"Mom is going to be so mad."

"What about Dad?"

This sidelong look glittered with tears. "Dad's dead."

Truth at last. "How old are you?" Ethan asked, more gently.

The answer was a mumble. Ethan raised his eyebrows.

"Eleven."

He blinked as he calculated. "That means you're not even in middle school."

The boy shook his head. "I'm in sixth grade. I left after lunch."

"It ever occur to you that the school probably let your mother know you'd disappeared?"

His mouth fell open in horror. "I thought since I was there in the morning when they did roll call…"

Ethan nudged him toward the parking lot. "I can pretty well guarantee somebody noticed you *weren't* there come afternoon."

"Oh, man." He raised desperate eyes to Ethan's. "*Please* don't tell her where I was! She *hates* guns. She'll freak!"

"What were you going to tell her if she found out you took off?" he asked, keeping his voice easy to encourage continuing confidences.

"I don't know." Back to mumbling. "Just that, like, I had a fight with one of my friends or something."

Ethan drew him to a stop beside his GMC Yukon. "Here's your ride."

His head turned back toward the light-rail station. "I'll go straight home, I swear! Please, mister. I mean, Detective."

Ethan shook his head. "We'll talk to your mom. She may be more understanding than you think she will be."

"She won't! You don't know what you're talking about!"

"In," Ethan said inflexibly, holding open the passenger door.

As he walked around to the driver's side, he watched through the windshield in case the kid tried to make a break for it. All he did was slump in defeat.

Once Ethan was in, he hit the button to lock the doors. "All right," he said. "No more dancing around. I need your name."

The kid jerked a one-shoulder shrug and mumbled again, although this time Ethan heard him. "Jake Vennetti."

"Vennetti." Oh, damn. Why hadn't he seen the resemblance right away? "Your father was Matt Vennetti."

Jake sneaked a look sidelong with those chocolate-brown eyes just like his father's. "Yeah."

Ethan opened his mouth and closed it before he could say aloud what he was thinking. *Oh, shit.*

Jake was right; his mother was going to freak. She had good reason to hate guns.

In fact, this boy, sitting beside Ethan, had to be the one who'd gotten his hands on his father's service weapon and accidentally shot another kid, who died. From there, the tragedy had cascaded. In the end, Portland Police Bureau Officer Matt Vennetti had ended up killing himself. Not with the same gun, but he'd swallowed a gun nonetheless. It all happened—Ethan wasn't sure. Five years ago? Six? He knew Matt's only son was a little boy and not to blame, which wasn't to say he didn't blame himself.

"I went to your father's funeral," he said quietly. Despite his rage at a man who'd leave that kind of burden on his wife and child. "Your dad and I rode patrol together early on."

Head ducked, Jake didn't respond.

Perturbed, Ethan said, "I can look up your address if I have to. Why don't you just give me directions."

"Like I have any choice," the boy spat.

Ethan started the engine. "You didn't do anything so bad today. I cut school in my time, too."

Jake turned his head sharply away. Ethan had a bad feeling it was to hide tears.

*WHERE COULD HE BE?*

Laura Vennetti paced, her phone clutched in her hand. Fear squeezed her heart. She'd be purely mad instead of scared if Jake had ever done anything like this before, but he hadn't. It wasn't like him at all. He was a good student. Never in trouble. She'd fear a kidnapping if a classmate hadn't reluctantly told the principal that he'd seen Jake get on a city bus.

He'd been gone *hours* now. School had let out. She'd called all his friends, none of whom would admit to knowing his plans, although it was hard to tell with preteen boys, who seemed to communicate primarily in grunts and hoots.

"I swear I'll ground him until he leaves for college." The sound of her voice was meant to fill the silence. Instead, it seemed to echo, leaving her even more conscious of being alone in the house. She reached the back door and swung around to stalk through the kitchen and dining room into the living room. "I won't *let* him leave for college. He doesn't deserve—" Her voice broke.

She'd thought it was dumb for a boy his age to carry a phone, but she had just changed her mind. If he was in trouble, how could he call her? There weren't many pay phones anymore, and he might not have money with him anyway, and she discouraged him from talking to strangers.

Maybe it was time to report him missing to the police. Her gaze went to the clock on the DVD player. No, it wasn't even four yet. Kids cut class all the time. Nobody would take her seriously.

Soon.

She heard a deep engine outside and rushed to the front window. A black SUV had pulled up to the curb in front of her house. The passenger side door opened and—

Laura clapped a hand over her mouth. *Thank you, God. Thank you.* She raced for the front door and flung it open. Her son lifted his head and saw her, then, ducking his head again, trudged across the lawn toward the porch. She was barely aware that a man had gotten out, too, and came around the big SUV to follow Jake.

She planted her fists on her hips in lieu of bounding down the porch steps and snatching him into her arms. "Where have you *been*? Do you have any idea how scared I was?"

He sneaked a shamed look at her. "I didn't think the school would call you."

The man came to a stop behind Jake and laid a large hand on his shoulder. She thought he squeezed, just a little, before letting the hand drop. Laura had to lift her gaze a long way to the man's face. He was…well, not a foot taller than Jake, but a whole lot taller. He had to be six foot three or four.

Her heart drummed for an entirely different reason now. Calm eyes she thought were hazel held hers. His hair was brown, but not as dark as Jake's, or as her Italian husband's had been. He might not be male-model handsome, but came close, with a strong jaw, prominent cheekbones and a high-bridged nose. He had broad shoulders and the long, lean build of a basketball player. Standing so close to him, Jake was dwarfed.

"Jake." She heard how sharp her voice was. "Come here. Right now."

The stranger arched dark brows but stayed where he was when Jake slouched his way up the steps onto the porch. She pushed him behind her into the house.

Only then did she see that the stranger wore a gun.

"Who are you?" She sounded hysterical, with good reason.

"Ms. Vennetti." He nodded. "I'm Detective Ethan Winter, with PPB."

A police officer had brought her son home. Dread closed her throat. She had to swallow before she could ask, in a harsh whisper, "What did he do?"

"Nothing more serious than cut school." That slow, deep voice was as calming as his steady gaze. "I was hoping to talk to you for a minute, though."

She bit her lip and gave a choppy nod. "Come in, then." She turned to find Jake hovering on the other side of the living room. "Go to your room," she said. "I'll talk to you later, after I've heard what Detective Winter has to say."

"I didn't do—"

"Your room," she snapped.

His expression stormy, he thought about defying her, but the moment lasted a matter of seconds before he bolted for his bedroom. The door slammed hard enough to make pictures on the wall bounce. Laura closed her eyes, prayed for strength and once again faced the police officer who had brought Jake home.

He stepped inside, his shoulder brushing her, his gaze skimming the room in what she guessed was automatic assessment.

"Please, have a seat," she said, and closed the front door.

He hesitated momentarily, making her aware none of the furniture was built on a scale for a man his size, then chose one end of the sofa. She sat in her favorite easy chair facing him over the coffee table.

"I knew your husband," he said abruptly. "We patrolled together for about a year early on in our careers. I'd been on the job a little longer than Matt had, but not much."

She suddenly felt stripped bare. All she could do was hold up her chin. "So I suppose you know our whole history."

A couple of lines deepened on his forehead. "Your whole history? No. I remember hearing about the accident, and I was sorry about what happened with Matt. I actually came to the funeral. You and I spoke briefly afterward."

She had been mercifully numb by that time. She remembered a succession of police officers, all in uniform, one by one expressing their regrets. Some she knew, many she didn't. She had been grateful they had come. If they hadn't, who would have? Her own family was so small. And Matt's—

Laura shook off that memory.

"Where did you find Jake?"

"The gun show out at the Expo Center."

"What?" She half stood, then made herself resume her seat. Oh, dear God.

"I didn't recognize him. I was only concerned because I thought he must have cut school."

"He did."

He bent his head in agreement. "He admitted he had. He says he's eleven? I guessed him to be older than that."

"He's tall for his age. And...mature looking." Jake's looks had come from his dad. The resemblance was becoming more striking all the time. She tried to hide how that made her feel.

Detective Winter sighed and rolled his shoulders a little. "I'll be honest. I might not have paid as much attention if he'd been looking at BB guns like you'd expect a kid to do. But he wasn't. He seemed a little too interested in the kind of handgun I carry. I thought you needed to know that he'd cut school because he wanted real bad to finger some Sig Sauers and Berettas and the like."

She looked pointedly at the big black gun at his hip.

"I carry a weapon because my job demands it," he said, more mildly than she probably deserved.

After a moment, she nodded.

"Were you aware of his interest, Ms. Vennetti?"

She started to shake her head, squeezed her eyes

shut and finally nodded. When she met his eyes, she knew she wasn't hiding her desperation. But she hadn't had anybody to talk to about this. Hadn't wanted anyone else to know. Certainly not her sister or brother-in-law. What if they decided Jake was a danger to their kids?

"I— He was only five and a half when it happened."

The kindness and sympathy in this man's expression made her feel shaky. She didn't want to be weakened, but...was it so bad, just for a minute, to feel grateful for someone who seemed to understand? "A little boy," he said. "Too young to know the difference between a real gun and a toy gun."

Her head bobbed. "Yes. Except... The boy who died was Jake's first cousin, Marco. They were best friends. It was really gruesome. The bullet hit him in the head." She hardly knew her hand had lifted and that she was lightly touching her cheek, letting him know where the bullet had entered Marco's head. "I don't think Jake will ever forget."

As if she could.

"No."

"He didn't see his father, thank heavens. At least Matt didn't do that to us," she said bitterly.

"But you found him."

She shuddered. "Yes."

Detective Winter swore, rose to his feet and came to her, sitting on the coffee table close enough for him to take her hands. "I'm sorry. You shouldn't have to carry something like that with you."

She had the oddest moment of bemusement. A man was holding her hands in a warm, comforting clasp. He leaned forward in concern, so close to her that she saw his eyes were hazel, mostly green streaked with gold, and that his lashes were short but thick. If she were to lift her hand to his hard jaw, she'd feel the rasp of his late afternoon beard growing in.

A near complete stranger was holding her hands.

She could not afford to think of him as a man. He wasn't here because he was interested in her. He was here because he'd caught Jake at a gun show.

All her fears rushed back. Even so, she couldn't make herself retreat from that comforting clasp. She looked down to see the way his thumbs moved gently, almost caressingly, on the backs of her hands.

"I put him in counseling, of course," she said in a stifled voice. "He…regressed, after Matt killed himself."

"Of course he would."

She nodded. "But he's done really well. He makes friends. He's close to a straight-A student. I thought…I thought we were through any danger period."

Detective Winter waited with seemingly limitless patience. *Ethan*, that was his first name, she thought, finding it fit the man.

"Only, recently I've caught him watching TV

shows he knows I don't allow. All he seems to want to watch are police shows. There's that reality one." He nodded. "And he's slipped a few times and said things, so I know he's seeing some pretty violent stuff at friends' houses. Movies I'd never let him go to or rent. And when the news is dominated by some awful crime, he'll stay glued to CNN or whatever channel follows it."

"He's a teenage boy. His father was a police officer. His interest might be natural."

"Why would he admire that, given what happened because his father carried a gun?" she said sharply.

Detective Winter's eyebrows twitched, but he didn't say anything. He straightened a little, though, and his clasp on her hands loosened.

"And then I was changing the sheets on Jake's bed," she went on, her voice slowing. "I found some gun catalogs under the mattress." She gave a sad excuse for a laugh. "*Playboy* magazine wouldn't have shocked me. These...seemed way more obscene."

"Understandably."

"And now this." She searched his face, as if she'd find any answers.

"Matt must have had friends Jake could talk to about some of this."

"Friends?" She huffed. "You mean from the department? No, they all did a disappearing act. He was probably their worst nightmare come true. Why hang around to watch the epilogue?"

The detective's dark eyebrows snapped together. "*None* of his friends on the job stuck around to be sure you and Jake were all right?"

"No. I quit hearing from the wives right away, too. I definitely embodied *their* worst nightmares." She didn't admit that, as angry as she'd been, Matt's cop friends and their wives were the last people she'd have wanted to hear from or see. She might have ignored their calls.

Had ignored some.

But there hadn't been all that many, and they'd tailed off within a couple of weeks. Nobody had been persistent enough to come by when she couldn't be reached by phone. Out of sight, out of mind.

"You have family?" he asked.

"My sister and her husband and kids. They're the only reason I didn't move away. Sometimes I think I should have."

Those eyes, clear as they were, had somehow softened now. "Fewer reminders."

"For Jake," she said briskly, sitting straighter and sliding her hands from his. She watched as he flattened them on his chino-clad thighs, long, taut muscles outlined beneath the cotton fabric. "I could move to Beijing and I wouldn't forget a thing."

He saw deeper than she liked. "Matt had a big family."

"Yes, he did."

His eyes narrowed. "I don't remember seeing them at his funeral."

"That's because they weren't there."

"His parents didn't come to his funeral."

"Nope." Anger had long since buried any pain at that loss. She lived with a whole lot of anger. "Neither did a single one of his three brothers and two sisters."

"They ditched you?" he said incredulously. "Because of a tragic accident?"

"Marco's father, Rinaldo, is the brother Matt was closest to. They had…a really horrible scene and never spoke again. I thought…after Matt died…" She grimaced. "But no. Either they held Jake responsible even if he was only five years old, or they blamed me." *For good reason.*

"*What* did you say?" This man, this stranger, was glowering at her.

She gaped at him.

"You think it was your fault?"

Oh, no. She'd said that aloud.

But it was the truth.

"I went outside to water the annuals in pots and left two five-year-old boys alone in the house." For five or ten minutes. That's all. But it had been long enough. "I should have checked first to be sure Matt locked up his gun. I'd gotten so I usually did, because he was so careless with it. But that one time… that one time…" Her voice wobbled. She couldn't finish.

He gripped one of her hands again. "Laura. It is Laura, right?"

"How did you know?"

He shook his head. "It stuck in my mind. The gun was Matt's. Not yours." His jaw muscles flexed, and his gaze bored into hers. "He'd carried it for years. He was a professional. He knew better. Him leaving that damn gun where his little boy could get his hands on it *was not your responsibility*."

There was so much grit in those last words, she quailed. Then she squared her shoulders. "I did a couple of things wrong that, coupled with what Matt did wrong, led to something horrible. I will not forget my part."

Ethan Winter just shook his head.

"Would you take advice from me?"

She eyed him warily. "It depends what that advice is."

"I saw Jake's expression when he looked at those guns today. Whatever is going on in his head is powerful. You're not going to be able to stamp it out by making guns taboo. I'd strongly suggest you consider enrolling him in a gun safety class—"

This time, she jerked back, pulling her hand from his and curling both hands into fists. "You think I should put a gun in his hands? No! No, no, *no*. I swore I would never allow one in my house again." She glared at his holstered weapon. "I shouldn't have let *you* in. Not carrying *that*."

His eyebrows drew together. The silence bristled

with too much said. After a moment he nodded and pushed himself to his feet.

"I'll leave, then. I think you're wrong, but you have a right to make the decision."

Her "thank you" rang of sarcasm.

He took a business card from a pocket. "My cell phone number is on the back. If there's anything I can do for you or Jake, call."

She was careful not to let her fingers touch his as she took the card, then looked down at it. *Detective Ethan Winter*. What did he mean by *anything*? Would he show up if she needed wood split next winter? A ride to work when her car was in the shop?

"May I say goodbye to Jake?" he asked.

He'd been...nice. She hadn't. Taking a deep breath, she nodded.

She stayed where he was when he went down the hall. Heard him rap on the door, then the bass rumble of his voice, but couldn't make out words or hear anything Jake said.

A minute later, the detective came back down the hall. She stood to see him out. He nodded politely as he passed her and crossed the porch, his expression cop-guarded.

"Detective," she said to his back.

He paused at the foot of the stairs.

She made herself say it. "Thank you. For bringing Jake home, and for listening to me."

He turned at that, searching her face. "I meant

it," he said. "If he does anything that worries you, or you need to talk, call me."

Why did he care? The fact that he so obviously did caused a lump to swell in her throat. Around it, Laura said again, "Thank you."

He dipped his head one more time, acknowledging her words, then crossed her small front yard with his long, fluid stride, got into his SUV and drove away without, as far as she could see, so much as looking back.

# CHAPTER TWO

THE WAITRESS SLID the plate with his food in front of Ethan, and he glanced up from his phone. "Thanks."

Damn, had her breast brushed his shoulder, or had he imagined it?

"Can I get you anything else?" she asked, her voice just a little sultry.

Maybe she couldn't help sounding that way.

"Not right now. Thanks."

The hamburger and French fries smelled really good. He set aside the phone, on which he'd been checking email. A day off didn't mean he didn't want to know what he was missing. Along with several other active cases, he had been working a disturbing series of residential vandalisms. Four so far. All the owners had last names that sounded Jewish. Most of the shit he dealt with these days was anti-gay, with some anti-Muslim and anti-black thrown in for variety. Anti-Semitic, that was more unusual, in this part of the country anyway.

The ironic thing was, only two of the families were actually practicing Jews. The husband and father whose home had been hit most recently had shaken his head in bewilderment. "I'm Lutheran. The family has intermarried so much since my great-great-whatever came through Ellis Island, calling me Jewish is like calling some mutt at the animal shelter a golden retriever when he's short-haired, has stubby legs and stand-up ears but just happens to be yellow." His face had hardened. "My last name is Finkel, but until now that didn't mean anything."

The swastika spray painted in red on his driveway had been blurred by water shooting from the firefighters' hoses, but he hadn't been able to look away from it. Ethan didn't blame him. He'd asked and learned that the Finkel coming through Ellis Island had emigrated in late 1937 from Austria. Just in time.

This was the first fire that had been set. The punk or punks doing this had used spray paint, thrown eggs and pitched rocks through the windows of the first couple houses. The third had included a mannequin left sprawled on her back on the lawn with her legs splayed, her head bald and her teeth removed. She'd worn a yellow armband with the Star of David. The implications and the threat were clear. These vandals had done their research.

Ethan still had that mannequin on his mind. No stores had reported a break-in or a display mannequin stolen, but he kept thinking that wasn't an easy thing to get your hands on, especially if you were a teenager. Order one online? What if Mom is the one home when it arrives? No. In pockets of time, he'd made calls to stores, asking whether they'd had one disappear. If he could find out, it would give him a string to pull.

The few witnesses thought, as he did, that the perpetrators were young. Late teens, maybe early twenties, losers who were desperate for a cause to give meaning to their lives. They were getting bolder, escalating with each exhilarating outing.

Ethan really wanted to get his hands on them before someone was injured or killed.

The fire had been minor and put out quick enough to avoid significant structural damage. A second detective from his unit had been assigned to work with him, Sam Clayton. He'd also now acquired an additional, temporary partner, Lieutenant David Pomeroy of PF & R—Portland Fire & Rescue—a fire investigator.

Right now, they were all in waiting mode, which he particularly disliked. There were a lot of names in the Portland, Oregon, telephone directory that might be construed as Jewish. How the particular victims had been targeted was one of the mysteries, although he suspected the phone book since all four home owners thus far still had landlines and none had unlisted numbers.

The part that had him most uneasy was that all four families hit had last names beginning with the letters *E* and *F*. What's more, the attacks had taken place in alphabetical order. Which meant the assailant/s could spell, too.

He'd scoured police reports and community newspapers in search of any hint that there'd been earlier instances of vandalism. Maybe more minor. Otherwise, damn it, why start with Eckstein? Why not Abrams? There had to be a reason.

He picked up the burger and began eating. His thoughts reverted immediately to Laura and Jake Vennetti, as they'd tended to do since he left their house earlier. He had a bad feeling he'd called up email in a deliberate attempt to distract himself.

What he'd been evading was the knowledge that he'd been instantly and powerfully attracted to Matt Vennetti's widow. The rational part of him knew he had nothing to be ashamed of; Matt had killed himself over five years ago. Given her looks, he had to wonder why she hadn't remarried.

Frowning, Ethan took a long swallow of beer. No, she wasn't a beauty, not exactly—he doubted guys trailed her around with their tongues hanging out, although given half a chance he might do just that. Shoulder-length hair was somewhere in that dark blond, light brown range that meant she'd definitely been blonde as a kid, and probably still would be if she spent any time out in the sun come summer. Sun-streaked or not, her hair was thick, straight and shiny. His fingers had itched to discover the texture. A few freckles dusted her nose and cheeks, giving her that girl-next-door look, belied by blue eyes darkened by pain and anger and fear. He wondered if they'd once been brighter.

She was taller than her son when she'd swept him behind her, which meant she was at least five foot eight or nine, no more than an inch or two shorter than Matt had been. Given that Jake was only eleven, it looked as though he'd gained his tall genes from his mother.

She had some serious curves, too, the kind men loved and women fought with never-ending diets. When she turned her back on him, he'd been riveted by a firm, generous ass and tiny waist. Face-to-face...

He grunted unhappily and took another swig of beer, his hamburger in his other hand.

Face-to-face...well, it wasn't her *face* he wanted to look at. Her breasts wouldn't tickle his palms, they'd fill his hands.

And it wasn't happening. His mouth twisted as he remembered the scathing way she said, *I shouldn't have let you in.* Yeah, safe to say he wasn't her dream man.

Clearly, he didn't need to do battle with his qualms about lusting after a—well, not a friend's— a fellow officer's widow. She'd made clear she would prefer he not come knocking on her door again. Which was fine; he'd been married to a woman who came to abhor his job. Once around was enough for him.

For the boy's sake, though, he hoped Laura changed

her mind, or at least thought about what he'd said. Ethan couldn't see Jake as likely to go on a shooting rampage, but if he didn't untangle his feelings, who knew what would happen? Hormones hadn't hit yet. Ethan hadn't liked the dark look on his face in that single moment before he raced for his bedroom.

*She* might not want a gun in the house, and Ethan could even sympathize. But Jake wanted, real bad, to get his hands on one, and where there was a will, there was a way.

Right now, Ethan doubted even Jake knew what he wanted to do with that gun once he had it. *Why would he admire that*, she'd asked, *given what happened because his father carried a gun?*

Who said admiration was what Jake felt? He'd been abandoned by his father in the most devastating way possible, shunned by his father's family. Self-loathing struck Ethan as a likelier possibility. And teenage suicide was all too common.

Ethan finished his hamburger and started in on the French fries, hardly tasting them. He was frustrated by his inability to get through to Laura, yet painfully aware he had no moral high ground here.

When he'd expressed anger at Matt's buddies on the job, she'd been polite enough not to say, *So where were* you? Ethan had almost opened his mouth to defend himself anyway, to say, *We weren't really friends. Damn it, he* had *friends.* But the truth is, at the funeral Ethan had looked at Matt's widow and small, bewildered son, and resolved to check up on them, be sure they were all right. Half the officers there had probably thought the same thing. He'd also vaguely assumed Matt Vennetti's closer friends would step in to help her out, but that was no excuse.

She'd have been right to paint him with the same brush.

Pushing his empty plate away, Ethan pictured her face. Not when she blazed with anger, but when she had looked at him with such vulnerability and bewilderment. The expression wasn't so different from the one he'd seen on her boy's face when he said with such despair, "Mom is going to be so mad."

Ethan sighed and scrubbed his hands over his face, then reached for his wallet when he saw the waitress bearing down on his table with his tab, a flirtatious smile on her face and a swing to her hips. Okay, he hadn't misread the tone of voice. *She* had plenty of curves, and he felt...nothing.

He was pleasant as he signed his credit card slip, then slid out of the booth and walked from the restaurant, noting faces, aware of people in the parking lot, passing vehicles.

Behind the wheel of his Yukon, he inserted the key but, still brooding, didn't immediately turn it.

He hoped Laura would think twice and call him—but if she didn't, he'd call her. Just to make sure she and Jake were okay. To let her know he'd meant it. And then he'd let a couple of weeks go by and call again.

This time, he wouldn't forget. She might not like it, but she needed someone, and he had a feeling there wasn't anyone else.

And damned if he was going to worry about the subterranean reasons behind the determination he felt to look out for this woman and boy.

"I'LL PROBABLY GET DETENTION," Jake grumbled.

Laura poured pancake batter onto the griddle. "You probably will." She refrained from adding, *And you deserve to.*

After she woke him up, he'd dragged himself into the kitchen this morning wearing pajama bottoms that hung low on his hips and carrying a T-shirt he pulled over his head as she watched. His chest and rib cage were ridiculously pale and skinny. Anyone looking at him would think she was starving him.

"Get the juice out of the fridge, will you?" she asked.

His bare feet were silent on the vinyl floor. Not until she turned her head did she see he had the orange juice carton tipped up and was drinking right out of it.

"Jacob Vennetti!" With her free hand, she grabbed a dish towel and snapped it at him.

He dodged it effortlessly. His grin made her heart hurt. He couldn't smile like that if he was really troubled, could he?

She flipped pancakes. "Grab the margarine and syrup, too."

He complied. He was enthusiastic about meals.

*And guns.*

How could that be?

She plopped a plate holding the first stack in front of him before turning back to make more.

Behind her, he whined, "If I have to stay home this weekend, what am I supposed to *do*?"

"I'm sure I can think of something." They'd been talking about scraping the several coats of peeling paint off the back deck and repainting. This was day three of dry weather, and they ought to take advantage of it, she reflected. April was a rainy month in Portland. As were…well, most months. Even in July, you took a chance planning something like an outdoor wedding around here.

Unfortunately, she was working today, as she did one or two Saturdays a month, and didn't have time to find what he'd need to start and give him instructions.

He stuffed his mouth full as she set down a platter with more pancakes in the middle of the table and pulled out a chair herself.

"I wish I was playing Little League," he grumbled.

"In February, you didn't want to sign up."

He shrugged discontentedly. She'd supported his decision, mostly because neither of them liked his coach last year and he'd have been on the same team this year. Maybe that was part of his problem, she thought, buttering her pancakes and adding a dollop of maple syrup. Maybe he had too much time on his hands. A couple of his better friends *were* playing baseball, which ate up a lot of their spare time.

"There are summer camps," she pointed out. "Baseball and basketball."

"I could do both," he said hopefully.

Laura barely hesitated. She'd worry about the money later. Camps weren't cheap, and she knew he'd need new basketball shoes *and* new cleats for baseball. All those calories he was packing in were being used for growing. "I don't know why not," she said. "See what Ron and Justin plan to do."

He bent his head and didn't say anything. Laura's eyes narrowed. He hadn't mentioned Ron recently. And…when had either boy last called? She ached to ask if something was wrong, but wanted to preserve this morning's tentative peace.

"How come you won't tell me what Detective Winter said about me?" he burst out.

She swallowed a bite. Pancakes would go straight to her butt and she shouldn't be eating them at all, but it was really hard to cook stuff like this and *not* eat it.

"You're ignoring me," he declared indignantly.

She met his eyes. "I'm refusing to repeat myself, that's all. But since you insist, one more time—I doubt he said anything to me that he didn't to you."

He looked sulky. "You talked to him for ages."

She didn't even want to think about her conversation with Detective Ethan Winter. Not when it included them holding hands. Not when she had imagined what it would feel like to have his arms around her. To lean against him, lay her head on his very broad shoulder. Feel his lips—

No, she hadn't imagined that until later, after Jake was in bed and she was alone. *That* fleeting fantasy had been especially vivid. It had horrified her to the point where she'd resolved not to think about him at all. If she ever got involved with a man again, he wouldn't be in law enforcement. He wouldn't carry a gun as casually as she did her purse.

Ethan Winter was off-limits, even assuming he'd been interested and not just…kind. Concerned about Jake. If his gaze had drifted from her face to her breasts, it was probably because he wasn't being straight with her and didn't want to meet her eyes.

Only, she didn't quite believe that, either.

"He said I could call him if I ever need him," her son said.

Jolted from her silent lecture to herself, she gaped at Jake. "He asked you to call?"

His face was set in stubborn lines. "He said I could if I want."

"Why did he think you'd want to?"

He shrugged.

"Are there things you'd say to him that you don't want to say to me?" She was proud of how calm she sounded.

"Maybe," he muttered. He stole a peek at her. "'Cuz he's a guy."

"So is Uncle Brian. And you like some of your friend's dads."

"Yeah, but they're not—you know."

*Cops.* They weren't cops. They didn't carry guns. Not a one of them even *owned* a gun. She hoped. She knew her sister's husband didn't.

"You know we can talk about your dad whenever you want."

He sneered. There was no other word for it. "You hate it when I ask about his job!"

"It's not that." Yes, it was. No, it wasn't, not entirely anyway. "Your father didn't like to talk about what he did," she said, although that wasn't quite right, either. He did like to brag, but he'd never talk about things going wrong, and she always knew when he was especially closed off that he'd seen something awful. He'd go out to a bar instead, to hang with his cop friends. Sometimes every night for days on end, stumbling home drunk, until she'd been forced to confront how peripheral her role in his life was.

Some of that, he couldn't help, she knew, given his upbringing. He'd been...old-fashioned, believing women were to be protected. He hadn't been crazy about her continuing to work, although thank God she had an employment history, given that suicide invalidated his life insurance policy. Had he given *that* a moment's thought before checking out on his responsibilities? she asked herself for the thousandth time, and knew the answer: no. Or if he had, worry about his wife and child's future hadn't weighed heavily enough against the shame he was facing. Guilt, too; she knew he'd felt it, but was petty enough to believe in the end what he couldn't face was the loss of everything that in his eyes made him a man.

Jake jumped up, his chair scraping back. "See? You won't talk about it! You never do."

He raced out of the kitchen. The slam of his bedroom door was becoming all-too familiar.

Appetite gone, she stared down at her half-eaten pancakes.

*Dear God*, she thought, *he's right.* There was so much she didn't want to say about Matt, it stifled her every time Jake asked questions. She'd told herself she was protecting him—but maybe it was herself she needed to protect.

Weary and discouraged, she stood and began to clear the table, scraping sticky lumps of pancake into the trash under the sink. Jake, she couldn't help noticing, had cleared *his* plate before he stormed out.

The dishwasher loaded, she leaned against the edge of the counter. She had to try to talk to him… but how was she supposed to know what to say, and what she shouldn't say? Sometimes she thought having a daughter would have been way easier—

but maybe she was wrong. It wasn't as though she understood herself very well lately, either.

Her gaze strayed to the wooden organizer at one end of the counter that held things like phone books, notepads, pens, paper clips and stamps. She'd dropped the card Ethan Winter had given her in one of the small drawers, telling herself she'd never want it but not quite willing to throw it away. She hated the pull it exerted on her.

He'd have that cop mentality, too. Just because he'd been concerned about Jake and nice to her didn't mean he was anyone she would ever turn to.

Maybe it was time for her to think about putting Jake in counseling again.

Filing the idea for the moment, she closed her eyes, girded herself and went down the hall to knock on Jake's door.

SHE'D FORBIDDEN JAKE to leave the house while she was at work, and was confident he hadn't. She'd called twice, and he answered the phone both times, but predictably was furious that she was "checking up on him."

Well, yes.

The week deteriorated from there. Sunday he helped her start scraping the deck, but complained so much she'd have rather done it alone.

He was mad that she insisted he go home after school with his cousins and wait there until she picked him up after she got off work. Why couldn't he just go home?

"Because it's going to take time before I believe you're trustworthy enough again," she said.

"Everybody cuts school!"

She gritted her teeth. "I don't care what 'everybody' does. You won't."

His bedroom door slammed at least once every day. Laura began to wonder if he was reaching early puberty, although she hadn't seen any other signs.

Her sister just grinned when she complained and said, "He's spoiled you because he's been such an easy kid."

"Tell me at least he's being polite at your house," she'd begged.

Jenn had given her a quick hug. "He is. He spent ages pitching to Benji."

Who was now in fourth grade, and any day now was going to demand his mother call him Ben before she humiliated him in front of his classmates.

Laura at least could be reassured that Jake was being nice to his younger cousins. Wrinkling her nose, she thought, *Oh, good. It's just* me *he's mad at.*

Saturday morning, a week after the gun show episode, Jake had gone back to his room after breakfast. Laura, grateful to be off for the day, was loading the dishwasher when her phone rang.

The number was her sister's, which was a surprise since they hadn't made plans for the weekend.

She dried her hands and answered. "Hey. I don't suppose you've decided you're dying to scrape paint off my deck."

"Not a chance." Her sister hesitated. "Laura, Benji just told me something kind of worrisome I thought you should know. Um, are you alone?"

As far as she knew, Jake was still in his room. Nonetheless, she stepped outside, sliding the door closed behind her. It wasn't raining, but the day was cooler than it had been all week and hinted that drizzle, at least, was on its way.

"Now I am," she said. "What did Benji say?"

"Did you know Tino and his wife moved last year? Laura, their kids go to Faubion, too."

Goose bumps of alarm rose on Laura's arms. Faubion, kindergarten through eighth grade, was Jake's school. And...Tino's son was a year older than Jake, which would make him seventh grade, and his next oldest, a daughter...fifth, she thought. Then Tino's kids stair-stepped down from there. They were a good Catholic family, and had already had three kids with Renata pregnant again the last time Laura saw them. They'd likely added a couple more since then.

"Why didn't Jake say anything?"

"It gets worse," her sister warned. "According to Benji, Tino's kids have been bad-mouthing Jake. Everyone knows about the shooting now."

"Oh, God."

"He said kids are whispering about him. He's

seen Jake alone at recess shooting baskets instead of hanging out with friends."

"And he didn't say a word to me," she said, stunned. "I'm sorry."

"Thank you for telling me." So much rage bubbled in her chest, she couldn't believe how calm she sounded. "I...needed to know."

"I thought so. Are you going to talk to him?"

"Yes. And *then* I'm going to talk to Tino."

"Laura? That doesn't sound like a good idea."

"That son of a bitch," she bit off, and ended the call with a single stab of her finger.

TOTALLY FREAKED, JAKE stared at the front door that Mom had slammed so hard, he thought it was still quivering.

Then, with a cry of fear, he leaped forward and wrenched the door open, racing after her.

He was too late. She was already backing down the driveway, looking over her shoulder. Even as he ran across the lawn, she reached the street and started forward without seeing him. Standing still on the sidewalk, breathing hard, he heard a squeal as she turned the corner a block and a half down. Mom *never* speeded, but she had to be.

What if something really bad happened? It would be his fault. Because of what happened back then. *Everything* had been his fault: Marco and Dad, and Mom sad for so long.

And now things might get really bad again.

He could call Aunt Jennifer. She might chase after Mom and…he didn't know. Stop her from talking to Uncle Tino?

But he'd heard the end of the phone call. Aunt Jennifer already *knew* what Mom was going to do. It didn't even sound as if she'd tried to talk Mom out of going. Jake pictured her, smaller, skinnier than Mom, nice but…well, nice. Too nice to stop Mom.

*What do I do?*

He didn't even know exactly where Uncle Tino lived. After finding out his cousins had started at his school, he'd looked in the phone book, but there was no Tino Vennetti there at all, not even at an old address.

As he ran back across the yard and into the house, his heart pounded so hard it felt as if it was going to burst like a water balloon when you dropped it.

And then his eyes widened. Detective Winter could stop her if he wanted. He'd make sure Uncle Tino didn't hurt her.

And Jake had the card with his phone number hidden under the base of his desk lamp so Mom wouldn't find it and take it.

He was in such a hurry to grab the card, the lamp fell over and the bulb shattered, but he didn't care.

SATURDAY MORNING, ETHAN was back to canvas neighbors of the Finkels he hadn't yet been able to talk to when his cell phone rang. He took it from his belt and felt a jolt when he saw who was calling.

He'd looked up Laura and Jake Vennetti's number last weekend and added it to his contacts list.

"Winter," he said, stopping halfway up the walkway to a handsome Victorian across the street and two doors down from the Finkels, whose house still had a blackened corner.

"Detective?" It was the boy, and his voice was high and scared. "Mom found out something, and… and I'm scared of what she's going to do."

That didn't sound good.

"What did she find out?" he asked, taking on the tone he used to soothe distraught witnesses.

"It's… See, we moved, after—you know, Dad died." His voice shook. "But a while back my uncle Tino moved near us, and his kids go to my school now. They've been, like, telling everyone about me."

Oh, hell.

"Only I didn't tell Mom, but my cousin Benji ratted to *his* mom, who told mine."

He had to untangle that. "His mom is…your mother's sister?"

"Yes!" This was a wail. "Mom is really mad. She just, like, roared out of here. She's going to my uncle Tino's, and…and I don't know what's going to happen!"

"Okay." Ethan had already leaped into his SUV and was calling up an address for Tino Vennetti. "I don't think anything that bad would happen. Your mom may yell, but it sounds like your uncle Tino deserves to be yelled at."

"Yes, but—" The boy gulped. "He punched Dad once. Dad fell down, and he was bleeding and he had a couple of broken teeth and..."

"Fortunately, I'm not that far away. I might even beat your mom there, if she just left."

"You'll go over there?" Jake's relief was vast and would have been heartwarming if Ethan hadn't been pretty sure Laura wasn't going to welcome his intervention.

"I'm on my way. Don't worry."

He pushed the speed limits a little, but hadn't lied; the Finkels lived in the Woodlawn neighborhood, which bordered the funkier, slightly less expensive Concordia where, apparently, *two* sets of Vennettis now lived.

Laura had already jumped out of her car and reached the sidewalk when he rolled up right behind her in front of the house on Northeast 28th. Her head swung around and she stared at him in astonishment that transmuted into fury as he got out.

"What are *you* doing here?"

"Jake called me. He was worried."

"Worried about what?" she snapped. "That I might hurt his uncle Tino's feelings?"

"I think he's more worried about you," Ethan said gently. "He remembers Uncle Tino slugging his dad. He said there was a lot of blood."

"Oh. Oh!" She pressed her fingers to her lips and then turned her back on him.

Ethan put his hands on her shoulders and kneaded. "I'm not here to stop you. I understand why you're mad. He…told me enough."

That lit a fuse. Laura wheeled around, forcing him to drop his hands from her. "Did he tell you his dear little cousin Gianna said her dad *ordered* them to make sure everyone knows what happened? To say that he's dangerous and shouldn't be allowed at school?"

"No." His teeth clamped together. It took an effort to relax his jaw. "He didn't tell me that."

"What would *you* do if this was *your* son?"

"Probably the same thing you want to do," he admitted.

Her eyes widened. "Do you have a son?"

"No. No kids. No wife." Not anymore.

Her eyes shot sparks. "Then you don't know."

He glanced sidelong. Curtains had been twitching in the front window since he got there.

"What I do know," he said quietly, "is that if you go in there screaming, all you'll accomplish is to ramp up the hostilities. Your brother-in-law will feel justified in spreading the word that you and Jake both are unbalanced."

If her glare had been a blowtorch, he'd be charbroiled by now.

"Then what am I supposed to do? Remind him timidly that Jake has feelings, too?"

His smile had her staring. "No." He let the smile go. "I'd shame him."

She didn't so much as blink. He absolutely couldn't tell what she was thinking. But then her fingers uncurled from fists and she gave a sharp nod.

"You're right." She turned and marched up the narrow concrete walkway.

Ethan was right behind her. He was damned if there'd be any bloodshed today.

Before they reached the porch steps, the front door of the nicely cared for house of 1930s or '40s vintage opened and a man stepped out. He advanced to the front of the porch, giving him the high ground. A dark-haired woman hovered just inside the house. Ethan kept his attention on the man, who was unmistakably Matt Vennetti's brother— and Jake Vennetti's uncle.

After barely flicking a glance at Ethan, he stared insolently at Laura. "What do you want?"

"Hello, Tino," she said with remarkable restraint. "Renata."

The woman faded back.

"I'm here to ask you why you're going out of your way to hurt a child. A child who is related to you."

His lip curled. "He murdered Marco."

Ethan laid a hand on her lower back. He felt the quivering tension in her muscles, but he also would have sworn she had leaned back into his hand, just a little.

"He was five years old, Tino." She raised her brow and again looked past him, where his wife was an indistinct shadow in the foyer. "Last I knew, you were expecting. Did you have a girl or a boy?"

There was a moment of silence. "A boy," Tino said stiffly.

"Who would be…maybe six now?"

His jaw muscles knotted. He didn't say anything.

"In kindergarten, I guess."

Still nothing.

"Probably six months older now than Jake was when he thought it would be fun to show off his daddy's gun to Marco. He wanted so much to grow up to be like Matt."

For all that she kept her dignity, the grief in her voice and on her face was shattering.

"Can you tell me that your little boy hasn't tried to get his hands on your tools, even when you told him he can't touch them?"

The expression on Tino's face shifted.

Ethan didn't know what he did for a living, but her shaft had struck home, he could tell that much.

"You didn't see Marco." She shuddered, and then steadied herself. "After. I did. You didn't hear Jake screaming. Do you know he didn't quit screaming until we had him sedated? Do you know he wouldn't talk for weeks? That he had nightmares for years?" Her voice had fallen to a whisper. She stared her brother-in-law in the eye, and then shook her head. "But no." She resumed a normal conversational tone, making sure the woman inside heard her, too. "Because you never again set eyes on him, did you? Nobody from your family did. None of you cared at all about the five-year-old boy, your own flesh and blood, who will be haunted for the rest of his life by the terrible thing that happened. A tragedy that was *not his fault*. Because he was playing. Until that unspeakable moment, all he knew about guns was what he'd seen on cartoons and that his daddy, the hero, carried one. Now, his own cousins are making his life so much harder." She shook her head and finished quietly, "You should be ashamed of yourself, Tino."

Then she turned, drawing Ethan with her, and started back to her car.

"Laura."

She paused. Ethan looked over his shoulder.

"You're right. I'm sorry," Tino said hoarsely. "Mama—" Then his throat worked and he bowed his head.

Laura resumed walking. When they reached her car, Ethan stopped her with a hand on her arm.

"Are you okay to drive?"

He felt her fine tremors, but she was steadier than he'd expected.

"Yes." She hesitated. "I think so." Her eyes met his. "Thanks to you. I...I might just sit here for a minute."

"Okay." He let one corner of his mouth tilt up. "You did good."

She almost smiled, but not quite. "Thank you. Um…have they gone back inside? I can't let myself look."

"Yeah. I think he's crying."

"Good," she said fiercely.

He smiled and hugged her, letting her go before she could protest. "I'll follow you home."

She took in the badge at his waist. "Aren't you working?"

"Doesn't matter."

Her eyes filled with tears. She took a swipe at them and hurried around her car. When she opened the door, he bent to see that she'd left her keys in the ignition and her purse on the front seat. From what Jake had said about the way she stormed out, it was probably a surprise she'd remembered to bring her purse.

"See you there," he said with a nod.

Over the roof of the car, their eyes met, and his heart skipped a couple of beats at what he saw in hers before color washed over her cheeks and she climbed in and slammed her door.

Feeling uncomfortably light-headed, Ethan got into his Yukon, where he sat looking at the back of her head and wondering what in the hell had just happened.

# CHAPTER THREE

LAURA PARKED IN front of the house instead of driving into the garage and waited for Ethan to get out of the big SUV that had ridden her bumper all the way. She was embarrassed to feel so grateful for his insistence on accompanying her home. She knew that, at the least, he'd listen patiently and that he was nonjudgmental.

She saw him putting his phone back on his belt as he walked toward her, which meant he'd taken a call during the drive. Her eyebrows pulled into a frown.

"If you have to go, it's okay."

He shook his head, wiping his face clean of whatever irritation or frustration he felt. "It was just an update."

"Oh."

"I assume Jake's home?"

She made a face as she led the way onto the porch. "Unless he's decided to run away."

He chuckled. "I kind of doubt that."

"I don't know." At least she'd remembered to lock the front door as she flew out. Inserting her key, she said over her shoulder, "He's been a real pain in the butt this week. It's like having a rabid teenager in the house."

Her reward was a deep laugh, so close behind it stirred the hair on her nape and made her shiver. "Sadly," he murmured, "my mother would know exactly what you're talking about."

Despite everything, Laura found herself smiling, too, as she opened the door. "She would, huh?"

Jake was waiting in the hall leading from the bedrooms, his mouth dropping open at the sight of her. "You're not mad anymore."

"I'm still mad. I'm just..." She tried to decide. "I did what I could. Monday I'll go talk to your principal."

"I thought Uncle Tino would hit you."

Laura crossed the room to gather him into her arms and press her cheek to his. "He wouldn't have done that. In his world view, it wouldn't have been manly."

"Really?" Her son's voice squeaked.

"Really." She smiled and kissed his forehead. "I don't know if I accomplished anything, but I didn't blow it as bad as I would have if Ethan hadn't showed up to talk some sense into me. So thank you for calling him."

His expression was so incredulous, it made her laugh.

"I thought you'd be mad."

"You mean, even madder." She grimaced. "I was. Until he talked sense into me. Now I'm not."

He exhaled a huge breath. "Oh." Then a frown crinkled his forehead. "What did he say? Uncle Tino?"

"Actually...not much. Mostly, I didn't give him a chance to talk."

"He said he was sorry," Ethan said quietly, and she turned.

"You were looking at him. Do you think he meant it?"

"Yeah. He was crying, Laura."

*"Crying?"* He'd said that, but it hadn't sunk in. Now, she tried to picture the oldest Vennetti son breaking down. *"Tino?"*

Jake looked stunned. "Wow."

Laura gave herself a shake. "Have a seat, Detective."

His eyes smiled at her. "Ethan."

"Ethan." Why had she even bothered to try to distance him? "Would you like a cup of coffee?"

"I'd love a cup of coffee."

"Sugar? Creamer?"

"Black."

He chose the same place on the sofa to sit as the last time he'd been here. When she went to the kitchen, she heard his and Jake's voices. Fortunately, she had some decent coffee on hand and returned reasonably quickly with two mugs.

Ethan took his with thanks. "I usually bring a travel mug with me. Kind of hurried out the door this morning."

"Jake said you investigate assaults and...bias crimes? Does that mean specifically anti-gay or whatever?"

"That's right. Did you know Oregon has a hate crimes law? It makes the penalty harsher for any given crime than it would be for one that wasn't motivated by dislike of someone's race, color, religion or sexual orientation."

She frowned. "There was something on KGW news about a fire and a swastika spray painted on the driveway."

He winced. "That one's mine. I'm...getting a lot of pressure on it. Do you know how many Portland residents have last names that sound Jewish or that some idiot could interpret as Jewish when really they're Polish or Russian or who knows what? City hall is getting a barrage of panicky phone calls, which means the police department brass are, which means..."

Understanding dawned. "You are." No wonder he'd had that expression on his face a minute ago.

"What's a swastika?" Jake asked, predictably. Normally he'd have watched the news with her, but he'd been sulking in his room.

Ethan explained, his tone grim. "The home you saw on the news is the fourth instance of vandalism within two weeks that included the spray painted swastika. First place it was painted was on the garage door, second house, on the front window, third, on the lawn. Those earlier ones were mostly garden-variety vandalism. Eggs, rocks thrown through windows, that kind of thing."

*Mostly.* She wondered about that, but didn't want to ask with Jake here. She thought Ethan would have said otherwise.

"Vandalism doesn't sound significant enough to justify all the anxiety, but the fire is a significant escalation," he continued. "We're afraid someone is going to be hurt soon. There's always the possibility a home owner with a gun will use it, too."

"But that's good, isn't it?" Jake said. "I mean, that's why people want guns. So they can protect themselves."

*Good?* Laura thought in shock. He *knew* how vehemently she opposed the whole idea, and still—

"It is," Ethan agreed, raising her ire, but went on before she could jump in. "The problem is, your average person hasn't practiced enough to be able to use their weapon effectively. They get scared and are more likely to freeze up than they are to shoot the right person at the right time. A dad panics, shoots and kills his teenage son who was sneaking into the house late at night. Or it's a burglar, Dad points the gun, but the burglar wrestles it away from him. And here's the bigger question…"

Laura was as mesmerized as Jake. Ethan wasn't saying what she'd expected from him. And, thank God, he'd been tactful enough not to include in his little litany, *Kids get their hands on their parents' guns and tragic accidents happen.*

"We have the death penalty in this state." He leaned forward, elbows braced on his thighs, and looked and sounded even grimmer. "Someone has to have been convicted of aggravated murder to receive death as a sentence. So, if we as a society agreed that's the *only* crime that we can justify putting someone to death for committing, is it all right for a home owner to shoot and kill someone breaking into his house?"

"But…it's self-defense, isn't it?"

Laura was glad to hear that Jake sounded unsure.

"It's usually ruled to be. And sometimes it is. A woman is certainly entitled to protect herself from a man who intends to rape her, for example. But the average burglar doesn't intend to hurt anyone. He's sneaking in, hoping to grab some hot electronics, maybe some jewelry, and sneak back out without anyone hearing him. If the home owner were to yell that he'd called 911, the guy would bolt. These idiots who target people with a Jewish last name were committing only vandalism until this last time, when they set a fire, too. Their form of vandalism was ugly and indefensible, don't get me wrong. But a capital crime? Not in my view."

"So…if you were, like, staking out a house and they showed up and started, you know, painting the swastika and throwing rocks and maybe setting a fire, you wouldn't pull your gun?" Jake asked in disbelief.

Ethan smiled faintly. "I would, because it would

give me the upper hand. I'd be less likely to lose control of the situation. I would use the weapon as a threat to achieve an outcome that didn't include violence."

"You mean, they'd put their hands up and do what you tell them. Like that."

His smile widened and he bent his head. "Just like that." But the smile was gone when he went on. "The difference between me and the average home owner is that I put in many, many hours at the range practicing. I know when and why I should actually pull the trigger. In that situation, with the vandals, I'd be prepared to defend myself, but otherwise I wouldn't shoot anyone."

"You'd let them get away?"

"I'd do my best to catch them." He flashed a startlingly boyish grin. "I also work out to stay in shape and make sure I'm fast. I can outrun most people."

Laura bet he could. He'd have a longer stride than most people, for one thing, and none of the clumsiness common to many large men.

"But no, I wouldn't shoot someone in the back to keep him from getting away. Vandalism isn't a death penalty crime, even when it's also a hate crime. Arson isn't a death penalty crime unless it's done to commit murder. Police officers rarely shoot except when they're being attacked or to keep someone else from being badly injured or killed."

"I never thought about that," Jake said. "Mom always says—" He sneaked a look at her.

She tilted her head, wanting to find out which, if any, of her oft-repeated pearls of wisdom had actually stuck in his head. "What do I always say?"

"That having a gun in the house is more dangerous than not having one." He flushed. "'Cuz things can happen. You know."

Ethan held her son's gaze. "I do know what happened, Jake. I've seen other tragedies like it. And let me say here that some law enforcement officers don't agree with me. And I'm not opposed to safe gun ownership. People who hunt, for example, who follow the rules and lock their weapons up when they're not carrying them. Target shooting can be fun. There's nothing wrong with it. Same caveats."

He had to explain what a caveat was.

"Dad always said he'd take me to the range when I got bigger." Jake sounded wistful. "You remember, Mom?"

She remembered. Even then, she had hated the very idea, but she'd never said so. Certainly not to Jake, but not even to Matt. "I do," she said.

"Did *you* learn to shoot when you were a kid?" Jake asked, earnestly pursuing…what? Justification for him to learn to handle a gun?

"Actually, no. My dad wasn't a hunter. He's in law enforcement, but he didn't encourage me to take that path."

"Is he still alive?" Laura asked.

Ethan glanced at her, his eyebrows climbing. "Sure. He's a US marshal, but not for much longer. He's taking retirement this coming year. Much to Mom's relief, he switched to guard duty at the courthouse these past few years. His knees aren't what they used to be."

"Is he why you went into law enforcement?" she couldn't resist asking.

His shoulders moved. "Partly. Of course there was always an element of glamour to it in my mind, like what Jake's talking about. But I had a lot of other interests. I didn't switch my major to criminology until I was a junior, and I had to add an extra semester to make up for lost time."

She wanted to ask why he'd changed his mind midstream, but couldn't help noticing how careful he'd been not to say. And really, he undoubtedly had better things to do today than exchange life stories with her.

He took a long swallow of coffee and set the mug down. "I've pontificated long enough. A piece of advice, though, Jake."

Her son gazed eagerly at him.

"Or maybe I should start by asking how you've handled the talk about you."

He hunched his shoulders, clearly unhappy to have the spotlight back on his own troubles. Turtle retreating into his shell. "Sometimes I say you don't know what you're talking about. Mostly I just, like, walk away."

"In other words, you're hoping if you ignore the whispers, they'll go away."

He jerked his shoulders. "I guess."

"Ignoring things hardly ever makes them go away, you know."

If *she'd* said that, Jake would have gotten sullen. But because it was Ethan instead, he screwed up his face. "I sort of know that."

"Well, here's what I'd tell them instead. 'Something really bad did happen, but I was only five. It was an accident. I never meant to hurt anybody. Five-year-olds don't understand much. I'd give anything for it not to have happened, but I can't go back.'"

Laura watched Jake's lips move as he silently repeated every word. Hero worship being born, she thought ruefully. And…she couldn't even be sorry. Ethan had been sympathetic without getting maudlin, practical and philosophically, well, not that different from where she stood.

Disturbed by the tenor of her thoughts, she reminded herself that he *did* carry a gun, and was fully prepared to use it at any time.

Ethan glanced down at his phone, and she realized it must have vibrated. He rose to his feet and said, "I do need to go now. Laura, will you walk me out?"

She nodded.

Neither of them said anything until they'd reached the sidewalk by his SUV.

"Maybe I should move again," Laura said suddenly. "Tino's two aren't going to rush around school on Monday telling everyone Dad says he was wrong, that Marco's death wasn't Jake's fault."

"Probably not. Kids don't want to admit they were wrong." His forehead creased. "What are his kids' names?"

"Names?" She blinked. "His oldest is Niccolo, although I think he goes by Nick. And the girl is Gianna. Then they had another girl...Maddalena, I think. She'd be...eight. Then the boy in kindergarten and, heck, probably at least one more if not two."

"Does Jake lengthen?"

"You mean, is it Italian? No. His full name is Jacob. Matt's parents were not happy. He was Matteo, you know. They blamed me, but it was all him. I'd have been fine with Rico or Roberto or something like that, but he refused. He kept saying, 'Mama doesn't want to admit it, but we're American now.'"

"Huh."

"What's that mean?"

"I take it that Mama Vennetti did not approve of her son marrying a woman who isn't Italian?"

"Mama did not, and she never tried to like me." At first Laura had been hurt, then mad. She'd become a damn fine Italian cook, she'd consented to raise their children in the Catholic Church even though she herself didn't take the sacraments, but she wasn't good enough and never would be. She wasn't a woman who would hover in the background, as Renata had done today. The irony was that Mama was a domineering woman who wouldn't hang back while her husband made decisions, either. Truthfully, what Mama didn't want was another woman in the family who would challenge *her*.

Ethan studied her thoughtfully. "So the setup was already in place after the shooting."

"For Mama to reject me? Absolutely. Matt…" She had to swallow and it was a struggle to go on. "That, I never would have expected—"

She wondered if being cut off by his family had devastated her husband more than her fury and inability to forgive him. Sometimes she almost hoped so, as if that would reduce the weight of her own sins.

"Hey." Given how hard Ethan Winter's face could be with its stark angles and planes, he had a way of looking remarkably gentle. Even…tender. "I didn't mean to depress you even more."

"What's happening with Jake tears off scabs," she said honestly. "How can it not?"

He didn't say anything, his eyes intent on her.

"I think you're right," she said in a rush. "About the gun safety class. Can you suggest someplace I can sign him up?"

She felt his subtle relaxation. "Yeah. In fact, I sometimes teach a session. Let me see what's coming up and call you, all right?"

Laura nodded. "And...thank you. For everything you said in there."

He smiled. "You're welcome."

His smiles made her feel and think things that weren't realistic. She looked away. "What can you do about the vandals? It is scary. I work for Lehman Fine Furnishings. The family that owns it is Jewish."

"What do you do there?" he asked.

"I manage the store. Uri Lehman started the store and hired me. He had a stroke two years ago. Neither of his kids was interested enough in the business to want to run it. So I got promoted."

"My ex-wife dragged me in there one time. Steep prices."

"Top quality," Laura countered.

His grin was devastating, his eyes warm. "I'll take your word for it. A cop's salary does not run to an eight-thousand-dollar sofa."

She laughed. "You didn't see any eight-thousand-dollar sofas in my house, either. Even with an employee discount, it's not happening."

They smiled at each other for a moment that stretched, before he sobered.

"I'm heading out to keep canvasing neighbors. I might catch people home we haven't been able to talk to yet."

"Wouldn't they have come forward if they saw anything?"

"People don't always. Maybe they think what

they saw wasn't significant. Or they don't read the newspaper or watch the local news and aren't aware the vandalism at the Finkels' wasn't an isolated incident. So we keep trying." His lips twisted. "Alternative is to wait until these punks strike again. The mayor doesn't like the idea of telling callers that the police don't have any leads to pursue and are having to wait until another attack occurs."

"Which is really what you're doing."

"Afraid so." His grunt might have been intended to be a laugh. "On that note…"

"Yes." She stepped back, unsure how she'd come to be standing so close to him. "Good luck."

Something moved in his eyes, but then he said only, "I'll call," and went around to get in behind the wheel.

Laura stood where she was and watched him drive away.

EVEN THOUGH HE had things he ought to be doing instead, once Ethan was parked in front of the Finkels' house again, he made a call to a gun range that offered youth hunter safety classes.

He waited on hold for barely a minute for Ken Rice, the owner. When Ethan explained, Ken said, "We have one scheduled for Saturday, but it's booked. So are the next three. We have a waiting list, Ethan."

"If you have range time for an add-on class but

no instructor, I'll volunteer as long as I can get this kid in."

There was a moment of silence. "And here I saw you at the press conference. You're not tied up?"

He gave a short laugh. "I'm always tied up. But this kid…" He hesitated, but he trusted Ken. "His dad left a gun out and he shot and killed another kid when he was only five years old. He's eleven now, and getting too interested in guns."

"A lit fuse."

"Maybe."

"Okay, let me see what I can do. I'll call you back."

He did, half an hour later. The classes at this range were usually eight hours and scheduled to take place in two sessions, but the only way he could see to get it in was to break it up into four parts. "We can do four consecutive Tuesday evenings, or maybe Sunday afternoons."

"Let's go for the evenings, if you think you'll get enough sign-ups."

"Oh, there's no doubt of that," Ken said drily.

"Okay." He hesitated. "First on the list is Jake Vennetti."

"The cop's son."

"Yeah. You remember?"

"Hard to forget."

"Thanks, Ken. I appreciate this."

"I appreciate you volunteering. I can't think of

anyone I'd rather have teaching here." He chuckled. "Even if you don't hunt."

Ethan decided he could wait to talk to Laura, and got out to start door-belling.

Nobody had seen a damn thing. Or they weren't home today, just like they hadn't been home the past three times he rang their doorbell.

Not until he took a break for lunch did he call her.

She was breathing hard when she answered.

"Did I catch you on the run?" he asked.

"No, I'm scraping paint from my back deck. It's an awful job. I was going to just paint it, but it was lumpy with a bunch of previous coats, so... One of the joys of home ownership."

"I live in an apartment." He didn't even know why he said that. He and Erin had bought a house but split up barely a year later and sold the place.

Laura huffed. "Right this minute, that's sounding good."

She made him smile more than he could remember in a while, a surprise considering how mad and/or upset she'd been during most of their interactions.

"The next youth hunter safety class with any openings starts Tuesday night. Two hours a session, four consecutive Tuesdays. I hope Jake doesn't have a conflict."

"No, but...hunter?"

"That's what's taught to kids his age. We get all the basics in." He hesitated. "With your permission,

I thought I'd spend a little time at the range with him myself, working with handguns."

"You're not teaching the class?" She sounded worried.

"I am." No way he was admitting he'd set the whole thing up for Jake's sake.

She expelled an "Oh!" that sounded relieved. "What time on Tuesday and where?"

He told her, and she promised to call to officially sign Jake up and pay the minimal fee.

"Can I offer you dinner Tuesday before the class?"

He wasn't fooled by how elaborately casual she sounded. Some anxiety vibrated in her voice. He couldn't help wondering. Did she want reassurance about Jake, about letting him handle guns? Or… was she asking because *she* wanted to see him, and feared it had never crossed his mind to make their relationship personal?

Man, he hoped the answer was number two.

"I'd appreciate that," he said. "That way Jake can go with me, unless you want to come along and watch."

The tiny pool of silence didn't surprise him.

"He'd probably rather I didn't come."

"He's a boy," Ethan said gently.

"I didn't even have a brother. Raising a boy is… challenging."

"If it's any consolation, my mother says my sister gave her more heartburn than I did."

"That's not what you said earlier." Her voice was teasing.

"Oh, I was a pain in the ass, but Carla was a mass of screaming hormones for at least two years. Even I was scared of her."

Laura was giggling when they signed off, Ethan smiling in satisfaction.

"NUMBER ONE IS the golden rule of gun safety. Anyone already know this?"

A girl who looked to be fourteen or fifteen raised her hand. "Never point your gun at anything you don't want to shoot."

Ethan nodded. "That's one way to put it. When you're handling a gun of any kind, point it in a safe direction. Not at a person, not at your dog, not at your mom's favorite lamp." He looked from one face to the next. "Safest place is at the ground, but not too close to your feet." Holding the unloaded .22 rifle, he demonstrated.

The kids were rapt, even though safety rules were pretty basic. Never touch the trigger until you're ready to shoot. Keep the gun unloaded until you're ready to use it. Check to see if the gun is loaded every time you pick it up. Don't rely on a gun's safety catch. Never try to take a gun away from someone by grabbing the barrel.

Never fool around with a gun. No Cowboys and Indians, Cops and Robbers games.

Ethan didn't look directly at Jake when he said

that one, but with his peripheral vision he saw him duck his head.

Ethan talked about some other dangers and rules, emphasizing that anyone handling a gun had to be aware not only of their target, but of what was surrounding that target and behind it.

"You might be accurate on the range, but shooting a deer on the run or a duck taking off from a pond is another story. You're tracking the movement, getting excited. What if there's another hunter on the other side of the pond? What if you're shooting tin cans off the fence at your uncle's farm and you didn't notice a horse wandering in the pasture behind that fence?"

He had them do some role-playing, let them handle several rifles he'd borrowed from Ken for the purpose, after elaborately checking to be sure they were unloaded even though he had, of course, done so before starting the class.

This first class, they talked about gun care, too. About trigger locks and gun safes. He paired them up and had each pair clean a .22 rifle, in part to help them understand what each part did, but also because a clean gun was a safer gun.

They all worked earnestly, although he could tell that, for about half the kids, he wasn't saying anything they didn't know and that they were already pretty comfortable handling the .22s. He appreciated their parents putting them through a class anyway.

He promised to give them a little time the next week on the range, and told them he was trying to book an extra hour at an outdoor range that would give them a different experience.

When the two hours were up, he spent another twenty minutes talking to parents. While he waited, Jake stared into the glass-fronted cabinets at handguns for sale.

Ken had hung around tonight, and he talked easily to Jake while Ethan was busy.

"See you next week," he said when they left, as if he hadn't noticed anything amiss about Jake's interest.

On the drive home, Jake grumbled about not having been able to shoot tonight, but he also asked some eager questions and talked about the other kids in the class.

"I didn't think there'd be girls. And one of them, Amber, says she already knows all this stuff. Her dad takes her target shooting all the time, and she says her mom hunts, too."

"There are quite a few women who compete all the way up to an international level in target shooting, too."

"Girls don't usually talk about guns."

Ethan laughed. "Better not say *girls* in quite that tone around your mom. And if you lived in a more rural part of the state, I think you'd find more girls interested. For men and women, hunting is a less common interest among an urban population."

"How come you don't hunt?"

"I take carrying a gun too seriously to want to do it for fun. Plus, I like animals. I don't want to shoot one."

"But you eat meat."

Ethan grimaced. "You've got me there. I'm probably a hypocrite. But the truth is I don't need to take a deer every year to keep meat in my freezer the way some folks do. If I'd grown up hunting, it might be different. As it is, I like to hike, I've done some mountain climbing, I love windsurfing, I play basketball, I run for exercise and do some weight lifting." He glanced at Jake. "Do you play any sports?"

"I did Little League until this year. And I play basketball. Mom said I might be able to do some sport camps this summer. Did you play college ball?"

"I did. Portland State. If it's okay with your mother, maybe this weekend we could find a hoop and play some one-on-one." Maybe Laura would want to play, too, or come watch. Offer to feed him lunch, he thought hopefully.

"I couldn't defend against *you*," the boy said indignantly. "You're really tall."

Ethan laughed. "No, but we can play Horse, practice our free throws and layups. Just have fun."

"Yeah! That would be cool."

"Good." He pulled up in front of Jake's house. "I'll call. And see you next week, if not before. Ask your mom about this weekend, but be warned that sometimes I end up having to work."

"You don't want to come in?" Jake sounded disappointed.

"I'd better not," Ethan said, even though there was nothing he'd have liked better. But…she'd had him to dinner. She'd blushed a couple of times. Once, their fingers had brushed when she passed him a dish, and she'd stopped talking midsentence and gone very still, a hint of yearning in her eyes.

Or so he'd convinced himself.

No, he wasn't going to push it.

And…he'd better think long and hard before he spent any more time with Laura Vennetti anyway. He had a hard time picturing her having casual affairs. Anything else—they had some major strikes against them. It really might be smarter not to start anything.

But he waited until Jake let himself in the front door, only then acknowledging how disappointed he was not to catch a glimpse of Laura.

And admitting how much he wanted to see her again.

# CHAPTER FOUR

ETHAN WAITED JUST inside Laura Vennetti's front door for Jake to change into basketball shoes. She hovered politely, giving him a chance to scan her dirty, ripped jeans and ragged flannel shirt—none of which disguised the lush curves he'd like to linger on but didn't.

"I'm feeling guilty," he said after a brief silence that had the potential to become awkward. "I could help scrape the deck instead of taking your helper away from you."

She sneaked a look over her shoulder toward the hall, and still lowered her voice. "Take him away. Please," she begged, surprising a laugh from him. "He whines more than he works."

Still grinning, he said, "Is this where I admit I don't blame him? It sounds like a crappy job."

Her freckled nose crinkled. "It is a crappy job, but I think I can mostly finish today. Especially if I'm left alone to do it in peace. Painting is bound to be more fun."

He looked past her to see Jake approaching. "You set?" Ethan asked.

"Yeah." The boy sounded eager. "You're not coming, are you, Mom?"

"And now I feel so welcome." She stuck out her tongue at him. "No, I'm not. But I was about to invite Ethan to stay to lunch when you get back if he'd like."

"I'd love to stay," he said without hesitation.

Her smile was more uncomplicated than any he'd yet seen. It lit her face. And, yes, he'd been right; her eyes were a brighter blue when she was happy.

"Good," she said, bumping her shoulder against her son's as he passed. "Have fun."

Talking idly about nothing in particular, they drove to Jake's school, which had the closest available outdoor courts. Despite the lack of rain, the sky was sullen enough they could have one hoop to themselves, Ethan was glad to find.

It felt good to palm a basketball, to feel the flow of muscles as he let loose of some long jump shots. He played often enough he hadn't lost the instincts, the reflexes. Funny, though, how long it had been since he'd played on an asphalt schoolyard court like this.

Ethan shot from way outside and watched as the ball dropped through the rim and Jake snagged it. Hit by memories, he said, "Man, I spent hours at a school near my house when I was your age, doing nothing but shooting. Half the time there wasn't any net. I was sure I'd be an NBA star."

"How come you're not?" Jake asked.

"I don't know if I'd have made it or not, and I doubt I'd have been a star no matter what. But by then I'd changed my mind. I loved playing college ball, though."

"You're tall enough to play pro, aren't you?"

"Probably. I'm almost six foot four. I played forward for Portland State, but I might have been able to move to guard." He shrugged. "There are a lot of good college ball players, though, who had the same dreams I did. It's probably just as well I'd moved on. If nothing else, pro ball isn't a career that lasts long. One knee injury can end it just like that." He snapped his fingers, and then beckoned for the ball, which Jake bounced to him. "Can you shoot from the free throw line yet?"

The boy grimaced. "Kind of."

They worked on it for a while, Ethan offering a few suggestions and Jake noticeably improving, before Ethan asked how his week had gone at school. "You try standing up for yourself?" he asked.

Jake gave a stiff shrug. "I said what you suggested to a couple of people. I don't know. Mostly people are still looking funny at me."

"They'll get over it." Ethan stole the ball from him, dribbled a couple of times and did an effortless slam dunk. Aware of the openmouthed stare from a group of boys playing a short distance away, Ethan felt some amusement at himself. *Showboating, were you?* He tipped his head toward the boys. "That anyone you know?"

Jake didn't look. "One is in my class. Another of those guys used to be a friend. Ron."

Ethan made an acknowledging sound. "What d'ya say we dazzle 'em, then?"

"Yeah!"

They played hard, Jake's layups getting smoother, his moves as he tried to steal the ball from Ethan sneakier. When they finally decided to quit, Ethan waited until they were walking past the other boys before he said easily, "Practice, and you'll play varsity, no problem. You're good for your age."

Jake flushed with pleasure. "Thanks. I mean— that'd be cool, you know?"

Ethan tapped him lightly on the back. They were past being in earshot of the little shits who'd snubbed Jake. "Looks like you might get some height from your mom, too. I don't think your dad was tall enough to seriously play basketball."

"He played baseball in high school." His forehead crinkled. "I think football, too, but mostly he was a really great first baseman."

Hearing how uncertain but also defiant he sounded, Ethan had to wonder how well the boy remembered his father. Ethan's own memories before age six or seven were pretty skimpy. Did Laura try to keep Matt's memory alive for his son, or had too much anger gotten in the way?

"I played on a baseball team with your dad one year," he commented as he buckled his seat belt and put the key in the ignition of his SUV. "You know, just for fun. Our team was made up of fire-fighters and police officers. You're right, your dad was dynamite at first base. Hell of a hitter, too. I'd kind of forgotten."

"I wish I'd seen," Jake said sadly.

Counting back, Ethan said, "If you were born at all then, you'd have been only a baby. Your mom might have brought you to games."

"You didn't see her?"

"If I met her, I don't remember." He had trouble now imagining how he could ever have set eyes on Laura Vennetti and forgotten her, but he'd been married himself then and not looking. In fact, if he'd really noticed her, he would have made a point after that of *not* looking.

"I bet you were a good baseball player, too."

"I wasn't bad, but basketball was always my sport." He flicked on his windshield wipers and said unnecessarily, "It's starting to rain."

"Mom won't like that."

Ethan grinned. "No, she won't."

When they let themselves into the house, she was just emerging from what he guessed was her bed-room down the hall. Her hair, loose now, gleamed, and she'd changed to clean jeans and a V-neck sweater snug-fitting enough to cause his body to stir.

"You quit before you got wet," she said, seeming pleased to see them. "I didn't even know the rain had started until I got out of the shower."

"You finished with the deck?" Ethan asked.

"It's as scraped as it's going to get. Who knows when I'll be able to paint now, though. The forecast isn't very promising."

"I noticed." He and Jake both followed her to the kitchen.

She turned to see them looking expectant and laughed. "I cheated. I called to order a pizza. It should be here any minute. What do you want to drink?"

They had a brief skirmish, but Ethan insisted on paying for the pizza when it arrived, and Laura didn't seem too disgruntled. Conversation flowed as they ate. Ethan nodded when told about the basketball camp Jake wanted to take that summer and repeated what he'd said at the school. Flushing with pleasure, Jake told her about how Ethan had dunked the ball.

"Like it was easy," he marveled. "And he makes baskets from way out. I wish I could do that."

"I couldn't when I was your age, either." Ethan reached for another slice of pizza. "You're not tall enough yet and your hands aren't big enough. Plus, it took a lot of practice."

"The school is too far for me to go over there whenever I want," Jake grumbled.

Ethan had had a thought about that, but figured it wasn't something he should say to Laura in front of her kid. He'd wait.

Laura talked about her week at work, and he did

the same. He'd made an arrest on an assault case he'd been pursuing for a while, and was working with the DA's office now to make sure there were no holes in the case that might result in an acquittal.

"I do enjoy arresting someone who thinks he's gotten away with something crummy," he admitted when Jake asked. "It's one of the pleasures of the job."

Jake leaned forward, his expression almost as avid as when he'd looked at handguns. "What else do you especially like?"

It was obvious Laura was alarmed by the question. Ethan was amused to meet her hard stare, daring him to give the wrong answer.

"Hmm," he said, giving himself a minute to think about how he would answer. It wasn't a common question. Probably a good thing, given that the satisfaction and frustration, boredom and adrenaline became so entangled, picking them apart was no easy task. "I meet good people along with the bad," he said at last. "I like helping people. Giving them justice even if I can't put everything back the way it was before the crime was committed." He smiled faintly. "Becoming a detective was my goal from the beginning because I enjoy puzzles. Putting all those pieces together until the picture is whole. That *aha!* moment can't be beat."

Jake looked appalled. "*That's* the best part? Not...I don't know...the way people look up to you?"

"No." Ethan's smile widened. "It's true that in

certain circumstances I need respect from people, even a little fear. But most day-to-day policing goes better if I can connect with people. Encourage openness."

The boy sneaked a look at his mother that Ethan didn't understand, then burst out, "Is that what Dad thought, too?"

"He seemed like a good cop to me, when we worked together." Ethan kept his voice relaxed, friendly, instinctively trying to ratchet down any tension between Laura and Jake. "People liked Matt. He had a gift for talking people down from whatever cliff they'd climbed up on. He could calm an enraged guy or a distraught woman like no one else I ever knew. I told him he should think about training to become a negotiator. I don't know if he considered that later."

"If he did, he didn't tell me," Laura said. "But he was really good at cooling tempers. I'd kind of forgotten. I'll bet family get-togethers have been way more tempestuous without him."

Ethan heard the wryness in that. The family hadn't had to do without their peacekeeper. They could have chosen to forgive his mistake, however terrible the result had been, to support him when he needed them as he never had before. Instead, they'd turned their backs, with yet more terrible results.

Jake seemed not to have heard the subtext. His face scrunched as he appeared to struggle to pull up memories of his father. "Mostly I remember

Dad being fun." His eyes focused on Ethan again. "Wrestling with me, laughing, helping me learn to throw the ball. Stuff like that. Oh!" He brightened. "And he had a motorcycle. Was it a Harley, Mom?" He saw her nod, but didn't see her expression. "He'd take me on drives. Just slow, like around the block, but *I* thought it was the best."

Laura's eyes shimmered with unshed tears. "I'm glad you remember," she said softly. "I wasn't sure you did."

"I wish you'd kept the motorcycle," Jake said discontentedly. "Then I could have had it someday."

"We needed the money I got for it." She gave a funny, broken laugh. "I have to admit, the idea of letting my teenage son head out on his Harley sends a chill down my spine, too. Maybe by the time you can afford to buy your own, I won't be so worried about you riding it."

"Didn't you go for rides with Dad on it?"

"We did in the early days." Having apparently conquered the tears, she smiled at him. "Before you were born. After that, well—" she laughed "—I'm a secret coward. I never enjoyed the open road the way your dad did."

"Really?" he marveled. He turned to Ethan. "Do you have a motorcycle?"

"Nope. I was never that interested in anything with an engine." Replete, Ethan pushed his plate away. "Now, windsurfing on the Columbia River, that's a charge. I'll take you this summer." He frowned. "You can swim, can't you?"

"Yeah!"

Ethan smiled at Laura. "Both of you." He'd really like to see her in a bikini. Even a tight-fitting one-piece. Although nothing would be even better.

He never had had that heart-to-heart with his common sense over whether getting too involved with both Vennettis was smart. Reaching out a hand to the boy, that was one thing; he could even think of it as part of his job. He remembered Ken describing Jake as a lit fuse. The spark could still be doused.

He felt a spark low in his belly every time he looked at Laura, too, but this one was entirely personal. He hadn't decided whether it would be better stamped out, too.

*It's not too late to back off,* he told himself, but had a bad feeling he was lying to himself, something he tried not to do.

His unease was such that he made his excuses right after Laura closed the box on the two remaining slices of pizza and, when he declined to take the leftovers, stood to put them in the refrigerator.

"Would you clear up the rest?" she asked Jake, and walked Ethan to the door.

"Thank you for doing this," she said, sounding more formal than she had since he first arrived.

"I like your son. I had fun, too. I don't take time to do something like shoot baskets often enough."

He grinned. "And, just so you know, the slam dunk was meant to impress some boys Jake knows who were ignoring him."

"Jerks," she muttered.

"Yeah, I figured they deserved to see that he has cooler friends than they do."

Her eyes sparkled and her laugh was a delighted ripple. "His friend isn't so modest, though."

Ethan shook his head. "Laura, Laura. You don't understand preteen boys. Modesty is not a virtue they admire."

That gained him another laugh. "Then thank you for the dunk, too."

"Ah, listen. I had an idea," he said. "I didn't want to say anything in front of Jake."

Her smile faded.

"Nothing bad. I was just thinking I could install a hoop above your garage, if you're okay with it. It would be healthier for him to be out shooting baskets than doing whatever he does in his room."

Laura made a face. "Probably computer games." She looked toward the garage. "Our driveway is flat."

"Pretty much perfect."

"If you mean that, I'll go ahead and buy a... backboard. Isn't that what they're called?"

"Yep. I could make one if I had time, but I can't promise right now."

In the end, she agreed to let him pick one up since she knew nothing about them and his vehicle was better suited for hauling something that might come in a huge box than hers was. She insisted on paying for it, though.

He was starting to turn away when she touched his arm. "I…wanted to ask you something."

Ethan tensed at the way she'd lowered her voice. "Sure."

"Please be honest with me. Do you, um…" She visibly squared her shoulders. "Are you carrying a gun?"

He felt a spurt of anger that he knew wasn't fair. For all she could tell, he might have a backup weapon; a lot of cops never got dressed without donning an ankle holster. He wasn't one of them. Maybe someday he'd be sorry, but he didn't think so.

"No," he said tersely. "Did you think I'd come to lunch or dinner at your house carrying, after you told me how you felt about it?"

Those shoulders sagged. "I'm sorry. I shouldn't have even asked. It's just…"

He got over his pique. "Hey. I do understand, Laura. It's a hot button for you, and for good reason. I respect that."

Desperate eyes searched his. "Thank you. I hope it's not uncomfortable for you. I mean, being un-armed."

He couldn't resist wrapping his hand around her upper arm and squeezing gently. "No. I'm not one of those guys who can't go to the john without his gun. I carry a backup only on the job, and even then only when I'm involved in something that might call for it." He managed a smile. "Didn't figure the playground was one of those places."

"I'm glad."

Somehow as he'd turned back to face her they'd ended up so close, only a few inches separated their bodies. Their voices had gone quiet, too; intimate. Her gaze was suddenly shy, her cheeks flushed. Ethan couldn't stop himself from bending to kiss her cheek, warm, soft and sweet-smelling. He heard her inhalation and went still for a moment. Man, he wanted to kiss her mouth, too, but he made himself straighten, let her go and back away.

"See you Tuesday."

"Oh! You don't have to pick him up, you know. I'd be glad to drive him."

No dinner invitation, then. He still didn't know if she was attracted to him, too, but thought she was. She'd have her own alarm system, though, and he had no doubt he triggered it.

"Why don't you bring him," he suggested, "and I'll run him home afterward?"

"Thank you. If—"

He mock-glowered. "Don't say, 'If you mean it.'"

She almost laughed. "I promise."

"All right." Even as he was loping across her front yard to the curb, he lifted a hand to her.

Once again, she remained in the open doorway, watching as he drove away.

SUNDAY AFTERNOON, LAURA spread bills out on the desk as she calculated what she could afford to pay and when. Her sister had picked up Jake to go with them to the Oregon Museum of Science and Industry, a perfect choice when rain was pitter-pattering down, so she had peace and quiet.

Her phone rang. She didn't recognize the number, but it was local, so she answered.

"Laura?" It was a woman's voice. "This is Emily. Emiliana?"

Laura's hand tightened on the phone. What was she supposed to say? Oh, how nice to hear from you after all these years?

"Matt's sister?"

"I'd forgotten your voice," Laura said coolly.

That opened a pool of silence. Finally Emily broke it. "Tino told us what you said to him. He's ashamed he encouraged his kids to talk about what happened."

"Is he? He should be ashamed. Him a grown-up, preying on a child. Did he mention that word has spread throughout the school? That Jake's friends have quit calling? That he hears kids whispering 'Murderer' as he passes?"

"I'm so sorry."

"Does Mama know you're calling? I'm sure she wouldn't approve. Or did you sneak out so Guido doesn't know, either? He never could stand up to her."

More silence. Then, "You have reason to be bitter, Laura, but…but we'd like to make it up to you for what we did."

"How do you make up for not returning your own brother's calls? For not attending his funeral? For not caring what happened to his only child after he died? Tell me that, Emily." What answer could there be? Laura didn't wait to find out. She gently touched the screen of her phone and cut off her former sister-in-law.

She wanted to turn off her phone, too, but couldn't when Jake was away from home. She wouldn't answer if Emily called back. Easy enough.

But so much rage boiled inside her that concentrating on the bills was impossible. All she could do was rerun the conversation through her mind, think of what she could have said and hadn't, wonder if she'd been wrong to be so ungracious.

*I can't accept an apology. Impossible.*

It was six years too late.

As angry as she'd been at Matt herself, she'd been stunned by the way his family treated him. He'd been so bewildered at Marco's funeral, never dreaming they wouldn't understand that he hurt as much as any of them. Not giving Laura or Jake the right to grieve for the boy they'd loved, too. Matt had been devastated by the shooting, but lost after the funeral, when every single member of his family turned their backs on him.

On Mama's orders, Laura had no doubt. She

wondered whether Mama knew Emily had called, or that Tino had cried.

Laura looked down to see her hands knotted in fists, and felt the bite of her fingernails pressing into her palms. *Yes, Emily, I am a bitter woman.* She had never known what hate was until the Vennettis— gregarious, loud, cheerful, quarrelsome, unfailingly supportive of each other—shunned one brother, his non-Italian wife and his shattered five-year-old son.

She choked on that fury now. It burned in her stomach, although in her heart of hearts she knew part of the fire that kept it alive was guilt, because she had turned away from her husband, too. If she'd said, "I forgive you," and meant it, might he still be alive? Might they have had other children?

She didn't know. Still couldn't forgive him. *He* hadn't had to see that child with his brains blown out. When he had raced back to the house after she called him, his fellow officers wouldn't let him anywhere near the small body in the kitchen.

*I stayed with him.*

No, she hadn't left him, but her first words on seeing him that day had been, "*You* did this." She could still see him, stunned and frozen as he stared at her.

Her phone rang again. Ethan's name came up on the screen, not her former sister-in-law's number again. Letting this call go to voice mail would be smart, given the anger still churning in her, but suddenly she wanted to hear his voice more than anything.

"Just thought I'd let you know I bought the hoop and backboard today," he said. "Did you tell Jake what we were doing?"

"No."

"I could try to put it up while he's at school, so it would be a surprise, but I was thinking he might like to help me."

"I'm sure he'd think that was way cooler than helping Mom paint the deck."

Ethan laughed. Laura closed her eyes, soaking that laugh in. It was low and rich, something like the tender touch of calloused fingers.

She had to quit thinking like that. He was so wrong for her, even assuming he was interested.

"Thank you," she said formally. "Jake and I are both lucky you saw him at the gun show."

The silence that followed had her shifting in her seat. She had a gift, it seemed. But what had she said this time?

"What's wrong, Laura?"

She blinked. "I… What do you mean?"

"You don't sound like yourself."

She closed her eyes. Even more than the need to hear his voice, *this* was why she'd answered his call. Because she could talk to him.

"Matt's sister just called. One of his sisters," she

amended. "Emiliana. She was closest in age to him of any of his siblings. Not much over a year older."

"What did she want?"

Laura tried hard not to let Ethan hear the hate burning in her. "To tell me Tino had talked to them. She wanted to say she was sorry."

"And what did you say?" His voice held amazing gentleness.

"That it's too late." The acid bubbled in her chest, rose in her throat. She couldn't help herself. "I almost suggested she visit Matt's grave and try apologizing to a dead man, but I restrained myself."

He was quiet for a moment. She wondered where he was. The apartment he said was home? Sitting in his SUV in the parking lot of whatever superstore sold basketball backboards? There was no background noise to offer a clue.

"What did you hope would come of talking to Tino?" he surprised her by asking.

"You know what I wanted!"

"To make him ashamed."

"That…wasn't my first thought." The truth shamed *her*. "I wanted to hurt him. Physically, I mean. Stab him, punch him, see blood gush." She made a face Ethan wouldn't see. "I guess I shouldn't say that to a police officer, should I?"

His chuckle comforted her.

"I wanted to make everything better for Jake, even though, well, realistically that wasn't going to happen. Nasty gossip can't be put back in the can."

"No, it can't."

She sighed. "I'm not sure I wanted anything but to tell him how angry I am and to make him feel terrible."

"I think you succeeded. It sounds like at least some of the rest of the family are ashamed of themselves, too. You could take pleasure in knowing they'll suffer, you know."

Hunched forward slightly, Laura realized she was rocking. "I'm not." Her voice cracked. "I was so angry when she said, 'I'm sorry.' So filled with—" *Hate. Why not tell him?*

"How does Jake feel about his father's family?" Ethan asked after a pause.

"I don't know." She swallowed. "We don't talk about them. Didn't until…you know. This thing at school came up."

"He must have been aware that they'd disappeared from his life."

"I doubt he noticed at first. You heard what I said to Tino. Jake was so destroyed, he didn't want to look at anyone. He wouldn't talk. It was a long time—" She broke off. "What are you getting at?"

"I'm no psychologist, Laura. I don't know what the right thing would be for you or Jake."

"But you're thinking something."

"It crossed my mind that their apologies might mean something to him, even if they don't to you."

"Why would they?" she asked, razor sharp. "Why would he want anything to do with them?"

"Maybe he wouldn't," Ethan said mildly.

"You weren't there." The moment the words were out, she regretted them. She sounded as if she was making an accusation. Saying, *Where were* you? As if Ethan Winter had owed her and Jake anything. "I'm sorry."

"No, you're right." He had become more distant again. "What do you think about the backboard?"

"Will you come to dinner Tuesday night?" she blurted, then cringed as she heard yet another silence.

Yep, she was definitely good at creating those.

"You don't have to," she said hastily. "I'm acting like you're our new best friend, and that's not fair to you. I just thought…" *I want to see you.* That's what she'd thought.

"I'd like to come to dinner Tuesday. But it's a workday for you. Why don't you let me take you and Jake out instead? How about Mexican? Do you two like it? I know a good place."

She closed her eyes in profound relief. "We both like Mexican. Are you sure—?"

"I warned you about that." Amusement infused his voice; she could see him shaking his head at her.

"Okay," she said meekly. "That sounds nice, Ethan. I have to admit that an evening off from cooking sounds wonderful."

"Good."

"And if you're willing to put up with Jake's help installing the backboard, I know he'd enjoy it."

"Okay," he said, in a tone that made a lump form in her throat. They set a time for Tuesday, and he was gone.

She was left with the scattering of bills, and the realization that the fierce anger was gone, too. In its place was a cautious sense of happiness.

# CHAPTER FIVE

SOMEHOW ETHAN WASN'T real shocked to discover, in the middle of dinner Tuesday evening, that he wished like hell Jake wasn't there.

He liked the kid. He did. But he wanted to get to know Laura as a woman, too, not only as a mother.

Was that even possible? He wasn't sure, but suspected that her parental imperative was even more powerful than most single mothers would feel. She had good reason.

And, on a practical note, how would he ever separate her from her son anyway?

"We get to shoot tonight, right?" Jake said eagerly.

Ethan tuned back in. That expression on the boy's face bothered him anew. A little excitement would be natural, but this was too intense, too...feverish. It reminded him why he'd gotten involved with the Vennettis in the first place. Jake, not Laura.

Ethan still believed the class was the right route. He hoped the experiences handling a gun now would eventually displace what was obviously still a deeply disturbing memory.

*God help me if I'm wrong*, he thought.

"That's the plan," he said. "We'll see how busy the range is. Eventually I'll take you on your own if you're still interested."

"I will be."

Laura was watching her son, too, and seeing what Ethan was, because worry shadowed her face.

"We'll see." He constructed a fajita, adding guacamole and sour cream before wrapping the tortilla. "Your dinners good?" he asked, before taking a bite.

"Wonderful." Laura's expression eased and she smiled at him.

"It's better than the place we usually go," Jake told him. "I really like the chips here."

Ethan swallowed. "Me, too. Hey, things going any better at school?"

Jake's "I guess" sounded less sulky than usual. "Ron—you know, the guy I said used to be a friend?" At Ethan's nod, he continued. "Ron came up to me yesterday and wanted to know who you are. I think he was jealous 'cuz I got to play ball with you."

"What did you tell him?"

"I said you're a cop. A detective." He seemed to savor that. "And that you played for Portland State, and maybe could've gone pro, only you decided not to do the draft."

"You think he wants to be friends again?"

Jake bent his head. He was quiet for a moment. "I don't know if *I* want to."

"I can understand that," Ethan said sympathetically. Like most adults, he'd learned to accept flaws in people and still call them friends, but at best forgetting a betrayal was hard, and sometimes there was no going back. If Erin had done a one-eighty after they separated and wanted to try again…he would have said no. Still, he felt obligated now to say, "You know, if you guys were good friends, he may have been hurt that you'd never told him what happened. If you had, he might have been able to help deflect the talk from the start."

Laura looked at him with a glow of gratitude and warmth that made him feel better than he probably deserved, considering he'd been wishing they could ditch her kid. Jake's expression was more dubious.

"But people would have *known* if I told *anyone*."

"That may be true," Ethan agreed, "but they know now anyway, don't they?"

His forehead crinkled. "Yeah, but—"

Ethan held up a hand. "You can't go back. I'm just saying, if it had been the other way around, wouldn't you have had your feelings hurt?"

Jake pondered that. "I don't know. Maybe." He turned those intense dark eyes on Ethan. "So you think I should, like, give him a chance?"

"Think about it. That's all." Ethan wiped his fingers. "How was your day?" he asked Laura.

"Oh, fine." She laughed. "I know you two will be riveted if I tell you about a new super high-end brand of mattresses I've decided to start carrying.

And what an amazing month of sales we've had. Record breaking," she said with satisfaction.

"Congratulations." He leaned back, smiling. "Feels good, I bet."

"Yes, it does. The family professes themselves to be delighted."

"Do you know what's made the difference? The economy is rebounding, but not to that extent."

"It is partly economic," she admitted. "When things are tight, people tend not to redecorate. On the other hand, people with lower incomes cut back first and most extremely. Wealthy people may not have as much disposable income, but they still have some." She made a face. "I'm almost embarrassed to say that I've been skewing the store increasingly toward people who can afford the best. There are a lot of furniture stores in the Portland area that are aimed at middle-income shoppers. I'm trying to distinguish us from those stores."

"And it's working."

"Yep." She grinned at him. "Putting the furniture I sell increasingly out of my own reach, of course."

"Do you mind?" he asked seriously.

"No. I have no ambition to be rich. We're doing okay the way we are, right, Jake?"

"Yeah!" His eyes narrowed. "Except, if you were richer, I could have a dirt bike, and we could go to Hawaii at Christmas like Aidan's parents do every year." He looked at Ethan. "His dad is some kind of software genius. They take the *whole* family, for *two* weeks. Like, grandparents and cousins and everybody."

"That does sound good," Ethan admitted.

Laura patted her son's hand. "You poor, deprived child."

Laughing with them, Ethan thought, *I could take them.* He had a flash, picturing the three of them on the beach, maybe setting out to take surfing lessons, or going out in a glass-bottomed boat. Windsurfing was such a high, he felt sure he'd like riding waves, too.

And Laura, of course, was wearing that bikini, the one that wasn't much more than a few strings failing to contain those lush curves...

"Hadn't we better get going?" she said suddenly. "You two will be late if we're not careful."

Good thing she'd interrupted what had been a high-risk fantasy. Because he'd been seeing the three of them as a family.

"You're right." Ethan signaled for the waitress, shaking his head when Laura offered to pay or at least split the bill. "You've fed me a couple of meals. If I'm lucky, you'll feed me more."

He liked the shyness in her expression as she said, "Of course I will." She wouldn't look like that if she saw him as nothing more than a mentor for her son, would she? Damn, he hoped not.

When they reached Ethan's vehicle in the parking lot, Jake said suddenly, "I should sit in front, right? 'Cuz we're just dropping Mom off?"

Laura raised her eyebrows. "What if I want to come and watch?"

"There weren't any parents there last time," her son lied. Actually, two dads and a mom had hung around. Ethan had approved; if he'd been putting his own kid in a class like that, he, too, would have wanted to be sure the instructor was competent.

She hugged Jake. "I was teasing. No, I don't want to come. And yes, I'll sit in back so you don't have to change seats when we get to the house."

"Cool," the kid said with obvious relief.

The flicker of passing emotion on Laura's face gave Ethan his answer: yes, her feelings *were* hurt. She wouldn't appreciate him calling her son on it, though, and he knew that kids excelled, however unintentionally, at hurting their parents. Jake was a little young yet to have hit the "I'm embarrassed to be seen with my mom" stage, but Ethan guessed that wasn't exactly what was going on here anyway. No, this had to do with guns, and Jake's acute awareness of how his mother felt about them and why.

*What made me think I could step in and make any difference?* Ethan asked himself. What if teaching the boy to handle a gun was the absolute wrong thing to do?

*Then it's on me.*

It was definitely too late to pull back, though. What's more, the way she smiled at him when he did let her out in front of her house gave him an odd sensation of pressure in his chest. It felt good in one way, uncomfortable in another.

"I'll bring him back safe and sound," he promised, looking over his shoulder as she climbed out.

Ready to close the door, she met his eyes for a fleeting moment, letting him see how scared she still was. He doubted she'd intended that.

"Have fun," she said to her son, then slammed the door and hurried up to the porch.

Ethan waited until she disappeared inside before starting away from the curb.

"You don't think she *wanted* to come, do you?" Jake asked suddenly, his face screwed up in consternation.

"No," Ethan said truthfully, "I don't think she did." He hesitated. "Does she usually like to watch when you're in an activity?"

"Well, she has to drive me. Like, to baseball practice. You know. So, um, I guess she usually does stay. And she always comes to games." He sounded worried now, as he should.

"No matter how much she enjoyed watching you at bat or playing basketball, I'm going to guess there've been a lot of times she wished she didn't have to stay," Ethan suggested. "But it's just been you and her. This gun thing makes her nervous anyway, and having me just take you away…" He shrugged. "It has to unsettle her a little." And maybe *he* should have been careful about making assumptions, too.

"I don't usually mind Mom being there. But this—" Jake took a deep breath. "You saw her. She hates guns! She'd be uptight, and I'd feel her watching and, I don't know, stewing."

Yeah, that's what she'd do, all right. He'd have felt her disapproval, too. Ethan felt one corner of his mouth tip up, even though nothing about this was remotely funny. "You're right," he conceded, and tapped his knuckles on the boy's thigh. "And she knows it, too, which is why she made the decision not to come. So let's not worry about it, okay?"

"Okay," Jake agreed with obvious relief.

Ethan shook his head. That was a kid for you— concern about Mom's feelings didn't come often, and was easily dismissed.

Unfortunately, Ethan wouldn't be able to forget the fear and sadness he'd seen in her eyes anywhere near as easily.

Realizing that he was walking through an emotional minefield should make him want to escape it as quick as he could. A woman who feared and detested guns and didn't seem to much like cops? And who, oh, yeah, had a kid haunted by the death he'd caused?

Why *aren't* I running? Ethan asked himself.

Parking beside the range, he was glad for Jake's silence.

*I'm not running because I want her.*

He could find another woman to want. He managed to find casual sexual partners without a lot of trouble.

*I like her. I admire her.*

Getting out, locking the doors once Jake was out, too, Ethan walked around the back of the Yukon.

*They need me.*

That knowledge wasn't new. Neither was his awareness that he empathized with Jake Vennetti in part because he, too, was haunted by a death he'd caused. Which made him the right person to help Jake…and the absolute wrong man for the boy's mother.

HEAD DOWN, JAKE walked down the hall toward his classroom, not making eye contact with anyone. He moved slowly, sort of dragging his feet, braced the whole time to hear his name or a whispered, "Murderer."

It didn't happen. The classroom door was opening, and he had to go in, but no heads lifted. Mrs. Lopez smiled at him and he hunched his shoulders and sat down really quick. Usually he hated that she assigned seats, but now at least he didn't have to wonder if someone would say, "You can't sit here," or yank the desk away when he tried to sit down. Assigned seats were non-negotiable. That was Mrs. Lopez's word. She said they needed to learn to get along with people of all kinds, so she reshuffled them on the first of every month.

He kept his head down, though, and didn't look

at Joel Snider, who was next to him, or Lisa Miller, who faced him. Because the bell hadn't rung yet, everyone was talking, guys yelling across the room, girls brushing their hair and whispering to each other.

He took out his binder and shoved his bag inside the desk. It really sucked not having friends, and what Ethan said sort of made sense, but the burning sensation in Jake's chest and belly didn't ease. He didn't want to say, "Oh, hey, it's all right, we can be friends again."

What he *really* wanted was for something to happen that made him so fabulously cool, everyone begged to be his friend, and he could shut down the guys who'd dropped him because bigmouthed Nick and Gianna called him a murderer. He pictured himself kind of noticing Ron and Justin waiting eagerly for a friendly word from him, and him just dismissing them.

Only, right now nobody was begging to be his friend. Things *had* gotten better this week. Even though he still felt like everyone was staring when he walked down the hall or went out to recess, he knew they weren't. No one had said anything really lousy to him in a while. When the teacher assigned him to work with other kids, they didn't go bug-eyed. It was kind of, almost, back to normal, except he was still alone at lunch and recess.

Maybe nobody was talking *about* him, but they weren't talking *to* him, either. He felt almost as though he was invisible. A ghost, like in *The Sixth Sense*.

And Ron *had* sounded jealous, which Jake really liked. He and the other guys who saw Jake playing ball with Ethan were probably talking about it.

Jake wished suddenly, intensely, that Ethan would want to hang out with him a lot. Like, practically every day, and guys from school would see.

That would be the best, he thought, and didn't even hear the bell ring or Mrs. Lopez start talking.

A HEADLINE IN the local section of the Friday edition of *The Oregonian* caught Laura's eye immediately: Arson Fire with Signature Swastika.

"Oh, no," she murmured, continuing to read even though she hadn't so much as poured her morning coffee.

This fire hadn't been spotted as quickly as the previous one and had therefore done more damage. Family members had escaped, but a five-year-old boy had been hospitalized for smoke inhalation. A new puppy had been shut in the laundry room and was killed. The perpetrator or perpetrators had spray painted a bloodred swastika across the back of the house. A spokesman for the Portland Police Bureau acknowledged this was the fifth in a series of hate crimes that appeared to be targeting home owners with Jewish names. Ethan expressed concern about the apparent escalation in rage. He was quoted asking for help from the public.

Jake's voice made her start.

"Why are you just standing there?"

"Oh." She set the paper down on the table. "There was another of those fires last night."

"The ones Ethan's investigating?"

"Yes." She set out bowls, cereal and milk. "We'd better hustle this morning."

Jake read the article while he ate, as she skimmed the front section, mostly taking in headlines. War, more war, suicide bombers, a scandal involving a state congressman, an alarming report on climate change. All per usual.

Jake slurped the last of the milk and cereal in his bowl. "You suppose he was up all night?"

"Probably." She wished they were good enough friends that she could call him later and hear his voice. Maybe say, *I read what happened and was thinking about you.*

"It's kind of cool knowing him," her son said.

"Because of his job, you mean?" Laura was careful to keep her tone casual.

He sneaked a look at her. "Well…yeah." He dutifully carried his bowl to the sink, rinsed it out and put it and the spoon in the dishwasher. "Did Dad ever talk about being a detective?"

A stab of discomfort made her realize how often she'd put Jake off when he asked questions like that.

He'd been right when he accused her of not liking to talk about Matt's job. Or maybe Matt at all. Now, because of Ethan, she was having to reevaluate the impact her reluctance had had on Jake.

"Actually, he did," she made herself say as she took cold cuts, cheese and mayonnaise out of the refrigerator.

"It's pizza day," Jake reminded her. That was the one day of the week when he liked to buy the cafeteria lunch.

"Right. I forgot. But I'm still going to make myself a lunch." She did most days; their budget was too tight to allow for a lot of eating out. "Your dad liked patrol. He said that's where the action was, but he figured eventually he'd move to the detective division." He'd also talked about applying to the Tactical Operations Division SWAT team, but she wasn't about to tell Jake that. Matt hadn't taken her terror at the idea seriously.

"It's not any more dangerous than what I already do," he'd said blithely, which was scarcely reassuring.

She sent Matt off to grab his pack, counted out lunch money from her purse for him and gave a private shudder as she wondered if Ethan had ever aspired to be on the SWAT team or—maybe even more frightening—the Gang Enforcement Team. Or undercover with Vice or Drug Enforcement.

*What am I worrying about?* she thought drearily. It wasn't as though Matt had been killed on the job.

Ethan remained in the back of her mind all day. As, she privately admitted, he was too often most days.

That didn't mean she was interested in getting involved with him. He was good for Jake. Full stop.

But when her phone rang that evening, after Jake had already gone to bed, her pulse bounced at the sight of Ethan's number. Chagrined, she thought, *Not interested? Remember?*

Somehow, the reminder failed to slow her accelerated heartbeat.

"Hi," she said. "I read about you in the paper this morning. Is that little boy all right?" She carried the phone to the living room in hopes Jake couldn't hear her. Choosing her favorite chair, she kicked off her shoes and curled her feet under her.

"Yes, but it was a close thing." Ethan sounded grim. "They have three kids. Each parent thought the other one had him. Dad tore back into the house, grabbed the boy and had to break the window because it was the only way out by that time."

"Thank God he got to him in time."

"Amen."

"They were Jewish, too?"

"Fischman. This isn't for public consumption, Laura, but this guy—or gang, we're not sure yet— is going in alphabetical order."

"But...why?"

"There's the question." He made a rough sound. "I really shouldn't have told you that."

"I won't tell. I promise." She frowned. "The last two victims both had names that started with *F*, too. Do they all?"

"No, we started with Eckstein and Eichler."

"Eichler sounds German to me. I wouldn't have assumed it was Jewish."

"Yeah, whoever this is has done some research."

The restraint in his voice had her eyes widening. "Or knows these people?"

"That's a possibility, too. Again, not one for—"

"—public consumption. I get it. But...do these families know each other?"

"So far, only two do. They attend the same synagogue." He talked then, his voice already hoarse, telling her that some of the targeted people weren't practicing Jews, and that the geographic cluster suggested other possibilities.

She speculated on that. "That whoever is doing this is staying close to home."

"Maybe."

"Don't you have any witnesses?"

A moment of silence suggested he might be regretting having said as much as he had, but then he replied, "A couple of people running away. Probably young guys. One with a leather jacket and possibly a shaved head."

Skinhead.

"But you've sounded as if you're only looking for one guy."

"Chances are, even if there's a gang, one member is the driving force. He's the one with a big-time grudge."

"Oh. That makes sense."

"Damn, I hoped we'd get them this time," he said with sudden force. "I've been warning people, speaking to Neighborhood Watch groups, hoping we'd get lucky."

"I'm sorry," she said softly, aware of the silent house and the intimacy of this conversation. Had he called just because he wanted to talk to her? "You sound tired," she said tentatively.

"Yeah, I'm beat. I'm about to hit the sack. I needed to let you know I can't make it tomorrow. Would Sunday work instead?"

Deflated, she realized that of course this was why he'd called.

"Yes." She made her tone bright, unconcerned. "Don't worry. As soon as I saw the article in the paper, I guessed you would have to work tomorrow."

"Okay. I hope you hadn't already gone to bed."

"No, I was just thinking about it."

"I shouldn't have dumped all this on you. I wanted—" He went quiet.

"You wanted?" Her voice was so hushed, it was nearly a whisper.

"To talk to you. That's all. Thanks for listening to me."

"You're very welcome. I...kept thinking about you today."

"Did you?" he said huskily. "Any chance I get lunch Sunday once the backboard is up?"

Fingers tight on the phone, she felt herself smiling. "Even if it isn't up."

"Deal." He sounded satisfied. "Ten o'clock okay?"

"Perfect."

"Good night, Laura."

"'Night," she murmured, and ended the call. She let her head fall back and thought again, *Oh, I am in such trouble.*

But...Ethan Winter wasn't like Matt. She did know that. They might do the same job, but they were very different men. So...it might be all right. Mightn't it?

He was amazing with Jake. Her forehead crinkled as she thought about that. He'd said he didn't have kids and was divorced. Otherwise... Wow, it was a fine moment to realize how little she knew about his personal life. He lived in an apartment. His father was a US marshal whose upcoming retirement would be a relief to his mother. That was about the extent of it. What if he had a girlfriend? *She* might have kids.

*Not my business.*

Yes, it was. He knew so much about her. Everything. Anxiety trickled through her bloodstream at the very idea he could be the kind of man who would spend time with her and Jake and deliberately fail to mention the really significant people in his life.

Along with something close to panic, Laura felt like a fool, because she had made some big assumptions. She could blame him for them, but she bore some responsibility, too. She hadn't been treating him like her new best friend, whatever she'd said; she had been acting as if they were starting a relationship. One that wasn't all about Jake, no matter what she'd told herself.

Now she was mad, and ashamed, and— Wait. If he had a woman waiting at home for him, why would he have called tonight? And said that, about wanting to talk to her? As if…he didn't have anyone else?

The relief was profound. Flooded with it, she drew her knees up and bumped her forehead against them. Too many emotions, too quick. This was like being on a roller coaster, and she didn't like it. She wanted off, but she'd probably stagger if she tried to stand up.

She moaned before she could stop herself.

*I could fall in love with him*, she thought in shock. *With a man who carries a gun every day.*

A man who *hadn't* carried it into her house since she'd told him how she felt.

Matt had scoffed at her fears about his carelessness with his gun.

Ethan, she knew without question, would listen to what she said, not belittle it. Moreover, he would never have been careless to start with.

Still.

He was good for Jake.

*And I can't seem to help myself.*

As she turned out lights, got ready for bed and finally lay waiting for sleep to take her, it was Ethan she kept seeing. Ethan, with a long, utterly controlled stride, huge hands that felt so gentle when he touched her, tousled brown hair, warm eyes.

Speculation on what kind of lover he'd make forestalled any hope of sleep. Instead, her body was rigid, tingling. Heat pooled between her thighs. She couldn't remember the last time she'd felt this way, or so much as thought about what it would be like to go to bed with a man. Either anger and grief numbed all sexual response, or she just hadn't met the *right* man.

Yep. She was officially in trouble.

ETHAN SPENT SATURDAY interviewing and reinterviewing the Fischmans' neighbors. Sam Clayton was tied up working an ugly gang rape, so Ethan was on his own for the moment. He also went by gas stations in the area, hoping someone had noticed a couple of tough-looking teenage boys filling gas cans. And, damn it, he called a dozen more clothing stores, department stores and boutiques, hoping to nail down where the mannequin had come from.

No cigar.

Despite his other investigations, he found himself eating, breathing and dreaming the swastika arsons. He had moments feeling as if the stench of smoke clung to him. Waking up Sunday, he realized how much he needed a real day off. Spending time with a sexy woman and a kid whose problems were still fixable.

He'd half expected Jake's enthusiasm for helping hang the backboard to wane partway through the job, but it didn't. He listened carefully to instructions, followed them well and understood Ethan's explanations.

When they were done, happiness all but blazed from Jake as he gazed up at the newly installed basketball backboard and hoop above the garage door. "This is so cool!"

Smiling, Ethan folded his tall ladder and leaned it against the house out of the way. It had to hang out the back of his Yukon, and he didn't want to leave his vehicle unlocked when he was in the house. Especially since he now made a habit of leaving his gun in the glove compartment. A locked glove compartment, but he suspected anyone determined enough could break into it.

"Go get your ball," he suggested. "We'll try it out."

"Yeah!"

Calling excitedly to his mother, the boy disappeared into the house. When he reappeared, Ethan was glad to see Laura accompanying him. She wore snug jeans and a pretty sweater with a deep U-neck that bared the uppermost swell of her breasts. He completely approved. The promised rain had yet to happen, and when he first arrived she'd told him of course she couldn't paint if there was any possibility at all that it *might* rain.

"Absolutely not," he'd agreed, straight-faced.

Her smirk made him smile even in retrospect.

Now she came to Ethan's side and gazed worriedly upward. "Is it the same height as one in a gym?"

His mouth quirked. If only she knew how many times he and Jake had measured and remeasured before drilling the first holes. "To the fraction of an inch. Conceding that the driveway isn't as flat as a gym floor. Wouldn't do Jake any good to practice his shot if this hoop was off. All he'd do then is throw clunkers when he got to the gym."

"Oh." She beamed at him. "That makes sense. So, have you tried it out yet?"

"Nope." He lifted a hand. "We needed a witness."

Jake bounced the ball to him. Without thought, Ethan dribbled it a couple of times, bent his knees and rose to lob in an easy jump shot. The ball swished through the net. Laura made admiring sounds that would have had him blushing if he hadn't caught her amusement. So, okay, he was showing off again.

Jake had grabbed the ball and laid it back up. *Swish.*

Laura retreated onto the lawn, and man and boy began to play more seriously. Ethan shot from everywhere but the middle of the street and every one went in. He had the golden touch today. Jake started rougher but became more assured. Ethan kept having flashbacks—himself playing in front of the family home. The smack of the ball on concrete as he dribbled, the thud of it hitting the backboard. Dad often coming out to play with him, undismayed when his kid started beating the crap out of him. Dusk deepening the sky, and Ethan playing on long after his father had gone in. Eventually Dad had installed a floodlight so Ethan could keep playing well into the evening. *Yeah*, he thought, *I might have to do that for Jake, too.*

He'd wait, though, to see if the boy spent anywhere near the time out here that Ethan had as a kid. Days were lengthening; night lighting wouldn't be necessary until the shorter days of autumn anyway.

Disconcerted by the long-range planning, he had to ask himself whether he'd still be around that many months away. No, he wasn't going to disappear from Jake Vennetti's life, no matter what happened with Laura. Too many people had already done that to him. It could get awkward, though, if things went sour with her.

*Then don't do anything stupid*, he thought.

Question was: What qualified as stupid? He wished he knew. Wished he thought he could resist the temptation she represented.

She went inside, and then popped out to call them in for lunch. She'd whipped up some really great black bean quesadillas, followed by a peach cobbler.

"I froze a bunch of peaches last year. This was my next-to-last bag, so you'd better appreciate what you're eating," she informed them.

Mouth full, he made some incoherent sound meant to express a great deal of appreciation.

Jake had just finished scraping his bowl clean when the phone rang. In Ethan's experience, kids tended to outrace their parents to grab a ringing phone, but this one ignored it. Laura answered, said, "Just a moment, please," and handed it to Jake, who stared at her in astonishment. "Ron," she murmured.

He took the phone from her, handling it as awkwardly as if he'd never used one before, then mumbled into it, "Uh, yeah, hi."

Both adults eavesdropped unashamedly until he looked up, taking in his audience, and stood, his chair lurching back. "Yeah" was the only other thing he said before he left the room and, a moment later, firmly closed his bedroom door.

"Ron is the friend who was hanging out at the school last week when Jake and I were there," Ethan said.

Laura grimaced. "Part of me wants Jake to tell him where to go."

Ethan grinned. "Really? After hearing my affecting speech on forgiveness and understanding why his friend might have reacted the way he did to the rumors?"

She blew a raspberry and he laughed.

Poking at the remnants of her cobbler, she said, "You know, I was thinking."

Intrigued by her overly casual tone, he cocked an eyebrow. "Do that sometimes, do you?"

This time, she stuck out her tongue. Then her gaze lowered to his bowl. "Would you like more?"

"I'm going to be sorry, but I would love more." Only good manners had kept him from licking the bowl.

He watched as she spooned another heap of cobbler into his bowl and added a scoop of ice cream. The whole while, he had an ear out for Jake's return, hoping he wouldn't.

"You were thinking?" he prompted, after she'd set his second helping in front of him and resumed her own seat.

"Oh… Only that I don't know much about you." She sounded unexpectedly hesitant. "You're so good with Jake, it occurred to me that…I don't know, you must have spent time with other kids."

Comprehension blinked into existence. She wasn't really asking whether he had…who knew? stepchildren or something of the kind. Or at least he hoped she wasn't. *I'm an idiot*, he thought.

# CHAPTER SIX

HE'D SAID HE wasn't married, hadn't he? But, of course, that didn't mean he wasn't involved with a woman, and one who might even have children. No wonder that hint of shyness was in evidence.

"No kids," he said. "I haven't even been in a relationship for a while. I told you I was married once, right? It's been…" He had to think. "Seven years since the divorce. No, six. It wasn't that long before—" He screeched to a stop. *Before your son shot another boy to death*, was what he was thinking. *Before I shot a man to death.* Good God. Was it possible the two events had happened the same year? He cleared his throat. "Before I met you the first time."

"You mean, at the funeral?" She frowned. "Why hadn't we met before that?"

"I can't swear we didn't, but I don't think so. I'm…good with faces." *You, I'd remember.*

"Jake said you played fast-pitch with Matt. I did go to a couple of those games, so I must have seen you, at least."

He nodded. He'd suspected as much. "You might have met my ex-wife, then. Erin."

"If so, I don't remember her." She moved a shoulder. "Did you two think about having kids?"

"By the time we got to where we'd have wanted to start a family, our marriage was on the skids." He watched her carefully in turn. "She had trouble with my job."

"Were you already a cop when you met her?"

"Yeah, but in theory turns out to be different than in practice."

Laura nodded her understanding. "Back then, I'd hear other wives—and a few husbands—complaining. I'd have sympathized more if they worried about the danger instead of the inconvenience of having to change plans at the last minute too often."

He grunted his agreement. "In the early days, Erin claimed to worry about me. As she got pissed because I missed dinner parties or couldn't get off in time even though we had concert tickets or reservations or whatever, she quit worrying and started resenting instead. It's a pretty common pattern. Cops have one of the highest divorce rates of people in any profession."

"I've read that, even though I don't understand it."

Surprised, he waited for her to finish the thought. "Either you love someone, or you don't. Isn't that what it should come down to?" She looked at him as if she really wanted him to answer.

"Yeah," he said gruffly. "That's the way it should be. In fairness, though, marriages fail because life wears us down. Little irritations mount. Cops do work long and erratic hours. It's almost worse when you become a detective. Forget end of shift. If you just caught on a case, you work until you're too tired to think logically, and then all you want is to go home and crash, not listen to someone else talking about her day or, God forbid, go out to dinner with your wife and another couple." He tipped his head and studied her. "You weren't ever aggravated at Matt because he didn't make it home when you were counting on him?"

"No." Grief darkened her eyes. "I was aggravated when he tossed his gun on top of the refrigerator or in the drawer beside our bed instead of putting it in the safe."

"I'm sorry." He covered her hand where it lay on the table with his. "He did it often?"

"Yes. It became…a battlefield, in a way. He dug in his heels at my nagging. If I'd handled it differently—"

"Whoa!" Angry at her husband, long dead though he was, Ethan stopped her. "What he did was on him, not you. I don't understand how he could leave a weapon out when he had a kid in the house. There's no excuse. Not a one."

She bit her lip and gazed searchingly at him

again. "No," she whispered, finally. "Thank you for saying that. There isn't."

"Thank you for saying what you did, too." His voice came out husky. "Implying Erin's the one who didn't love me enough. I still ask myself whether it wasn't the other way around. If I'd cared enough, I could have quit the job and found something else to do. In the end, I guess I didn't."

"No, it wasn't the same thing," she said stoutly. "She was asking you not to be the man you are. The man she knew you were when she met you. Do you really think your marriage would have survived the resentment you'd have felt if you'd given up the job you loved for something that would always pale in comparison?"

He was shaking his head before she finished. "No. I know it wouldn't have. That's one reason I refused."

Her lips curved into a soft smile that made his heart go *bump.* "Then you were smart." Before he could say anything, she frowned. "I wonder why Jake didn't come back?"

"Still on the phone?"

She gave him a look. "Come on. You were his age once upon a time."

Oh, yeah. Eleven-year-old boys weren't given to chatting at all, and especially not on the phone. Calls were reluctantly made when required to set up a meet. Having to make conversation with a parent, however momentarily, was torture.

"I'll go find out," he said, pushing back his chair. "Assuming I can still heave myself to my feet."

She chuckled. "I have faith."

Carrying the picture of that last smile in his head, he went down the hall to her son's bedroom and rapped his knuckles on the door. "Jake?"

"Yeah?"

Well, at least he hadn't sneaked out.

"I might take off now," he said.

"Oh." The door swung open. "I didn't think you were going yet. I just, uh, was thinking. You know."

Ethan propped a shoulder against the door frame. "About your friend?"

"Yeah. I told him about you putting up the hoop. He wants to come over and try it."

"What'd you say?"

"That I'd ask Mom."

"I see. So what's the conclusion?"

His face screwed up in a pained expression. "I don't know! I'm still mad, but—" He shrugged.

Ethan clapped him on his shoulder. "Tell you what. Call him back and say sure. If you want, I'll hang around a little longer. I'll blow him away by dunking the ball a few times. I won't go home until the little snot is worshipping at your altar, because clearly you have *way* more amazing friends than he does and don't need him anyway."

Jake's big grin made Ethan blink. The kid looked so much like Matt, it was rare when an expression echoed Laura's instead.

"Can I?"

"If it's okay with your mom."

The boy rushed to the kitchen to find out if he could ask Ron over. "Ethan says he'll stay for a while. You know, to shoot some more baskets with us."

Having meandered after Jake, Ethan reached the kitchen in time to see her smile at her son. "We have no plans. By all means, put Ethan on display." Her dry tone and the laughter in her eyes had him smiling.

Jake hurried back to his bedroom to get the phone, leaving the two of them momentarily alone.

"Thank you," she said quietly. "I'm sure you had better things to do with your afternoon."

He shook his head. "I can't think of one." Realizing how true that was came as a hammer blow. *Yes, I want to hang around with two eleven-year-old boys, maybe give them some tips to make them better ball players. Hope one of the boys' mothers comes out to watch.*

Yep, why didn't he go for broke and take off his shirt while he was at it? he asked himself in amusement. Of course, given that this was the first week of May and it was all of about sixty degrees out there, she'd probably laugh at him instead of gazing in awe. Goose bumps weren't all that sexy.

Bouncing with excitement, Jake reappeared. "He's on his way! He only lives a couple blocks away and he's riding his bike."

"Then let's go on out." Ethan patted his stomach. "Now I wish I hadn't had that second helping of cobbler."

"You can still dunk, though? Right?"

Laura laughed, giving her son a quick hug in passing. "He's just trying to scare you. I think he can still get himself off the ground." She gave him an impish look. "Unless he's getting too old for that kind of thing. Maybe his knees are going, like his dad's."

"Now you have to come out there and let me dazzle you, too," he murmured as he passed her.

For a moment, he saw a kind of vulnerability and naked honesty in her eyes that stunned him. "I think you already have," she admitted before waving them on, her cheeks pink.

Following her kid out, Ethan felt like his feet were barely touching the porch steps or paved driveway. One blush and quiet admission, and he knew he could fly, no problem.

THIS HAD BEEN the best Sunday Laura could remember having in years. She ought to feel guilty for even thinking that, given that church attendance hadn't been part of their day, but she couldn't.

Truthfully, their church attendance had already become sporadic. Growing up, her parents had mostly taken her and her sister only on special occasions like Easter. Laura had turned her back on the Catholic Church the day after Matt's funeral.

Maybe it wasn't fair to blame the Vennetti family's priest for their sins, but no way was she continuing to attend the same services as his family. Her promise to raise any children within the Catholic Church had been given to Matt, not the rest of the Vennettis anyway. *He* had abandoned her. Petty as it was, she had to find a way to lash out at him in return, and this was one way.

Instead, she and Jake had started attending the same Congregational church her sister's family did. Only, the minister lacked charisma, and Laura's faith had been damaged by first Marco's death and then Matt's, with the result that she felt as if she was only going through the motions Today, Ethan's willingness to do something that mattered for Jake had seemed a lot more important than she and Jake dutifully sitting through a sermon that probably would have bored both of them anyway.

So, okay, she did feel a little guilty at that thought, but not enough to puncture the bubble of happiness that had buoyed her all day.

He wasn't married! He couldn't think of anything he'd rather do than hang around with her and Jake! He'd thanked her for believing he'd been right to refuse to quit the job he loved to save a marriage on the rocks. He'd come down solidly on her side when she tried to take a share of the responsibility for Matt's carelessness with his gun.

He loved her cooking, too.

But most of all, he smiled at her. He touched her,

and his eyes heated pretty much whenever she felt herself melting down inside. She couldn't be mistaken, Laura thought. He was attracted to her.

In the important ways, he wasn't like Matt.

She hadn't felt anything like this sense of hope and possibility in so long, she'd hardly recognized it when it first bloomed.

After demonstrating admirable patience and entertaining the boys for an hour or more, Ethan had finally jogged up to the house to say goodbye to her. He didn't touch her; they could both hear the ball still slapping the pavement in front of the house, a catcall from one of the boys. She quite desperately wanted him to kiss her, even though she knew he wouldn't. She just hoped she remembered how it was done if the chance ever came her way.

Once he was gone, Laura stood unmoving for several minutes, breathing and remembering the way his gaze lowered to her lips before returning ruefully to her face. If she'd been a teenager, she'd have let out a squeal.

That evening, she tapped on Jake's door to say good-night. A year ago, he'd rarely closed it and *privacy* wasn't really a concept to him. Now...well, she didn't know if his new desire to have time to himself had to do with his worrisome fascination with guns, or whether she was seeing the onset of puberty.

"Come in," he called, and she did.

He was already in bed, but had his iPod in his hand.

"Good day?" she asked.

His smile was the most uncomplicated, the *happiest*, she'd seen in a long time. "Yeah, it was really cool. Ethan said you paid for the backboard, and, well, thanks. It's great."

"I'm glad you think so." She bent to kiss the top of his head. "I hope you thanked him for getting it and putting it up, too." A sense of fairness made her add, "It was his idea, you know."

He grinned at her. "Yeah, I kind of thought it was."

"Come on," she teased. "I do nice things for you."

"I know. You're pretty cool. For a mom."

Laura laughed and smoothed his hair back from his forehead even as he ducked. "Sweet dreams."

"I want to be just like Ethan," he said, as she crossed the room.

Feeling a hint of apprehension, she turned back. "Not an NBA star?"

"Well...I'm not going to be tall enough, am I?"

She hated to squelch any dreams, but realistically... "Probably not. Odds are, you'll end up taller than your father, because my father was over six feet and I'm reasonably tall for a woman. But nobody in the family can give you Ethan's height."

"He says he's six four, and he sounded like that was barely tall enough for a pro." He shrugged. "I want to be a cop, like he is."

"Like your dad."

He didn't say anything.

She managed another smile, said good-night again and closed his bedroom door behind her, the way he'd had it.

*I will not worry*, she decided. There were plenty of years for him to change his mind about what he wanted to do with his life. And…would it be so terrible if he followed in Ethan's footsteps?

She made a small, strangled sound. In *Matt's* footsteps, not Ethan's. That was what she'd meant. Matt had loved his son. It would have made him proud to know Jake was thinking he wanted to be like his dad.

But Ethan was the one here now, the one stirring unexpected changes in their lives. Mostly for the good, but also some that scared her.

Turning out the hall light and going into her own bedroom, she reminded herself of how worried she'd been about Jake before Ethan brought him home that day from the gun show. No, the changes had all been positive, compared to what she'd feared then. She'd been right to put off finding a therapist.

This was the best day she *or* Jake had had since she couldn't remember when.

ETHAN CHECKED OUT his phone when it rang, but didn't recognize the number.

He'd intended to take Monday off, but had several ongoing investigations that were like an itch he needed to scratch. As a result, he had just pulled up in front of the home of a man whose assault might or might not have been racially motivated.

Honesty compelled him to admit, if only to himself, that if Laura and Jake had had today off, too, he wouldn't be working.

Maybe it was just as well they didn't. After all, he was seeing them tomorrow.

With an effort, he pulled himself back to a work mind-set and answered the phone. "Detective Winter."

"Detective," a woman's voice said. "This is Cheryl Brown. I'm a neighbor of the Fischmans. You knocked on our door Saturday."

"Yes, I spoke to you and your husband." He couldn't picture either of them offhand, but recalled the name. "Have you remembered something?" he asked.

"Well, it's actually my daughter who said something." She sounded apologetic. "The thing is, she's only five, so you may not think it's worth talking to her."

"I've sometimes found children to be excellent witnesses. Do you have reason to believe she saw something?"

"Becky has been scared to go to bed the past two nights. She kept asking if *our* house would burn down. I've been reassuring her, but this morning at the breakfast table she said, 'What if those two men come back?' I asked her if she'd seen two men at the Fischmans, and she said yes."

"Then I'd definitely like to talk to her," he said, already glancing over his shoulder and pulling away from the curb. "If it's okay, I can be there in about fifteen minutes."

"Oh, thank you," she said, her relief obvious.

He made it in closer to ten minutes. Beaumont-Wilshire was a family oriented, prosperous neighborhood bordering Concordia where Laura and Jake lived. As he'd told Laura, the swastika incidents were clustered in a semicircle of neighborhoods in the northeast quadrant of the city.

The Browns' home, a brick two-story, was around the corner from the Fischmans'. He'd rung their doorbell because you never knew, but with low expectations. The only way they would have seen anything was if they'd happened to be looking out an upstairs window at the back of their house at the right time—in the middle of the night. Turned out the master bedroom looked out at the street. Neither Mr. or Mrs. Brown had even awakened until they heard the sirens.

They had two kids, he recalled, bounding up their porch steps. A toddler boy, and the little girl. The girl had seemed so unlikely he hadn't asked to interview her.

Cheryl Brown answered the door so quickly, he guessed she'd been hovering by the front windows.

She was a tall, attractive blonde whose lean muscles suggested she might be a runner.

"Thank you for coming," she said, stepping aside to let him enter. "Becky is watching TV in the family room."

He followed her to the back of the house, where what he guessed had originally been a library had been converted to a comfortable room with a large-screen TV and lots of toys. The toddler stood in a playpen, a thumb in his mouth while his free hand gripped the top rail. His gaze was riveted on the TV where ponies with rainbow manes and tails pranced and…sang?

"Hey, sweetie," Mrs. Brown said gently. "The man I told you about is here to talk to you. I can stop your movie and then you can finish watching it when we're done, okay?"

The girl, a small version of her mother, looked unblinkingly at Ethan. "Okay," she said finally, sliding off the sofa to her feet. A sparkly pink shirt topped purple leggings bagging at the knees and those kid shoes with flashing lights.

Mom grabbed the remote and the screen went dark. The toddler squawked in protest, but she scooped him out of the pen and carried him on her hip as she led the way into the kitchen.

Ethan declined the offer of a cup of coffee, but waited patiently as she poured a glass of juice for her daughter and mixed some with water in a sippy cup for the little boy. Then they all sat down at the table.

He smiled at the girl and said, "I'm sorry I didn't talk to you the last time I was here. I bet your bedroom window looks out at the backyard, doesn't it?"

"Uh-huh." She gave a decisive nod. "Only, I got *two* windows."

"She has the corner bedroom," her mother murmured.

He hid his smile. "Then I *definitely* wish I'd talked to you and not just your mom and dad." Seeing her satisfaction, he asked if the fire truck sirens had woken her up, but she shook her head.

"I heard… I don't know. Something. And when I looked up, there was this funny light. It was on my ceiling."

"Kind of orange?"

"Uh-huh. So I got up and looked out the window. And…and there was a fire! A *big* fire."

He kept the pace of questioning easy, and circled around several times to see if he could shake her story, but she remained firm: she'd seen two men there on the side of the house by the fire. Except maybe they weren't really *men*. Possibly older boys or teenagers, she agreed.

Her forehead crinkled. "'Cuz one of them had something funny on his head. Like Ashley's boyfriend," she told her mom.

Mrs. Brown cringed slightly. "Ashley is a neighbor girl," she said to Ethan. "She started babysitting for us when she was thirteen, but now she's sixteen and into sort of a Goth look. Her boyfriend has a Mohawk."

Ethan pulled out his notebook and sketched a head with a Mohawk. Yes, this very bright little girl agreed, that was what she'd seen. Could he have been Ashley's boyfriend? Uh-uh. She was sure of that. *His* hair was the same color as hers. Both these boys had brown hair. Or black or something, but not blond.

That same boy had worn especially baggy pants. She regarded those contemptuously. When she saw them run away, he'd had to pull his pants up so he didn't trip, an observation that amused Ethan to no end until she added that he'd had something in his other hand. They determined it was sort of square, and when he gestured to indicate a size, she nodded firmly. Gas can.

They concluded that the second boy's appearance had been more standard issue, since she couldn't think of anything distinguishing about it except that he'd worn a T-shirt with short sleeves. She saw the pale flash of his arms. And he'd been carrying something, too.

"Like Daddy's flashlight," she said, but doubtfully. "'Cept it wasn't on."

He was betting that what she'd seen was a can of paint, the one that had been used to spray the swastika on the side of the house. He kept hoping one of these times a paint or gas can would be left behind, but so far they hadn't gotten that lucky.

Eventually, he thanked Becky Brown and, at the front door, told Mrs. Brown she had a very smart daughter. He gave her another card and asked that she call if Becky thought of anything else. The little boy, still sucking his thumb as he clung to his mother, studied him gravely until the door closed between them.

Striding to his Yukon, he reflected with satisfaction on what he'd learned. It wasn't much, but it confirmed some of his suspicions. The only other witness, and that to one of the early incidents, had been sure she'd seen a whole gang of hoodlums. He'd increasingly discounted the likelihood of more than two or three perpetrators. Young men in a crowd would have egged each other on. They couldn't have stayed so quiet, the reason for the frustrating lack of witnesses.

And five-year-old Becky said she didn't hear a car.

So either they'd parked a block or so away…or they lived close enough they'd hoofed it. The incidents had all taken place within about a mile-and-a-half radius. He thought these boys were either young enough not to own a car, or, if they did have access to one, had to be cautious driving away from home in it in the middle of the night without a parent hearing.

His mouth tipped up at one corner. Hey, maybe they were walkers. Either way, he thought there was a real good chance they lived within that radius, which would place them…in the Alameda neighborhood, maybe Irvington or the south end of Concordia.

He would definitely be intensifying his warnings.

And now…back to talk to the severely injured young Iraqi immigrant who had been cornered and beaten by a bunch of idiots sure anyone who looked Muslim had to be a terrorist. By God, Ethan looked forward to arresting them. All victims he interviewed were traumatized, but this one had clearly believed he'd made it safely to the promised land, where violence would be nothing but a fading memory. Putting the pieces of that dream back together might take years, or it might not be possible at all.

His mood darkening as he remembered his first interview with the young, bewildered guy, Ethan wished this was Tuesday, so that he could look forward to seeing Laura. He rarely talked about the job with anyone except fellow officers. His father, occasionally. That was it. Erin hadn't wanted to hear about the grim parts of his job, and increasingly he'd had to wall off what he'd done all day and the emotional toll it took.

So it was strange now to feel this urge to talk about the things that disturbed him with another person. A woman.

FEELING LOWER THAN an earthworm, Laura lifted her son's mattress to see if he'd added to his stash. This had been such a good week, she almost skipped her search. He'd come home ebullient from the Tuesday night class, and had then been excited about Ethan coming over to hang the backboard. Since Sunday morning, his every spare moment had been spent with a basketball out on their driveway. She was almost starting to find the irregular *thumps* as the ball struck the backboard soothing.

But here she was stripping their beds to change the sheets, and she couldn't resist taking a quick peek. And...oh, damn. On top was a magazine with a cover she didn't recognize. She tugged it out. *Guns & Ammo Handgun*, this month's issue, with a huge picture of a hideous black pistol. Fear filled her as she stared at that cover, more obscene than a pair of inflated naked breasts on a men's magazine.

Where had Jake gotten it? She gave him an allowance, of course, but was he spending the entire amount on magazines like this? She wasn't even sure where he'd found it to buy. Or... Oh, God, was he shoplifting, too? Now that she thought about it, he had disappeared for a while the last time she took him to the store with her. He could have either slipped away to purchase the magazine, or to tuck it inside his jacket after making sure no clerk was looking his way.

Horrible thought.

Confront him? Or keep hoping his interest would wane?

His attitude did seem to be better, she reminded

herself. And she hated to admit she had been spying on him. So…it made sense to let it go for now, right? To let him continue with the gun safety class, resume his friendships, maybe gain new interests? Ethan was doing him so much good.

She made a face, thinking, *I'm such a coward.* But it was all true, so… She began putting the bottom sheet on.

Jake came thundering down the hall. "Mom, what are you…?" Breathless, he swung himself to a stop in the doorway. "Oh. I can make my bed. You're always saying I should."

She'd said that until she hit on his secret. He evidently hadn't noticed clean sheets were still appearing on his bed.

"You can finish if you'd like," she said casually, dropping the still folded top sheet and pillowcases on the bed. "I'll go do my own."

"Sure," he said with suspicious willingness. "Ethan's gonna be here pretty soon. You didn't forget, did you?"

As if. "Nope," she said over her shoulder. "Dinner's in the oven."

"Oh, okay. 'Cuz tonight's my class."

"I'm well aware." If her tone was dry, he didn't seem to notice. A glance back told her he was clutching the top sheet and waiting for her to leave the room before he continued making his bed.

Not more than ten minutes later, the doorbell rang, followed by another thunder of footsteps and then Jake's eager voice. Laura looked at the casserole she'd just removed from the oven and grimaced. Her pulse had rocketed at the sound of the doorbell. *I'm as bad as Jake*, she thought in dismay. Maybe worse, because her interest in their guest wasn't nearly as innocent as his.

Carrying the casserole to the table, she felt a spurt of anxiety on top of everything else. If he didn't like her cooking, he might not want to keep coming back. This was a favorite of hers and Jake's, but, well, it was just a hamburger, cream cheese, tomato sauce and noodle bake. An everyday meal.

Too late to worry.

"Hey," he said behind her. "Smells great."

Pinning on a smile, Laura turned, to find he was as big and impressive and *male* as ever, shortening her breath. "It's nothing fancy," she warned.

His eyebrows rose. "It's not out of a can or the freezer case."

Her smile became more genuine. He had that effect on her. "You can't tell me you never cook."

"I know how, but I don't very often." He grimaced. "Don't tell my mother."

"That's an easy promise, since I've never met her."

"You will," he said in a low voice imbued with… something.

They stared at each other for an unguarded moment, before a hissing sound recalled her to what she was supposed to be doing. She hastened back to the stove where the asparagus was boiling over.

Taking the pan off the burner, she poked the asparagus to find that, thank goodness, she'd rescued it in time. Jake popped into the kitchen then, wanting to know when dinner would be ready, and after she poured drinks they all sat down.

Jake dominated the conversation at first. His mood was almost hectic. He bragged about how much better his outside shots were getting, and how Mr. Nichols the PE teacher had let *him* choose teammates today, because they were playing basketball right now. Had he told Ethan that? "So it's really great that I can practice whenever I want."

"I'm glad you're enjoying it," Ethan said easily.

Having gobbled his dinner, though, Jake got twitchy and wanted to know when they were going to leave.

Seemingly unperturbed, Ethan glanced at his watch. "Not for half an hour. We can't have the room early, so there's no point in getting there."

"We could use the range, couldn't we?"

Ethan shook his head. "It would take too long to set up. And, to tell you the truth, I wouldn't mind taking it easy for a little bit. I've been on my feet most of the day."

Jake's face fell.

Ethan just grinned at him. "Go play a computer game or shoot some baskets, since you're so full of energy. Let me talk to your mom for a bit and have a cup of coffee."

Laura kept her expression pleasant with an effort when she was thinking, *Yes! Go away.* Did that make her a terrible mother? She didn't care.

"Oh, fine." Jake dragged out.

The front door closed a minute later. Laura took a bite.

*Thump.*

Ethan chuckled. "That one wasn't all air."

She rolled her eyes. "I wish they all were. Although if he was too quiet, I'd have to go check on him, and this way I know he's alive and present."

*Thump.*

He winced. "Yeah, I'm acquiring new sympathy for my parents."

They smiled at each other, another of those lingering moments that had her heart thudding loud enough in her ears to drown out the basketball ricocheting off the backboard.

"Things going okay?" Ethan asked quietly.

"Yes, except…" She found herself telling him about the damn magazine, grateful to have someone in whom she *could* confide. Most things she'd talk to her sister about, but not this.

Ethan listened, his gaze never leaving her face. He listened really well, never seeming restless. Maybe it was a skill he'd developed on the job, it occurred to her. God help her, maybe his mind was wandering the whole time she vented her worry aloud.

But he frowned a little at the end, and then said, "Giving him time makes sense. I'm not seeing any lessening of his interest in guns. That's one reason I didn't want to get there early tonight. Given an extra minute, he heads right for the case that holds the handguns for sale and pores over them. I don't like the way he looks at them. He's still pretty obsessed."

She hated to say this, but had to. "You don't think the class and you offering to shoot with him is, well, condoning his obsession?"

"I don't know, but ignoring it wasn't working."

After a moment, she sighed. "You said that to him." About the gossip at school, but the principle was the same. Sticking your head in the sand was pretty useless as a strategy.

Now his eyes held a smile. "And you nodded approvingly, as I recall."

That called for her to make a face at him, and he laughed. "Don't you hate it when you have to admit someone else is right and you're wrong?"

She drew herself up haughtily. "Did I say anything like that?"

"You didn't have to." His smile faded and his gaze became...intent. "I kept thinking about you today." His mouth twisted. "Yesterday, too."

"Really?"

"Really." His expression softened. "Maybe I

shouldn't complicate things, but…I guess I need to know whether you're thinking about any of the same things I am. I'd really like to kiss you, Laura."

She couldn't have looked away from him to save her life. "I've…been thinking about that, too," she admitted, in a voice that was soft and shaky.

*"God."* Ethan shoved back his chair and surged to his feet, the heat in his eyes searing her. "I want to kiss you *now.*"

Her knees weren't sure they wanted to hold her, but she managed to get to her feet, too. All she could say was, "Oh, Ethan," but it was enough.

His arms closed around her.

# CHAPTER SEVEN

ETHAN STILL DIDN'T know if this was a good idea or not, but he couldn't seem to help himself. He had it bad for this woman, and when he'd heard her tremulous admission that she'd been thinking about the two of them together, too, that was it. He had to find out what she tasted like, whether her response was as shy as her eyes sometimes were, her skin as soft as he imagined.

His mind registered a distant *thump*, identified and dismissed it.

Laura got to her feet, only then all but fell into his arms, as if her legs didn't want to hold her. That was fine by him. He wrapped her tight, savoring the feel of her body leaning into his, and bent his head to kiss her.

Leashing the need roaring through him wasn't easy, but he was determined to take this slowly. There had to be a reason she often seemed shy about her response to him. A single mother, who knew how often she dated?

So he brushed her mouth with his, loving the way her lips quivered. He gently nipped her lower lip, and then stroked it with his tongue. She made a tiny, surprised sound. Ethan smiled and kissed her again, slow and careful. Only when he felt her relax did he stroke his way inside with his tongue.

She tasted as good as he'd dreamed. He was hardly conscious of the dinner they'd both eaten, or the milk she'd drank with it. The something indefinable was what he sought. It was woman; it was *her*.

He teased her with his tongue until she teased him back, and then deepened the kiss, a rumble rising in his chest. Laura answered eagerly, going on tiptoe as if she'd found her strength. Her arms had come to be wrapped around his neck. One hand gripped his nape, kneading like a cat. God, that felt good. His hands were busy exploring and positioning her to suit him. He was too tall for her, of course; his erection pressed her belly instead of being cradled by her thighs the way he wanted. If the table had been cleared, he'd have lifted her onto it so he could move between her legs. As it was… Damn, it was too soon, he knew it was, but urgency had grabbed him and felt hot and sweet, running through his veins.

And he had some of his answers. The skin he'd found beneath her blouse was pure silk, the muscles taut and her vertebrae delicate. Her response was… not shy, but a little clumsy, as if she didn't have a lot of experience. A widow with a child. He'd have to think about that when he *could* think.

He came up for air and looked down at her flushed cheeks, pink, slightly swollen lips and dazed blue eyes. "You're beautiful," he said hoarsely, then went back for more.

They moved in a slow circle, a kind of dance. Instinct had him searching for a surface to back her against. A way to lift her higher. He wanted her legs around his waist, her riding him—

A sharp sound brought his head up. Hell—it was the front door opening.

Laura looked startled by the interruption but uncomprehending. Part of him reveled in knowing he could make her forget her own son.

"Jake," he murmured, and forced himself to let her go. Ethan managed to resume his seat just before the kid burst into the room. He might be young enough not to notice when a man was blatantly aroused—but he might not, too.

Standing where Ethan had left her, Laura blinked at her son as if her brain still wasn't working.

"What's wrong?" Jake asked, gaping at her.

Oh, hell, Ethan thought, seeing her cheeks not only flushed but rasped red by his stubble. His body hardened even as he knew he had to distract the kid.

"Anxious to get going, are you?" he asked, hiding his wince when his voice came out with a little extra gravel.

The boy tore his gaze from his mother, whose eyes widened in alarm as her brain resumed function.

"Oh!" she said. "I just need to clear the table. Darn, I meant to offer you some cookies."

"Cookies?" Jake said hopefully. "We could take them with us."

"We could." Ethan mimicked the hopeful tone, although he could care less about food right this minute.

It gave her something to laugh about, though, and she scurried to grab dirty dishes to carry to the sink. Apparently she got a look at the clock on the microwave because she said, "Oh, my. You do need to be on your way."

*Think about cookies*, Ethan told himself grimly. Handling guns. Shooting at the familiar paper target as a herd of kids watched. Kids whom he would soon be certifying as safe to handle hunting rifles even though he was inclined to think the words *kid* and *rifle* qualified as an oxymoron.

Thank God, his erection was subsiding as long as he could keep his eyes off Laura.

Even when he didn't look directly at her, he remained conscious of her bustling around, though, her delicate face as pink as if she'd been standing over a hot stove instead of being kissed blind. God, he thought—what he felt was more than lust. He'd just stepped into dangerous territory.

"You look weird, Mom," her son proclaimed.

"Well, thank you very much." Her laugh sounded artificial to Ethan, but then he was in the know.

She handed Jake a ziplock plastic baggie full of obviously homemade cookies. Okay, they did look good now. As Ethan rose, she said, "Hold on, let me get you a cup of coffee since we never got around to having any. I'll send you with one of my travel mugs. Jake, pour yourself some more milk if you can take it without spilling it in Ethan's truck."

"Mo-om!"

Only once, as she saw them out the front door, did Ethan let himself meet her eyes. What he saw there was pretty much what he felt: astonishment edging into shock, aching regret that they'd been interrupted and yearning.

His instant attraction to her hadn't been one-sided. And, despite his profession and her initial hostility, she was willing to act on it.

Yeah, triumph was part of the mix he felt, too. That, and a deep ache in his chest he hadn't felt in a long time, if ever.

"I'll have him home at the usual time," he said, a little gruffly, lifting the travel mug in an abbreviated salute. "Uh…thanks for dinner."

"You're very welcome," her lips said while her eyes begged him to tell her when she'd see him again.

Or so his ego decided.

"Come *on*," Jake whined, and Ethan perforce followed him toward the street.

"I'll call," he said over his shoulder, not caring if the kid wondered why.

She waved in acknowledgment and shut the door.

Kids, he reminded himself. Guns.

*Damn it.*

EVEN AS HE sank his teeth into a cookie, Jake cast a suspicious glance at Ethan. Something had been weird with Mom *and* Ethan. Had they been talking about him? Or were they fighting? Or—

He choked on a piece of cookie and had a coughing fit. One hand still on the steering wheel, Ethan whacked him on the back.

Once he could suck in air again, Jake reverted to the thought that had made him breathe at the wrong time. Did Mom *like* Ethan? Did he like her? Boyfriend/girlfriend kind of liking?

He couldn't imagine. Mom never even went out with guys. Cody's mom was divorced, and she did all the time. Jake hadn't told Mom, but once when he was spending the night, a strange man had come out of Mrs. Boone's bedroom in the morning. Jake could tell Cody didn't like it, but he'd shrugged and said, "Yeah, guys stay sometimes."

What if *Ethan* started staying overnight and coming out of *Mom's* room in the morning?

Oh, gag. Some of the girls at school were starting to whisper about boys, but Jake couldn't imagine ever wanting to kiss one or anything. He knew he would; guys not that much older than him said they did. And Ron had stolen a *Playboy* magazine, and the two of them had stared for a long time at the pictures before Ron finally hid it in a drawer and said, "Big deal."

Sometimes, after he turned out his lights, Jake found himself remembering those pictures and feeling…he didn't know. Restless, maybe. And sort of fascinated.

But…*Mom* naked? No way!

He sneaked another look at Ethan. Had he thought about Mom naked?

No, he decided, that was dumb. More likely they'd been arguing about him. Mom was probably saying he shouldn't be going to the gun range and Ethan had disagreed. That would explain the tension Jake had felt in the room. Sometimes it was like that when he and Mom had a fight. His skin would prickle, like during a lightning storm.

When he and Ethan walked into the range, most of the kids were already there. He wished they'd come earlier so he could at least look at the guns in the glass case. There were some majorly cool ones there. He'd recognized some from his magazines. But all Ethan had wanted to do was sit and talk to Mom. *He could at least have come out and played basketball with me*, Jake thought, feeling resentful.

So maybe Ethan *did* like Mom.

Tonight, a couple of mothers and a dad hung around the back of the small room used for classes. If their kids minded, Jake couldn't tell. If Mom had insisted on coming, *he'd* have been pretending for all he was worth that she wasn't there. But maybe the girls, especially, didn't feel that way.

The talking part of the class was boring. Jake slumped in his seat and didn't really listen. They were supposed to spend most of the session on the range, but really it only ended up being, like, half the time. And then Ethan only let them shoot .22 rifles, which was fun but not what Jake wanted. What he really wanted was to try Ethan's Glock, which he wore on his hip as he went from student to student, correcting their stance or the way they held the rifle. Because Jake was in the next lane, despite wearing earplugs *and* earmuffs he heard Ethan talking to a girl who shut her eyes every time she pulled the trigger. Since they were all wearing eye protection, too, Jake didn't know how Ethan could tell except she wasn't hitting the target.

Something else Jake didn't like: the targets were sort of vaguely deer-shaped. He wanted to use the ones he'd seen in movies, a man's torso and head, because he knew that was what cops would be shooting at.

Tonight was the first time since the day of the gun show Jake had seen Ethan with the Glock. He hadn't even worn it to the other two classes, and because Mom was so freaked about guns, he didn't when he came to Jake's house. But tonight, as soon as they left the house and he got in his big honkin' SUV, he'd used a key on his ring to unlock the glove

compartment and taken the gun and holster out of
it. He took a moment to snap his holster back on
his belt even before he started the engine.

Jake had wanted really bad to hold the gun. Just
looking at it made his chest feel tight in a way that
was good and bad, both. He couldn't remember exactly what Dad had carried. He'd only been five, too
young to pay attention to stuff like that, but knew
Dad's had looked a lot like Ethan's. And Ethan said
the Glock was a common weapon for cops to carry.
There was no way Jake could ask Mom what gun
it was he'd fired that day.

So part of him was thinking now with a kind of
horror, *Was that what I used to kill Marco?* And
part of him was conscious of how powerful that
gun was. The memory of the way it had leaped in
his hands as if it was alive was embedded in his
very bones. But he'd been little then. Now he was
almost as tall as Mom. He could control it. *He'd* be
powerful holding it.

He didn't know why, but he badly wanted to re-
live the experience of holding a gun like that. It tangled him up inside sometimes, because Mom would
never understand. He wasn't sure anyone would.

Having run out of his allotted ammunition, he
stepped back from the counter, leaning the .22
pointing down against it, and started to lift off his
earmuffs.

Ethan moved to his side, shaking his head and
frowning. He bent close and said loud enough for

Jake to hear, "Leave those on until everyone is done and we leave the range."

"Can I have more ammunition?"

"No, everybody gets the same amount."

"I bet Mom would buy some extra—"

"No." Like it wasn't even worth talking about, Ethan walked away to help some other kid. Jake was left bored, and now mad, too.

Finally they finished, turned in the rifles and eye and ear protection, and walked out. All around him, kids were talking to their parents about how cool the class had been, and calling goodbye to each other, and some of the parents wanted to talk to Ethan so Jake had to just stand there and wait.

It seemed like forever before it was just the two of them in the Yukon. Jake fastened his seat belt, watching as Ethan did the same.

"How come you never came to help me?" he asked as if the question had been bottled inside without him realizing it.

Ethan glanced at him, one eyebrow raised. "Because you didn't seem to need help. Some of the other kids did."

"Oh." He slumped lower. "You said we could go sometime and shoot handguns, too."

Ethan was looking over his shoulder to back out. "When I think you're ready."

"If I didn't need help, doesn't that mean I'm doing it right?"

"You are doing fine. Fine doesn't mean you're ready to handle a Glock."

Anger built in him until it had to burst out. "So you get to decide?"

"I do." Ethan looked at him, a single, somehow dismissive glance. "What's with you tonight? I had the impression you weren't paying attention in class, and you seem mad."

"I don't care about .22 rifles. They're, like, for *girls.*"

"They're great for boys, too," Ethan said mildly. Like he wasn't taking Jake seriously. He was stopped at a red light, and his fingers tapped on the steering wheel. "Not a lot of kick, fun to shoot and a good way to build accuracy."

"You *said* you'd take me shooting with just us."

The light turned green. Accelerating, Ethan said, "Even if I were otherwise inclined to, I don't think I'll have time this week. I have a couple of investigations that are getting intense."

"So you don't have time to come over?"

"I came over tonight, didn't I?"

"So you could talk to Mom," he mumbled.

He got another raised eyebrow look.

"Come on, that's not fair, Jake. We all talked during dinner, and I took you to the class, not your mother. She and I spent all of twenty, thirty minutes talking."

They'd told him to go do something else, like they were trying to get rid of him.

"You promised," Jake said stubbornly.

"I'm a law enforcement officer. You know that. A lot of the time, my work has to come ahead of doing fun things. My friends have to understand that."

He did, but he was still mad without knowing why. Jake jerked his shoulders and didn't answer. They were passing under a streetlight, and out of the corner of his eye he saw the way the muscles in Ethan's jaw flexed.

Jake's eyes burned and he felt sick to his stomach. The way he was acting, Ethan would probably never want to do anything with him again.

And now they were home, and Jake would have to get out and not know whether Ethan would come back and shoot baskets with him again or anything.

"I'm sorry," he said suddenly. "I guess I just liked you being *my* friend, and tonight it was like you were everyone's."

Ethan came to a stop in front of Jake's house and set his emergency brake before he turned in his seat. "I am your friend," he said quietly. "I'm teaching the class because I wanted to do it for you. But once I committed to doing it, I have to be fair-minded. You handled the .22 well tonight. You *didn't* need any extra help. Other kids did."

"Then why did you say that, about me not being ready to try a handgun?"

"You know how dangerous they are. The only way you're going to be able to handle one is when you're being closely supervised."

"But I could *try*!"

"Your attitude sucked tonight." Ethan's tone said, *We're done.* "Work on that, and we'll talk about it again. Now scoot." He nodded toward the house. "Tomorrow's a school day."

Mad all over again, Jake fumbled enough to have trouble releasing the seat belt, and he almost fell when he slid down from the Yukon. But he slammed the door really hard without saying good-bye first and ran up to the porch. Feeling as though he wanted to explode, he let himself in the house without looking back. And when Mom stepped out of the kitchen and asked how the class had gone, he said, "It was okay," and kept going until he was alone in his bedroom, the door shut.

WHEN ETHAN DIDN'T accompany Jake to the door after the gun safety class and didn't call the next day, Laura felt as miserable as a thirteen-year-old girl who'd been snubbed by the boy she thought liked her. She swung between humiliation—he had lost interest after kissing her because she was so bad at it—and the only slightly more mature realization that he might be having second thoughts because he must know she couldn't be into casual sex and he didn't want anything more complicated. Especially, she thought unhappily, with a woman who had an almost-teenage son with as many problems as Jake had.

To make matters worse, Jake had been sullen ever

since Ethan dropped him off Tuesday night, and he wouldn't say why.

"You know what?" she said finally, after watching him stuff his face at the dinner table Thursday evening while never once looking at her and barely mumbling minimal replies to her conversational forays. "I'm sick of your moods. No TV. If you have homework, please do it. Otherwise, go to your room. I'll expect a better attitude from you tomorrow morning."

He did lift his head. Shock was quickly supplanted in his eyes by something so dark, it lifted the hairs on her arms. *Hate*, she thought, then immediately corrected herself. No, of course not hate; he was mad, no surprise, and maybe he *was* heading into puberty, because he was sure acting like it.

His bedroom door slammed. She was left alone with a chilling silence.

*And maybe I didn't handle that very well.*

She could only pray she hadn't been taking her mood out on him.

*Gee, and I wonder why Ethan has done a disappearing act.*

Which, of course, he hadn't done. A small moan escaped her. He'd had dinner here Tuesday. Kissed her passionately. Spent the rest of the evening teaching a class she suspected he'd signed up for solely for Jake's sake. And now she was sulking because he hadn't called yesterday.

Given that she hadn't kissed a man in six years,

she supposed she could forgive herself for not having a clue how relationships got up and running these days. But, really, did she have to revert to complete insecurity?

Clearing the table and scraping half her own dinner in the garbage, she talked sense into herself since she refused to let herself call him. Ethan definitely wanted her; he hadn't even tried to hide how much. He was the one who'd made the move on her, not the other way around.

He was also a very busy man who'd somehow found an astonishing amount of time to give to a boy he must know needed someone. He might well have been working all-out the past two days. He was a detective; it must happen. And, insecure she might be, but she refused to be as shallow as his ex-wife.

After cleaning the kitchen, she sat down to go through catalogs to study furniture her buyers had recommended. Concentrating was hard. Her ears strained for the slightest sound. An occasional car passed outside; a dog barked. If Jake was doing anything but lying on his bed glowering at the ceiling, he was doing it silently.

Her heart clenched as she had the thought that, if he had access to a gun, she'd be scared right now.

Ridiculous.

*I'm depending too much on Ethan*, she thought. *I need to quit hiding my head in the sand. Jake needs counseling.*

Something she couldn't do anything about right this minute. Eventually she calmed herself down and was able to focus.

Mostly underwhelmed by the pictures she'd flipped past, she did like a line of finely made, solid wood dining room furniture. Much of what her store carried was traditional in style, but with a difference. She didn't want anyone walking in the door to see the same things they had already seen at three other furniture stores. This line used inlays and contrasting stains along with clean lines for a look that was elegant and distinctive. She'd do some research on the history and reputation of the small manufacturer—

Her phone rang.

Her heart gave a disconcerting little bump even though the caller might very well be her sister or a store employee who'd come down sick or—

*Ethan Winter.*

She took a couple of deep breaths before answering, making sure her tone was pleased and just a little surprised. "Ethan."

"Hey," he said. "Hope I didn't catch you in the middle of something."

"Like what? Supervising Jake's toothbrushing?"

His chuckle was a lovely sound, low and just a little husky. "I suppose you had to do that, once upon a time."

"Baths, too," she told him. "He hated having

water in his face, so hair washing was a challenge until he was, oh, four or five."

In the tiny silence, she inevitably thought of what else had happened when Jake was five.

Ethan didn't let her dwell on it, though. "Did you and Matt intend to have more kids?" he asked, both surprising her and sounding as if he really wanted to know.

Because he hoped for children of his own?

Oh, boy. She was getting way ahead of herself, and after a single kiss.

"Yes, but it would have meant me quitting work because of the cost of day care. So we thought once Jake started school, but then it didn't happen."

"Did Mama Vennetti know you were using birth control?" His amusement was plain.

As was so often the case with him, she found herself smiling, her mood suddenly sunny. "I think she began to suspect when I didn't pop out a kid two years after the first one, like her daughters and her other daughters-in-law did."

He laughed, and then said abruptly, "I wanted to call you last night, but I didn't get home until damn near midnight."

"I'd have been long since asleep."

"I figured."

"Was it the swastika case?"

"No, something else I've been working. It was one of those shit hitting the fan things that actually

turned out well. As in, the asshole is now in lockup."
He made a sound. "Sorry for the language."

"It doesn't bother me," she said truthfully. "I've been known to use bad words, believe it or not. Plus, I don't want you having to watch what you say to me."

"Same goes."

"Are we talking about swearing?"

"And anything else," he said, in that comforting rumble.

Laura blinked against the sting of tears. How did he know to say what she needed to hear?

"Like the fact my son is currently sulking in his bedroom after hardly speaking to me since getting home Tuesday night?" she said, almost lightly. "Did something go wrong?"

"Yeah, I think it did. I'm not a hundred percent sure what, though. He seemed at a simmer during the whole class. I could tell he wasn't listening to a word I was saying in the classroom part of the evening, which irritated me. Then he developed some major attitude. He admitted on the way home that he was jealous of the time I spent with the other kids, but he was also in a snit because I wasn't willing to reserve time at the range for him to handle my Glock. I told him I'd decide when and if I thought he was ready."

She closed her eyes. "Oh, God."

"Honestly, I don't see it happening in the near future." He was quiet for a moment. "I'm not sure what's going on in his head, Laura. I thought things were going well, then suddenly—"

He didn't have to finish.

"I think," she said, "he was excited when you came along. Flattered. And…he really has enjoyed the time you've spent with him. But inside, that need he has to handle a gun like yours is burning, and maybe it's more important than anything else. His initial excitement might have…" She wasn't sure how to say this.

"Been like flying on a roller coaster?" Ethan understood. Of course he did. "And now we're clanking slowly up the tracks, and maybe there'll be another thrill and maybe there won't, but it's out of his hands."

She lowered her voice and cast a glance over her shoulder to make sure Jake hadn't silently slipped out of his bedroom to eavesdrop. "He had this expression tonight when he looked at me—"

"He scared you?"

"Oh, only for a minute. But I had the thought…"

"I can imagine. Damn it, Laura—"

"I'm going to make some calls tomorrow." She'd already made the decision. "He needs counseling. I didn't love the therapist he had back then, but I'm sure I can find someone good."

"I think that's smart."

When he didn't immediately say anything, she had a moment of panic. Was he figuring out how to tell her he obviously wasn't what Jake needed?

She wouldn't blame him—but also knew abandonment by Ethan would devastate him.

*And me.*

"There's only one more session of the class," he said, sounding thoughtful. "I vote we finish it. I'll keep playing basketball with him, maybe do some other things as the weather improves, but hold off on going back to the range until we both feel better about it."

"You're...still going to spend time with him?" Appalled, she heard how shaky that had come out.

"You think I'd ditch him?" Ethan sounded offended.

"You don't owe us anything."

"I'm not spending time with either of you out of obligation." There was a small pause. "I want to."

Laura swallowed. Her "Thank you" came out small.

"Damn it, don't thank me! Which part of 'I want to' didn't you hear?"

Her lips parted; she closed them again when she realized what she'd been about to say. *Thank you.*

"Can I thank you for listening, at least?" That sounded almost steady. "I've felt so alone. And... since you came along, I haven't."

"You don't need to," he said roughly. Then, "I wish I could see your face."

Laura wished he was there so much, she ached with it.

"Yes. I wish I could see yours, too."

"Crap," he muttered. "Can we have lunch tomorrow? If I can get away?"

A smile trembled on her mouth. Tears dripped down her cheeks. "Yes. Please. But I'll understand if you can't."

"I'll be frustrated beyond belief if I can't. Okay, sweetheart. Do you keep your cell phone with you? I'll call midmorning and we'll set a time."

He was gone a minute later, leaving her to mop up her face and deal with the swell of intense emotions he'd awakened.

*Sweetheart.* He'd called her sweetheart.

# CHAPTER EIGHT

TWO KISSES AND counting had Ethan feeling as giddy as a kid on Christmas morning. He wouldn't have labeled himself as an optimist, but he kept catching himself grinning at random moments for no apparent reason. Just because he felt good.

Following a meeting with Sam Clayton and Lieutenant Pomeroy, the fire investigator, he'd managed to duck out on the job long enough to take Laura to lunch Friday. Afterward, he'd dropped her off at the back of the store, which, being windowless, meant they had complete privacy and he was able to kiss her.

Tuesday night's kiss had been mostly gentle, slow—a promise. Friday's got a little more heated, on both their parts.

What Ethan hadn't yet figured out was how he was going to separate her from her kid long enough to get her in bed with him. Down the line, he'd enjoy a nooner. His apartment wasn't so far away as to make it impossible. For a first time, though, his every instinct said *no*. Emphatically. He'd become almost certain that his earlier suspicion was right on: whatever sexual experience Laura had was long ago and far away. As in, she hadn't had sex since her husband blew his brains out. Maybe hadn't even kissed a man.

Come to think of it, it might have been even longer ago than Matt's death. She'd been furious with her husband. He bore responsibility for his nephew's death—and for the memory of trauma his own son would have to live with. Did that kind of anger allow for marital relations? Ethan kind of thought not.

Of course, he wasn't crazy about imagining her *having* marital relations. Which was completely idiotic, he realized. He probably wouldn't have given it a thought if he hadn't known her husband. The fact that he *had* known Matt, and pretty well, was what stirred up an unfamiliar feeling he could only label jealousy.

Something he was doing his damnedest to suppress and had no intention of sharing with Laura. Considering he had been married back then, too, it was especially irrational. He'd get over it, he told himself. Wild, irrational feelings just seemed to be part of this giddy knowledge that he was in love, whatever he'd vowed on that subject since his divorce.

Saturday night, he couldn't dodge having dinner at his parents'. He'd been using the work-has-me-swamped card for several weeks now. Since he'd happened on Jake Vennetti at the gun show, come to think of it. What a coincidence.

Since he planned to spend Sunday with Laura and Jake instead of his parents, going to their place Saturday evening wasn't much of a sacrifice. There was a limit to how hard he could press Laura. *Can I move in with you?* would definitely be pushing it.

Particularly since he was still occasionally rational enough to feel his feet getting cold. *Take it slow,* he kept telling himself. *Be sure.*

"So what are you working on that has you tied in knots?" his father asked at the dinner table. His eyes were narrowed in suspicion.

Joseph Winter had passed on his genes to his son. A little shorter than Ethan—maybe six foot two, although right before the surgery he'd growled that, thanks to his damn crumbling knees, he was probably shrinking by the minute—he had much the same broad-shouldered, long body. He'd played basketball for the Arizona Wildcats. Ethan's dark hair came from his father, too. Dad's eyes were brown, though; the hazel came from Mom, who was something like five foot ten inches herself, still slim and blond-going-white.

Usually Mom would have given Dad a minatory look. She'd encouraged independence in their offspring more than he had. But now she trained a nearly identical gaze on Ethan. She, too, suspected he hadn't been entirely honest about his reasons for being too busy for them.

"Uh...the swastika shit." He flicked a glance at his mother. "Stuff." Dad's comments were few, but to the point. When Ethan felt the need to brainstorm, there was no one better.

"How are the knees?" he asked.

"My bionic knee is 100%." As good a way as any of describing knee replacement. "Had a cortisone shot in the other right before I saw you last." He didn't like admitting he'd needed one. "They're as good as they get."

Maybe.

He looked down at his plate. Apparently he'd been eating without actually tasting his food. Too bad, since it had been a favorite of his. Mom made great pot roast.

*Give it up*, he decided. His parents knew him too well.

"I'm seeing someone, too," he said abruptly, then winced. He really hadn't meant to start this.

"No one you want us to meet?"

"We aren't quite at that point." He hesitated. "Her name's Laura Vennetti. I knew her husband on the job." He looked at his father. "You might remember. He left his service weapon out where his five-year-old son could get it."

"And the boy shot and killed another kid," his father said slowly.

Ethan nodded. "Matt Vennetti killed himself a couple of months later. We weren't close enough friends for me to follow up with his widow. Turns out, nobody did. She's been on her own. Really on her own. Matt's family turned their backs on him and Laura and the boy, too. It's actually Jake I encountered." He told them about the gun show and his unease about a boy who clearly hadn't dealt with his complicated feelings about the tragedy.

"Did you know this Laura back then?" his mother asked.

He shook his head. "First time I remember seeing her was the funeral."

"So you're dating now?"

"Kind of." He grimaced. "It's a little tough, with her a single mother. I don't think Jake knows yet that his mother and I have…uh, started something. I'm still spending as much time as I can with him."

His mother raised her eyebrows. "Be careful not to keep him in the dark too long. Especially if he's already volatile."

"You're right. Laura and I are taking it slowly, that's all. She's come as a surprise to me."

"Because you thought you'd vaccinated yourself against getting serious," his father said sardonically.

Ethan grinned. "Something like that." Sobering, he said, "You know Toomey is on wife number three now?" Chad Toomey was a fellow detective. "Cochran and his second wife just separated." He listed four more cops with whom he worked closely. None had been able to manage a lasting marriage. And that didn't include the others who let the job get to them to the point where they developed drinking or anger management problems that would put the *finis* on marriages. "The chances are grim. You know that. I wasn't sure I wanted to lay myself out for that again."

"Despite the fact that your own parents succeeded." His mother sounded sad.

He met her eyes. "Sometimes exceptions prove the rule."

"I didn't raise you to be a cynic," she said firmly.

His dad grinned.

"Tell us about her," his mom invited.

Between bites, he did. When the pot roast was gone, apple pie appeared in front of him. Thinking how good it was, he had a minor revelation. "She's a good cook, too."

His father laughed. "That was one of my requirements."

Mom whacked his shoulder without looking away from her son. "You're both sexist pigs. Ethan is every bit as good a cook as Carla is. I made sure of that."

So, okay. He could cook; he just didn't, except on an occasional day off.

He shouldn't have relaxed too soon. Joe Winter's gaze speared him. "Would you have been interested in this woman if you hadn't met her the way you did?"

He stiffened. "What's that mean?"

"If she didn't have problems? If she didn't make you feel needed?"

Initially irked, Ethan made himself give the question some real thought. Dad was sharp. When he raised a point, Ethan made a practice of thinking it through.

Finally he said wryly, "You've got me there. But not for the reasons you're thinking."

Dad had leaned back in his chair, coffee cup in hand, and waited patiently. Mom had begun clearing the table, but stayed within earshot.

"What am I thinking?" Dad asked.

"That I have a white knight complex."

"Actually," his father said mildly, "what I was thinking is that you would have shied right away from a woman who was obvious marriage material if you'd seen that as an honorable alternative."

Ethan gave a half laugh. Damn, Dad was good.

"Part right, mostly not," he said. "If I'd met Laura some other way, I'd have asked her out without hesitation. In fact, I hesitated *because* of the past. Because she'd been the wife of a fellow cop. Because she needed my help with her troubled kid and I didn't like the idea she might say yes to keep me around."

His father nodded acknowledgment.

"Because she has a real problem with guns and anyone who carries one," Ethan said more slowly.

The lines on his father's forehead deepened a

little. He knew what had gone wrong in his son's first marriage.

"The problem with guns, I can see," he said after a minute.

"Ya think?" Ethan grimaced. "I don't wear it in her house, but that would have to change if we got to a living-together stage."

"She must know that."

"I suspect I'm way ahead of her in my thinking. She's pretty focused on Jake. She's scared for him."

"Is she right to be?"

"I wish I knew." Yes, Jake was angry, and obsessed with guns. But, from what Laura said, he was also a good student, and had had plenty of friends until the crap Uncle Tino had instigated went down at school. The friends seemed to be drifting back. Ron had appeared to be an upstanding kid to Ethan. Ethan's instincts said Jake had things to work through but was basically a polite, good boy who loved his mother and enjoyed sports. "She's putting him back in counseling."

Mom had quietly resumed her seat to listen. Dad nodded.

"So can Laura take being married to a cop?" he asked, blunt as always.

"She's been through it once. She didn't walk out on Matt." Not even when the worst happened. "Yeah," he heard himself say. "I told her about Erin. She said the lousy hours are part of the job, and the job is part of the man. She topped that with saying, either you love someone, or you don't."

The creases in his father's forehead smoothed. He lifted his cup in a salute. "Bring her to meet us."

"Glad I have your approval," Ethan said, not coming off as sardonic as he'd intended. He was close to his parents, the past month notwithstanding. Even to his sister, although with her finishing law school in Seattle and starting a family, too, they often had to resort to phone calls one or the other made out of the blue. His parents had wanted to love Erin, but he'd always known they felt some reservations.

*My family would be good for Laura and Jake both*, he thought.

*Gettin' ahead of yourself again, buddy.*

He liked the view ahead, though.

"Can I help clean the kitchen?" he asked his mother, who gave a delicate snort.

"Don't be silly. You think I didn't notice the bags under your eyes? Shoo," she said, flapping her hands. "You might even want to think about going home and getting a good night's sleep."

Laughing, he pushed back from the table, circled it and kissed her cheek. Her arms came around him in a hard, compulsive hug. "Love you, Mom," he murmured.

"Of course you do." She let him go, smiling.

Dad walked Ethan out, but didn't say a lot more. A back slap took the place of the hug, and "Thanks,

Dad" replaced "I love you" but the actual meaning was understood by both parties.

Ethan felt pretty damn good about life as he drove home.

ETHAN STAYED ALMOST all day Sunday. Jake responded to his presence the way a flowering annual did to a dose of fertilizer and a stretch of sunny weather. Whatever had made him grumpy seemed to be forgotten.

Because a bunch of the guys from school had said they were going to be playing on the outdoor school court, after lunch Ethan and Jake decided to go down there, too. Although she'd have loved to watch, Laura cheerfully waved goodbye, changed into her grungiest clothes and took advantage of semi-decent weather to paint the back porch boards. As such jobs went, it was fun. She had to be careful where the porch met the house, but otherwise she could just slap the paint on. It went fast enough, and she was almost done when she heard their voices in the kitchen. As the slider opened, she turned in alarm.

"Don't come outside!"

With his broad shoulders, Ethan filled the opening. "Wouldn't think of it." His smile was slow and sexy. "You might put me to work."

Laura made a face at him. "Hard to do when you managed to go out the door right when I would have recruited you."

The smile widened. "Yeah, don't know how that happened."

Jake peered past him. "Awesome, Mom. Except I see a spot you missed." Scanning, he pointed out two or three more.

"Oh, gee. Thanks. I did plan a second coat. I'm going to do it first thing in the morning. I can afford to take a few hours of personal time."

"You still have to do the railing, too," her son reminded her.

"I'm well aware. It's going to be a different color."

"Oh. Cool. Like to match the trim around the windows?"

She smiled at him. "Exactly. Did you two have fun?"

They had. They waited until she finished and circled the house to come in through the garage, having put the lid on her paint can and wrapped her brush in a plastic bag. Then they told her with great enthusiasm about this pickup game they'd played, which was *awesome*—a current favorite word when Jake was high about something—because a couple of high school guys had come by, and when they saw Ethan they wanted to play, too.

Ethan's enthusiasm, Laura saw, was tempered by amusement he gave away with crinkles beside his eyes. Fortunately, there was no sign Jake had noticed.

Since Laura had made lunch, he wanted to take them out to dinner. She went off to shower, returning to find the TV on and the two of them seemingly absorbed in a Mariner baseball game. What she ought to do was leave them to it and go pay bills, but she had this greedy desire to spend as much time as she could with Ethan.

Ethan and Jake were seated at opposite ends of the sofa. Seeing her, he shifted to the middle cushion and patted the one beside him. She settled down with a sigh, keeping her gaze on the TV but oblivious to what was happening. All her awareness was focused on Ethan. She'd have given almost anything to be able to snuggle against his side and feel his arm come around her. For him to kiss her.

He was so big, so male. With an apologetic glance at her, he stacked his enormous feet on her coffee table, an act that Jake immediately copied. The well-worn denim of Ethan's jeans didn't disguise the powerful muscles in those long legs. Below the short sleeves of his faded Portland State T-shirt, his forearms were tanned, strong and dusted with dark hairs. She fixed on his hands, both splayed on his thighs. As she watched, the one closest to her curled into a fist and, when she turned her head, it was to find him watching her. His eyes were knowing and heated with the glow that was becoming familiar to her.

Very casually, still holding her gaze, he lifted his left arm and laid it along the back of the sofa behind her shoulders. "Hope I'm not too ripe," he said, in a rueful undertone.

She'd reached the pathetic stage where she loved the smell of his sweat. It aroused her. Feeling his warmth so close aroused her. Looking at his big long-fingered hands—one now dangling so close it was *almost* touching her—aroused her.

When his fingers lightly brushed her upper arm, she jerked, and then saw the corner of his mouth curl.

"What?" Gaping at the TV, Jake half rose to his feet, then sank back down. "That's such crap. He was safe!" He turned to Ethan. "You saw it."

Laura certainly hadn't, even if she was ostensibly watching.

"Looked safe to me, too," Ethan agreed, then flicked a half grin at her that told her, no, he hadn't been paying any more attention than she had.

Blocked from her son's sight by Ethan's big body, his fingers started playing with her. Sliding up beneath the cap sleeve of her knit shirt to stroke her collarbone. Squeezing her upper arm. Skating along the sensitive skin of her neck, making her shiver.

He twined a lock of hair around one finger, tugging gently, then smoothed it behind her ear, after which he traced the outline of her ear. She couldn't do anything but sit there, frozen, hoping she was hiding the tiny shivers, that her bra was doing its job and her nipples weren't too obviously poking out.

To all appearances, Jake missed the byplay, enjoying the game, coaxing Ethan into talking about players and the Mariners'—probably nonexistent—chances of making the play-offs.

Just before the game ended, Ethan very casually removed his arm, using the chance to trail his fingertips across the back of her neck, then leaned forward and reached for the remote on the coffee table.

"How's pizza sound?" he asked. "I made reservations at Apizza Scholls, just in case."

Jake cheered. Laura was so turned on by that time food was the last thing on her mind, but said, "We love it."

"I figure I can kick your butt at some video games," Ethan told Jake as he rose to his feet and stretched, his hands touching the ceiling. Laura got an up close and personal view of his partial erection, nicely cupped by denim.

She stood and brushed that erection with her hip not-quite-accidentally as she said, "Let me grab my purse. Who's driving?"

His expression was pained but amused, too. "Me."

"Control freak."

"Absolutely," he agreed, straight-faced.

If Matt had had his way, she'd have never gotten behind the wheel of a car. When they went somewhere together or as a family, she'd had zero chance of driving. So, okay, Ethan *did* have something in common with Matt besides the job. Which, come to think of it, shouldn't come as a surprise. Cops might come in a variety of configurations, but "laid-back" probably wasn't one of them.

And…Ethan had an innate sense of confidence that contrasted with what she had eventually realized was a smidgeon of swagger in her husband that hid some insecurities. She blamed Mama Vennetti for those. She'd had a gift for tiny pinpricks that smarted. Laura would put Ethan, however, up against Mama any day.

She joined in the video games at Apizza Scholls, enjoying the experience of trouncing Jake, who was stunned, and Ethan, who flexed his fingers and said with determination, "Rematch." The humor in his eyes told her she'd been right about his ego, though; it could stand up to losing to a woman.

When he beat her the second time they played, she just smiled and said, "Had to let you win to regain your sense of masculine prowess."

Jake hooted.

They all agreed on a plain pie with ricotta, garlic and fresh basil added. Ethan ordered a second one. "It'll give me dinner for a couple of nights."

"But…aren't you having dinner with us Tuesday?" Jake sounded momentarily bewildered.

Ethan's eyes, heavy-lidded, met Laura's. "I haven't been invited yet."

She smiled at him. "Consider yourself invited."

"And I accept," he said in a low, husky voice.

"Wow, it's the last class," Jake exclaimed, apparently unaware of anything going on beneath the surface.

Thank goodness, Laura thought. What was she *doing*, flirting in front of her eleven-year-old son?

Having more fun than she'd had in years?

*Well, yeah.*

Ethan declined to come in when he pulled into their driveway. Jake had ridden in front with Ethan on the way to the restaurant; on the way home, Laura had claimed the front seat. Now, impatient that she didn't move fast enough, Jake reached over her shoulder and snatched the keys out of her hand. Apparently there was something he wanted to watch on TV, and she wasn't about to object although she did call after him, "Did you finish your homework?"

"Duh," he said over his shoulder, and then raced away.

Neither adult moved until he disappeared inside. Then Ethan groaned and reached for her. "I had a lot of fun today, but, *damn*, I want to be alone with you."

"Ditto." She pressed an openmouthed kiss to his throat.

That spurred him to grip the back of her head, tilting it up so he could devour her mouth. Nope, this was *not* a laid-back man, not right now anyway. He wanted her, and if they hadn't been sitting in the driveway not far from a streetlight, if her son hadn't been liable to pop out of the house to find out why Mom hadn't followed him, if the steering wheel didn't keep Ethan from dragging her onto his lap, she thought things might have gotten really serious. His tongue wasn't playing, it was thrusting in a mimicry of what he really wanted to be doing to her, and the hand that wasn't positioning her to suit him was kneading her breast. That hand felt so good, she arched to push herself at him, which had him growling—she thought—and finally wrenching his mouth from hers.

Panting, he rested his forehead against hers. "We can't do this," he said hoarsely.

"No." Had she ever even made a decision that, yes, she was going to make love with Ethan?

Maybe not consciously, but there seemed no question the decision had been made. If it had been possible, right this minute, she'd have been reaching for his belt buckle.

"Damn," he muttered.

They stayed like that for a good two or three minutes, their breathing slowly becoming something approximating normal. She hadn't realized how tense his body was until she felt the muscles easing.

Finally he lifted his head, his eyes dark in the dimness. "I'll walk you to the door."

"You don't have to." She had the presence of mind to release the seat belt, which, come to think of it, had been slicing between her breasts and across her belly. "Jake would notice."

"Don't you think it's time we tell him we're, uh…"

"What? Making out behind his back?"

He smiled at the old-fashioned term. What should she call it? Getting it on? To her regret, they hadn't yet managed that.

"Let's call it dating," he said. "Tell him I'm your boyfriend."

"Are you?" Dismayed, Laura heard how breathless she sounded.

"Yeah." He kissed her again, quick and firm. "If that's okay with you."

She had to close her eyes against the unexpected sting. "Yes," she whispered. "It's okay."

"Good."

He straightened away from her, and she opened her eyes to see him unfastening his own seat belt and opening his door. Laura grabbed her purse and got out. He gently put her in front of him instead of trying to stay beside her on the narrow, concrete walkway, but kept his hand resting on her shoulder.

"You don't mind if I wait to tell him until, I don't know, it feels like a good moment?"

"Nope. I won't say anything until you do."

Climbing the few steps to the porch, they both saw the flicker of the television. Ethan kissed her one more time. "Lunch tomorrow?"

"Are you taking the day off?"

"I don't think so. Too much going on. So I can't promise, but I'll call, okay?" At her nod, he reached past her to open the front door.

Laura smiled shakily. "Good night." It felt as if

they'd just crossed some threshold, and not the one in front of her.

She loved his smile. "'Night," he murmured, then raised his voice. "See you Tuesday."

"Yeah!" Jake called back.

Laura couldn't help turning to watch Ethan lope back across the yard to his SUV. She saw the flash of white that was his grin when he got there and saw her.

Clutching a very warm, fuzzy feeling to herself, she went in.

MONDAY, SAM CLAYTON and Ethan divided up tasks. Sam took Ethan's lists and continued making calls in pursuit of the stolen mannequin. He agreed with Ethan's belief that they'd find a connection between the store from which it had been taken and their perp.

Meantime, Ethan made the round of synagogues in search of disaffected boys. He found rabbis reluctant to disclose names, but a few did and others inadvertently gave away enough that he was able to speak to temple members who were willing to talk. Back at his desk, he researched fourteen names, a couple of whom he decided were worth speaking to personally. No one name lit up for him.

Pomeroy was frustrated because he couldn't offer any useful information. If the fires had been set inside the homes, they'd be more likely to find some kind of trace evidence. Any kind of device would give them something to work with. But anyone could splash a little gas and toss a match or lighter. Of course, those same somebodies were taking a serious risk of getting burned when the vapor in the air caught fire, but so far that apparently hadn't happened. Pomeroy had checked with emergency rooms across the city in search of burns treated the night of the fires or the following days, with no leads.

"The idiots have just gotten lucky so far," he growled, and Ethan agreed.

Unfortunately, he, Clayton and Ethan all had other investigations competing for their attention, and Ethan wasn't sure what they could do but hadn't already. The simpler a crime, the more likely the perpetrator was to get away with it. Their best hope was an honest-to-God witness, somebody who got a license plate number, for example, but the fires were being set in middle-class neighborhoods where few people were out and about at night.

Frustrated, Ethan knew he had no choice but to devote the next day to a different investigation. Plus side—he'd be having dinner with Laura and Jake.

"Why can't we go now?" It was Tuesday night, and Jake stared in disbelief at Ethan, who was leaning comfortably back in his chair and who'd just agreed he'd like a second cup of coffee.

Despite his apparent relaxation, there was no flexibility in the hard look he was giving Jake or in his voice. "Like I told you last time, I see no reason to get there early. I've already put in an eight-hour day. This is my break. I'm enjoying talking to your mother. You don't need to spend half an hour drooling over weapons you're not old enough to handle."

The explosion of rage Jake felt scared him. "You said you'd let me try them." His voice shook.

"When I think you're ready. This attitude tells me you're not."

"You're some guy who teaches the class. You're not my mom or dad." Part of him was horrified at what he'd said and at the way Ethan's eyes narrowed. Part of him was glad. Sometimes he'd caught himself wishing Ethan *was* his father, but that made him feel sick.

"I'm the guy deciding when—or *if*—you spend any time at the gun range. Whether you go tonight, in fact."

So much swirling inside him he couldn't name, Jake was vaguely aware his mother stood beside the table with her eyes dark with shock. Her silence gave Ethan the right to say what he had.

Jake whirled and raced from the room. There wasn't anywhere to go except his bedroom, unless he took off.

He wasn't stupid enough to think he could get away with that. Where would he go? Any of his friends' parents would just call Mom. If a police officer saw him, he'd get picked up, same as when Ethan spotted him at the gun show.

Frustration and the inchoate need he didn't understand tangled inside him.

*I'll tell him to forget taking me. He's never going to let me shoot anything but the dumb .22 at the range anyway.*

Outside his bedroom, he hesitated, but if they were talking, he couldn't hear their voices. Because they hadn't heard his bedroom door. Understanding, he opened it and, an instant later, slammed it. As if he'd gone in.

Now he could sneak back and listen to what they were saying about him.

Only, then he had an idea. A breathtaking idea.

Mom had hung Ethan's jacket on the coatrack inside the front door. Jake had heard the car keys in the pocket rattle.

The key to the glove compartment was on that ring, too.

He could sneak out. Just…hold the Glock for a minute. Kind of…look at it. Remember.

He heard the low rumble of Ethan's voice, the higher sound of his mother's. Last week, they'd talked until it was time to go and never once checked on him. They'd never know.

Jake crept down the hall.

Mom was talking. "I haven't told him yet I scheduled…"

Peering from the shadows, he saw that Ethan's back was to him and he was blocking Mom's sight line to the hall.

Jake hurried past, slid a shaking hand into the pocket of Ethan's leather jacket, gripped the keys tightly and opened the front door as quietly as he could.

# CHAPTER NINE

"WHAT DO YOU want to do?" Laura asked.

"I'm sure as hell not in the mood to take him, but…shit." Ethan exhaled. "He already thinks I'm not keeping promises. It's understandable that he resents me calling him on his behavior. In his view, taking his father's place."

"Understandable?" Face pale so that her freckles stood out, she looked at him like he was nuts. "He's admitted to me he wouldn't remember Matt's face if not for pictures."

"And he probably feels guilty for that." The thought nudged another one. "If he blames himself for his father's death, too…"

"Then he believes he has to cling to whatever memory he does have of Matt," she said with a sigh. "Be loyal to him."

"That's my take," Ethan agreed, although he didn't like the understanding. Face it: he *had* been trying to step in as a father figure. If he and Laura were going anywhere serious—and, if he had his way, they were—part of that would be Jake accepting him as a stepfather, at least.

Plus…Jake needed more than a distant memory of the father who had both betrayed him by leaving that goddamn gun out and then abandoned him by killing himself. A hell of a lot more.

Witness his struggles now.

Suddenly uneasy for no reason he could put his finger on, Ethan cocked his head. "I don't hear him."

"He's sulking. He does that quietly."

The prickling sensation on the back of his neck was something he never ignored. "I'm going to check on him." Ethan made sure the chair didn't scrape back, and from long practice he was able to walk silently the short distance to the boy's bedroom. There, he rapped lightly then without waiting opened the door.

The room was empty.

He swore and spun on his heel, running to the front door.

"Ethan?" Looking scared, Laura appeared from the kitchen. "What's wrong?"

He dug his hand in his coat pocket and found it empty. "Jesus," he breathed, and tore out the door.

With sunset over an hour away, he saw the boy right away, sitting on the passenger side of the Yukon. His head was bent until he must have heard the front door of the house and he looked up. For a moment he went completely still, his mouth forming a circle.

Ethan hadn't been kidding when he'd told them he

moved fast. He reached the SUV and was wrenching the passenger door open before Jake could slam the glove compartment.

Ethan closed a hand hard around the boy's thin wrist. Checking to be sure the Glock was pointed away—it had no safety—he squeezed inexorably until Jake's hand opened and the gun dropped with a faint *clunk* to the bottom of the glove compartment.

"So much for trusting you." He loosened his grip slightly but didn't let go. What he did do was close the compartment, lock it and take the keys. "Back in the house," he said grimly, and pulled him out of the vehicle.

The boy didn't say a word. He hunched like a turtle and wouldn't look up. Laura waited on the porch, her fingers pressed to her mouth. Ethan towed him to his mother, and then all but tossed him inside.

"Sit," he ordered.

"I don't have to!" the boy blazed.

Ethan got his hand on the thin shoulder and pressed him down on the sofa. "Yeah, you do. You're in deep trouble here. I could arrest you and haul your ass to juvie."

"What?" His head shot up. "You wouldn't!"

"Try me." He couldn't remember being so mad, and that was something considering the shit he saw every day. This was different—it was personal.

"Ethan—" Laura said behind him.

He shot her a narrow-eyed look. By God, if she

jumped in on the kid's side, he just might *have* to arrest him.

Looking stunned, she closed her mouth on whatever she'd been about to say.

He crossed his arms and stared down at the defiant boy. "What were you going to do with that gun? Shoot me? Shoot your mother? Shoot yourself?"

"No!" Jake half rose, then sagged back onto the sofa. He scooted back, as far as he could get from the man looming over him. "I just wanted to see it!"

"You had it out of the holster, in your hands. That's not looking."

"I just wanted— I don't know what I wanted!" he cried. "But not to shoot anybody!"

Ethan shook his head, and then scraped a hand over his face. "Damn. I don't have time to deal with this. I owe it to the other kids to show up at the range." He backed away. "You violated my trust. You're out of the class. Right now, I'm going to leave you in your mother's hands." Deliberately, he turned his back on the boy. "Laura, I'll call you later. We need to talk."

"I… Yes." Her voice was small, shocked.

All he could do was nod, snag his jacket and walk out.

LAURA HAD NEVER felt as out of her depth as a parent as she did right now. It was all she could do not to run after Ethan and plead for him not to leave.

But she knew he was right; he had made a commitment and needed to keep it. And Jake was *her* problem.

She was used to dealing with her problems on her own.

He started to leap up again, undoubtedly with the intention of racing to his room to shut himself in.

"Sit down!" she snapped.

He took a scared look at her face and complied. "What were you thinking?"

"I just wanted to look at it! I told you."

She shook her head. "You went to the gun show to look. How many handguns did you see there?"

He didn't say anything.

"Then there are all the pretty pictures you keep under your mattress." She raised her eyebrows at his expression. "You thought I didn't know?"

No answer was necessary or forthcoming.

"You will start counseling." She made sure there was no give in her voice. "Dr. Redmond recommended a therapist. You have an appointment Thursday after school."

"Maybe he likes to shoot guns!" her son cried.

"If he does, we'll find someone else."

"Ethan shoots them," he said disagreeably. "It was *his* gun."

Yes, that bothered her. The knowledge that he usually carried one was an ever-present niggle she'd been able to avoid acknowledging until now. But she refused to let Jake see her unease.

"His gun," she agreed, "which, to comply with my wishes, he had locked up in his vehicle. Which was *also* locked."

Dark color stained her son's cheeks. After one wild look, he bent his head as if hoping she couldn't see his face.

Laura sank wearily onto the coffee table in front of him. "Jake, don't you understand that this... compulsion is troubling? Can't you see why it worries me?"

After a moment he nodded.

"I'm going to take those magazines and catalogs."

His head came up fast enough to get him whiplash. "You can't—"

"I can and I will." She lifted a hand. "I won't throw them away yet. Recycle them," she corrected herself. "Not until we've talked to this new therapist. Instead, I'll be hiding them. I'm asking you now not to get any more. No buying, no picking up the catalogs wherever you have been."

His chocolate-brown eyes, the same color as Matt's, were so dilated they appeared black. Again, she felt a shudder of fear that she knew was really for him.

This was her fault. She'd let herself be lulled into complacency. Stopped the sessions with a counselor after a year because she didn't think they were doing any good, without understanding that she should have found another one. Jake had seemed to be doing so well. He was so young. She'd deceived herself that events had become blurred to him; he'd been too young to know what had really happened.

*I was wrong.*

"Your dad would be glad to know Ethan is spending time with you."

"He's trying to act like my dad and he isn't!" he said violently.

"No, but—" *He could be.* "He's been good to you," she said instead.

"He lied to me."

She knew better, but tried reason. "Did he say, 'Jake, I'll let you shoot my gun at the range in the next two weeks? Three weeks?'"

His sullen look said no, Ethan's promise hadn't included a time frame.

"You're old enough to be more patient than this, and to understand that you have to earn some privileges."

His shoulders jerked. "I don't care. I don't want to go with him."

Oh, God. This was definitely not the moment to say, *Oh, by the way, Ethan and I are dating, so he's going to be around whether you like it or not.*

Maybe she should cool things until… She didn't know when. Jake became more accepting? With him so troubled, was this the time to introduce the concept of Mom having a boyfriend? Oh, God, she didn't know, but— *I need him.*

*Jake needs him, too*, she told herself, and believed it, except that, clearly, Jake also resented Ethan.

"All right," she said, pushing herself to her feet, wishing she felt steadier. "Come with me."

He trailed her down the hall, thank heavens. Increasingly she'd asked herself: What could she do if someday he said no? He was almost as big as she was now. She had no doubt that in another year he'd shoot past her in height.

*Shoot.* The word made her wince. *Grow* past her.

He watched in dark silence as she hefted his mattress high enough to pull out the entire collection and dump it on the carpet. Then she straightened and looked at him. "Is this all of them?"

He thought about lying, she could tell, then apparently realized that he'd be in even bigger trouble if she actually searched his room. Without a word, he went to his closet, pulling down a box that held some once-loved childhood toys he hadn't wanted to get rid of. Laura shuddered at the sight of an issue of *Shooting Times* lying atop a well-worn Pooh bear.

She snatched it and several others and dumped them on the floor with the rest.

"Did you steal these?" she asked.

"No!" His outrage seemed genuine. "I have my allowance money!"

"Which I am suspending until I have more faith in you."

He glared. She glared right back, then scooped and gathered up the entire pile of slick magazines and catalogs.

"You won't throw them away?" he begged.

"For now, I won't."

"You mean, you still might?"

Her heart squeezed at the panic in his voice. He was willing to humble himself to protect this hideous, awful collection.

His pornography.

"We'll talk to the therapist about it," she said.

"Why can't I—?"

"Not another word. Go clean the kitchen."

She heard a couple of strangled sounds, but he apparently thought better of whatever protest he'd started to make. As in, *You were gonna do it because I was supposed to be at my gun safety class?*

Yeah, that one wouldn't have gone over well.

For the moment, she took the pile to her bedroom. She was stymied over where she could successfully hide them. Somewhere in the garage, maybe, but she'd wait until she was sure he was asleep to slip out there. For now, she dumped them in the middle of her bed, then went to the kitchen where she grabbed a plastic trash bag she took back to her room. She was happier once she couldn't see any of the covers.

Then she had a very quiet emotional breakdown as she remembered in graphic detail the past two times she'd seen a semi-automatic pistol that wasn't in a holster, as Ethan had worn his.

To kill himself, Matt had apparently sat down on the kitchen floor with his back to a wall. Because he hadn't liked the idea of falling off a chair? Or because this was the closest he could get to where Marco had died? She didn't know. He hadn't said in the brief note he'd left her. The gun had fallen away from Matt's hand as he slumped sideways. Blood had dripped from gun and wall both.

And then, of course, there was the one she had snatched from the hand of her five-year-old, who had been frozen staring, stupefied, at what was left of his best friend and cousin's head.

She sat on the edge of her bed and shook.

ETHAN CALLED LAURA as soon as he said goodbye to the last of his students and their parents in the parking lot outside the range. A last "thank you" rang out just as he pulled his door closed and reached for his phone.

Laura answered immediately, as if she'd been waiting with her own phone clutched in her hands. "Ethan?"

"Yeah, it's me," he said. "You okay?"

"No. Yes, of course I am. Just…" She let that trail off.

"How's Jake taking this?"

"He's mad and freaked and…" She stopped again. "I don't know. I used to be able to tell what he was thinking. Not being able to—" Her breathing was audible. "It freaks *me* out."

"Yeah, I can see why." Intensely focused on every tiny sound coming from the phone, Ethan stared straight ahead at the painted cinder-block wall of the range, a sickly mustard color under the sodium lamps. "Can I come over?" he asked.

"I think it might be better if you didn't. I don't want to antagonize him."

What the—? Ethan went rigid before he could reason with himself.

She was right; hearing Ethan's voice out in the living room or kitchen would cause the kid's resentment to boil. He'd lie there in bed wondering what the two of them were saying about him.

*So what?* was Ethan's immediate reaction. Let the boy stew. There was something even more seriously wrong with him than Ethan had suspected if he was now sleeping like a baby and *not* filled with anxiety and rage and a whole lot else.

"You going to cater to him?" he asked, a fraction of a second before thinking better of it.

"What's that supposed to mean?" she fired back.

"It means Jake is in deep shit, and he needs to know it. It means you shouldn't be tiptoeing around him."

"I'm not tiptoeing! I took his magazines away from me and broke it to him that he's going to start seeing a therapist Thursday. And that he isn't getting his allowance until I'm convinced he won't spend it on the next issue of *Gun Porno*."

His mouth quirked. As tart as she was sounding, she'd be mad if she could see him smiling.

"Okay," he said. "That sounds like a good start."

"Gee, thanks. Any other advice on parenting from someone who has never tried it?"

He wasn't smiling anymore. "Is that criticism for how I handled him?"

"No! But you don't have to sound so condescending, either!"

"I didn't mean to be—"

"Forget it." Snappish, she said, "Can we not talk about it tonight?"

He closed his eyes and leaned back against the headrest. "I'm sorry. Are we still on for lunch tomorrow?"

The silence was long enough to crank up his tension. Then, "I guess so," she said, sounding less than enthusiastic. "We do have to talk."

That wasn't what Ethan wanted to hear. Common sense told him not to jump on her words or tone right now, though. She was stressed, and had reason to be. What's more, she was a mother. Jake's problems and what to do about them had pressed on Ethan for the past two and a half hours, a weight he felt no matter what else he'd been doing or saying. They'd been pressing on her without relief for years. Plus, tonight she'd been left alone to face down the storm that was her son.

"Then I'll call you in the morning," he said, but knew that nothing was going to get in the way of him having lunch with her. Nothing. He swallowed, bumped his head a couple of times on the back of the seat, and said as gently as he could, "Go to bed,

Laura. Get some sleep. We knew this was coming to a head. Nothing all that bad happened."

"No." An odd sound might have been a hitch of breath, or a suppressed sob. "No, you're right. Thank you, Ethan. Good night."

He said good-night, too, and then she was gone, leaving him more unsettled than he'd been in a long time.

LAURA TALKED TO him over lunch the next day, but something was different. Off. She was reserved in a way he had yet to see, Ethan finally decided. Not unfriendly, but treating him more like an acquaintance than a man she'd passionately kissed. One she was supposed to be introducing to her son as her boyfriend.

He almost snorted at the word, even though he'd suggested it. He hadn't been a boy in a long time.

"Thank goodness I already had the appointment," she said. "I think I'd go nuts if I had to wait a week to get him in to see someone."

"The doctor who recommended this guy understands what the issue is?"

"Yes, apparently he—his name is Randall Lang, by the way—specializes in working with kids who've suffered a trauma. I haven't met him yet, but we have an hour and a half long appointment. The first half hour is just me and him." She made a face. "Jake won't like that, but tough. Then he talks to the two of us together, then with Jake alone."

She'd told him all this last night after dinner, before his early warning system had kicked in and he'd started wondering what Jake was up to. Ethan didn't say anything, though; she needed to talk, and he was glad to listen.

"Does Jake seem open to this?" he asked.

Momentarily, her expression revealed worry and despair. "I don't know. He sort of nodded when I asked if he understood this compulsion he has is worrisome."

Ethan hoped she knew that "sort of nodding" did not translate to agreement. "I still think at heart he's a good kid."

She flashed him a grateful look. "I do, too. But… I'm still scared."

"I don't blame you." He reached across the table and took her hand in his. "But you're doing what you can." He hesitated. "What did you do with his stash?"

"I sneaked out into the garage in the middle of the night and hid it in a box of Christmas ornaments."

"Do you have enough clutter in the garage that he won't find it right away?"

She made a tiny sound. "He's going to my sister's after school this week. I don't want him home alone."

Ethan waited.

"No. There aren't that many good hidey-holes out there, but I couldn't think of a great place in the house, either."

"Do you want me to take them?"

Hope dawned in her eyes, but she shut it down fast, shaking her head. "I promised him I wouldn't throw any of it away. That…we'd talk to the therapist and see what he thinks."

He grunted. "Boys do like guns and shooting things, and violence has an appeal. Has it occurred to you that some of his friends may share his interests?"

Laura looked aghast. "No! Oh, my God. How do I find out?"

"Do you let him play any of those shooter video games? Halo, say?"

"No!"

"He may be playing them at friends' houses."

"But…aren't they rated Mature?"

"Sure. That doesn't mean some of his buddies don't have big brothers who own games like that, or the parents don't pay any attention to ratings. You know that, Laura."

She appeared shell-shocked. Ethan didn't see her as naive, but she'd definitely been practicing denial.

"Oh, my God," she said again, sounding short of breath. "I need to call his friends' parents and make sure."

"Normally, I'd say it's not that big a deal for a boy." He ignored her glare. "Jake's case is different. I don't like the idea of him having the illusion of firing a lethal weapon. At his age, I don't know how he'd integrate what he's seeing on the screen with his memory of the real thing."

She exhaled as if someone—*he*—had punched her and bent forward slightly, crossing her arms as if to protect her vulnerable midsection.

"I'm sorry, Laura." He wanted to touch her, but he couldn't draw her out of her chair in the middle of a restaurant the way he could at home, and her body language didn't suggest she wanted to be touched anyway. That stung a little, but he pushed the knowledge away. "These are things you might want to talk to this counselor about. I don't know if you even want to isolate Jake from what's normal for other boys. I'm damn sure you can't succeed a hundred percent."

"No." Her whole face looked pinched. "I need to get back to work. I know this hasn't been fun, but thank you for listening."

"I'm available any time you need to talk." He made sure she could tell he meant it. "Middle-of-the-night panic attack, call me." Then he signaled the waitress and took out his credit card.

While they waited for it to be run, Laura perched on the edge of her seat, all but quivering with her readiness to get out of there. Worried, he watched her, not liking the way she evaded his gaze or the fact that she hadn't said, "Better be ready for your phone to start ringing at 2:00 a.m." In fact, he realized, she hadn't responded at all to the last thing he'd said.

There wasn't a whole lot of conversation of any kind as they left the restaurant or during the short drive back to her store. He kissed her, but briefly, gently, knowing she wasn't up to anything more… and suffering from an uneasy feeling she'd reject more. Him.

"You'll let me know how the counseling session goes?" he said as she reached for the door handle.

Her eyes fleetingly met his. "Oh! Yes, of course. I might wait until after Jake has gone to bed."

"Okay."

She hurried to the door, unlocked it and disappeared inside without so much as a glance back.

No invitation to dinner, either.

Maybe he was the one who had to make that move. Show up Saturday and say to Jake, "Let's work on those layups." Or maybe they needed to talk first.

Either option, he'd need to clear first with Laura. *Tomorrow night*, he told himself. He couldn't do anything until then.

Didn't mean getting his head back into his job was easy.

"I CAN SEE why you're alarmed," Dr. Randall Lang told her, his expression kind. "Jake obviously has some issues we need to work on, but from what you're telling me you've kept him well grounded, too. I'd be more concerned if he were having angry outbursts at school, getting into fights, even assaulting you when you insist on limits. We'd be facing a bigger challenge if you'd waited until he got into the teenage years. Taking action now is absolutely the right thing to do."

She had liked him immediately. He was young, maybe mid-thirties, wore chinos and a rumpled sports shirt with the sleeves rolled up, and had the lean athleticism of a runner or biker. A baseball sat on his cluttered desk. He'd insisted she call him Randall, and said he'd ask the same of Jake. She'd felt immediate relief, knowing Jake would respond best to someone young and "cool." What's more, along with an engaging smile and a relaxed style, Randall Lang projected calm, as if his aura had washed over hers.

Ethan could do that, too, except…his aura was different. Maybe it was the fact that she could never forget his capacity for violence. He wouldn't be able to do his job if he lacked the ability to switch gears in a millisecond from seemingly relaxed ease to intense mental and physical preparedness. She shivered every time she remembered how he'd exploded out of the house when he realized what Jake was up to.

Then, she'd been glad, but in retrospect she was scared by that glimpse of the man he was on the job.

*Not now.*

Jake had to be her focus.

"Do you deal with angry, violent teenage boys?" she asked.

Randall smiled. "Sure."

"Have you ever worked with a child who accidentally killed another one?"

His eyes held hers. "Yes. Accidents of all sorts can result in similar feelings of responsibility and guilt. And with the prevalence in gun ownership, tragedies like his are inevitable. I'm currently seeing one other boy who also shot and killed someone else by accident, and I've had other clients like Jake in the past."

They talked about Jake's magazine collection, and he advised holding off on shredding it for now. "We don't want to damage his sense of trust in you, and our goal is to reach a point where he'll either lose interest in those magazines or will conclude himself that they aren't healthy for him."

Eventually he went out and called Jake back to join them. No surprise, Jake slouched into a chair, hung his head and, in response to questions, mumbled monosyllabic replies. When Laura opened her mouth to say something to him, Randall gave her a slight head shake and she subsided. Of course he was right. Jake was shy and scared.

Liking the way Randall interacted with Jake, she ended up going out to the waiting room early, giving the two of them something like forty-five minutes alone together. She pretended to flip through a magazine, her tension level climbing, one nail-biting inch at a time. Part of her wanted desperately to be a fly on the wall. What if Jake was in there blaming her for his problems? Maybe she'd only deceived herself that they had a good relationship. His current resentment might have been simmering for ages and she'd been blind to it. She had this awful picture of herself dressed in a cheerleader uniform, bouncing and kicking and waving pompoms, Ms. Perky oblivious to the debacle happening on the field behind her.

*I'm not* that *bad.*

There was a momentary lull in her head, followed by a timid addendum: *Am I?*

No, damn it, she was a good parent! And she and Jake were a lot closer than most mothers and sons. She refused to believe anything different. So Dr. Randall Lang could *stuff it* if he decided to blame her, she decided, fury spilling through her.

Laughter from down the hall penetrated her absorption, and she squeezed her eyes shut. She was officially going nuts. That was the only explanation.

*I'm available any time you need to talk. Middle-of-the-night panic attack, call me.*

How about a late-afternoon panic attack? she thought ruefully. No, she couldn't call Ethan this minute. Whatever he'd said, right now he would be working. Heaven only knew who he was with. Besides, she wasn't alone, either. An older woman kitty-corner from her in the waiting area had scarcely looked up from a book since Laura sat down, while a very young woman seemed to be texting nonstop on her phone, her fingers flying.

*I'll call him later.*

Yes, but…

It was the *but* that shook her. *But*, it had been his gun Jake had gone after. *But*, he was a man who carried one day in and day out, just as Matt had. *But*, violence was a part of his life.

*But*…was getting involved with him smart, especially now?

*I don't know*, she thought miserably.

# CHAPTER TEN

"YOU HAVEN'T SAID much about the session today,"
Mom said in her bright, encouraging voice.

Much? More like nothing, Jake thought.

They were eating dinner, and she gave him this
big insincere smile. "I really liked Randall, didn't
you?"

He made the mistake of meeting her eyes, which
were so anxious he couldn't stand it. "I guess he's
okay."

"Did you have a good talk?"

Jake shrugged. *He* had hardly talked at all. Well,
not about guns or Dad or Marco. Mostly the guy
had rambled about sports and school and stuff he
enjoyed doing, and he lured Jake into admitting he
played basketball and baseball and his favorite subject in school was social studies because he especially liked history. The history part Mom probably
hadn't already told him, but Jake had no doubt she'd
given him a list titled My Son's Favorite Activities.

Once Randall mentioned the hunter safety class,
and Jake had mumbled something about it being

boring and he didn't want to hunt anyway. He *liked* animals.

"This Detective Winter who taught it. Is he a hunter?"

Jake had shaken his head. "He likes stuff like wind sailing and mountain climbing."

"Oh?" the guy asked, all innocence. "Why was he teaching the class, then?"

Like he didn't know. "Because he thought I'd like it." But that wasn't exactly right; it was more that Ethan had thought it would be good for him somehow, Jake didn't know how.

"Good guy?"

He'd bobbed his head, feeling a shaft of pain because Ethan had been really mad and probably didn't like him anymore. And it was his fault.

*Everything* was his fault, whatever Mom said.

"Your mother says Detective Winter is a heck of a basketball player." The counselor or psychologist or whatever he was sounded admiring. "She said he had the chance to go pro."

He'd mumbled something about how Ethan maybe could have.

At the end, walking Jake out, Randall laid a hand on his shoulder and said, "It's good to start getting to know you," and Jake had stared at him for a minute thinking they didn't know each other *at all*. But sure. Okay. The guy was getting paid to say things like that.

Now Jake looked up at his mother. "I don't want to go every week. It's not going to do any good."

She dropped the fake smile and her eyes got steely. "Not going isn't an option. And you'll get out of it what you put in it."

She always said stuff like that. Like always, he ignored it.

"You must have told him about Ethan," he challenged her. "How come?"

"How could I not, when Ethan's the one who found you at the gun show, and taught the gun safety class—"

"*Hunter* safety."

"—*and* it was his gun you went after," she went on, as though he hadn't said anything.

He got this churning feeling in his stomach. "It wasn't his fault."

"I didn't say it was."

"You *sound* like you think so."

She looked at him for a minute, and he could see her trying to decide what to say. "I'm responsible for the fact that he was having dinner at our house. And I knew he carried a gun on the job and probably had it locked in the car."

"So?"

"So, you knew that, too. It was a…temptation. In the past, I've never invited a friend over who was a gun owner."

He stared at her in shock. "He's not a gun *owner*. He's a cop! He *has* to carry one."

"I realize that's true," his mother said, sounding prissy, "but nonetheless…"

"You don't want him around anymore, do you?" Jake felt sick. Then he felt even worse when he remembered the last expression he'd seen on Ethan's face. "Not that he'll want to be around after what I did. So I guess it doesn't matter, does it?" He jumped up so fast, his chair fell over. That made him so mad, he kicked it, then ran for his bedroom.

Inside his nose burned, like he was going to cry, but he didn't let himself. *My fault, my fault, my fault.*

*Why did I do it?* he cried inside, where no one else could hear, and didn't know the answer any more than he ever had.

It had been so cool, having Ethan for a friend. Sort of a friend. Why did he have to start acting like a father instead of a friend? Like he could give orders and assign punishment and be disappointed in Jake? Why couldn't he have just kept playing basketball with him and hanging out and taken him to the range to shoot the way he *promised*?

And why, somewhere deep inside, did Jake wish Ethan *was* his father?

But that answer, he knew: because Ethan was sort of like his real father, only better. Stronger. *He* wouldn't have left his gun lying around where a little kid could get to it. *He* wouldn't have killed himself, either, without thinking how his son would blame himself.

And that made Jake feel awful, because he had a father who'd loved him. And maybe he wasn't perfect, but Jake bet Ethan wasn't, either. So he shouldn't pretend he was, and make Jake want... something.

To his horror, he realized hot tears were running down his face. He flipped over and buried his face in his pillow so Mom wouldn't see if she came in.

*My fault, my fault, my fault.*

PULLING UP IN front of Laura's house, Ethan felt a lot of the same apprehension he had that first day, when he'd had a sullen boy at his side and had known how unhappy the mother would be when she found out what her kid had been up to.

Now...damn. He had no idea whether Jake would welcome him or not. The part that really got him was that he was just as uncertain whether Laura wanted him there or not.

Thursday night, when she called to tell about the counseling session, he'd said, "I'd like to come over and spend some time with Jake Saturday, if you don't have other plans."

She was quiet just long enough to tweak his insecurities, then said, "Jake's hardly talking to me, so I don't know whether he'll be happy to see you or not. But, if you're willing, it's worth a try."

And, yes, she'd offered him lunch, too, but the reserve he'd sensed the other day was still there.

The only positive was that after a week of drizzle, it wasn't raining today.

He muttered a profanity and got out.

It was Laura who came to the door. Her hair was pulled into a ponytail that, along with her freckles, made her look about seventeen years old. Old jeans and a shapeless T-shirt were paint-splattered.

He raised his eyebrows. "The deck railing?"

Her look of polite inquiry dissolved when she scrunched up her nose. "What else? I am going to be so glad to be done. I'm aiming to do a coat this morning and, if the rain holds off, a second one this afternoon."

"Jake know I'm coming?" he asked as he stepped inside.

She closed the door. "Yes. He looked sort of…" Her hesitation was obvious. "Shocked," she finally concluded.

Ethan shook his head. "He and I have some things to get straight on. Did he think I was dumping him because he did something that disappointed me?"

"You looked pretty mad." The restraint in her voice cranked his tension a little tighter. And, yeah, made him mad.

"You never get mad at him?"

"Of course I do!"

They pretty much glared at each other for a minute, until they both heard Jake's bedroom door open.

"Mom? Oh. Uh, hi."

Ethan gave the boy a crooked smile. "Hey. You ready to play some ball?"

The expression of naked hope on his face reminded Ethan uncomfortably of the one he'd seen over lunch Monday on Laura's face.

"Yeah," Jake said. "I mean, if you want."

Ethan had to clear his throat. It took an effort not to look at Laura. "Of course I want. Big question is, do we go to the school or use your home court?"

Turned out, Jake didn't know if anyone else was going to be at the school, and he peered dubiously out the front window at the gray sky and said they could get out of the rain quicker if they stayed at the house.

Ethan laughed. "Grab your ball, then."

Laura backed away. "I'd better go paint quick, too."

Jake's skill level had regressed a little, maybe because the rain had kept him inside, maybe because he'd chosen to sulk in his bedroom instead of getting out there this week.

Ethan limited conversation to a few remarks like "Loose in the knees, remember?" and "Good one" until they were both warm and had just completed a vigorous game of Horse—which, Ethan having handicapped himself, Jake had won.

Holding the ball, he asked, "How'd the counseling session go?"

The flash of anger took him aback. "Didn't Mom already tell you?"

"Her perspective and yours might be polar opposites," Ethan said mildly.

The kid's shoulders sagged. "Sorry," he muttered. "It's just...she keeps asking me, and I wish she wouldn't."

"I probably shouldn't say this, but you know you don't have to tell her."

Jake's brown eyes widened. "That's not what *she* thinks."

Ethan allowed himself a grin. "You're wrong. She knows it won't work if you don't feel like you can say things to the counselor and be confident none of it will get back to her. She's just worried about you and wanting to fix everything. You know that, right?"

"Yeah, yeah." He sprang forward and stole the ball, sending it up in an arc that shocked them both by catching nothing but net. "Hey!" he exclaimed.

Ethan jogged forward and retrieved the ball, then offered a high five. "Good job. That was from behind our free-throw line." He'd measured and they had determined that one of the seams in the concrete was close enough to the free-throw distance.

If only for this moment, Jake was high on himself. "It was, wasn't it?"

"So, the counseling," Ethan reminded him.

"Do I have to tell *you*?" The question was more honest than spiteful.

Ethan shook his head. "Nope. Not a word if you don't want."

"Oh." Jake watched as Ethan drove in for an over-the-shoulder layup, dribbled it back out and shot from the foot of the driveway. *Swish.*

"The guy seemed okay," Jake said unexpectedly. "His name is Randall. He's a doctor, but he said to call him by his first name. Like with you."

Ethan nodded.

"I think he wanted to know about you." This sounded shy.

"Because he wonders what kind of influence I am on you?" A thought struck him. "Or because the gun was mine?"

"I don't know." That came out worried. "It was me, not you. Why would anyone blame you?"

Ethan shook his head, but he was wondering— No, damn it, he knew. Laura blamed him. She'd remembered everything threatening that he represented.

"Are you upset with me?" he asked.

Jake shook his head. "It was me." And then he mumbled something that Ethan only half caught.

"What was that?"

The boy twitched a little, and then mumbled it again. Ethan just waited. Finally Jake yelled, "It's always me! Okay?"

"No." Ethan set the basketball down on the grass and walked over to the boy. He gripped his upper arms and said, "Look at me."

The tumult in those brown eyes made Ethan's chest constrict. Defiance and pain, old and new.

"This is the kind of thing you need to talk to that counselor about. But I'm going on record right now to say it's *not* always you. What you did Tuesday night, that was on you. You chose to do something you knew you weren't supposed to. You need to take responsibility for your own wrongdoing." He held that wild stare. "But your cousin dying was *not your fault*. You may not like me saying this, but the truth is your father was to blame."

"I'm the one who thought it would be fun to play with the gun."

"You were five years old. Jake, Monday at school take a look at the kindergarteners. There must be some who ride your bus, or you see them going out to recess."

He swallowed hard and nodded.

"They are little kids. That's how old you were. All you'd ever done was play. You had no idea what could really happen if you pulled that trigger. How could you?"

"Dad said never to pick it up," he whispered.

"That's good enough when a parent is talking about something breakable. A glass vase that was a Christmas present from Grandma. If you pick it up anyway and it gets broken, you feel really crummy and next time maybe you steer away from things Mom or Dad tell you not to pick up."

Jake was listening.

"A handgun is a deadly weapon. Your dad carried a Glock that didn't even have a safety. It didn't allow for an 'oh, oops,' for you to learn a lesson. He didn't mean anything bad to happen, either, but he was the adult. A law enforcement officer, no less. He screwed up. It doesn't mean you can't love him, that he wasn't a good man. But that one terrible thing was his fault."

Tears filled those brown eyes. "I never meant…"

"I know you didn't." Ethan pulled him into an embrace. As the boy sobbed against him, he knew he was crying, too.

"If I hadn't done that, he'd be alive!" Jake wailed.

*Damn you, Matt, wherever you are.*

"Jake." Ethan gave him a small shake. "Stop. Listen."

The shudders and sobs slowed, and finally Jake pulled back and swiped furiously at his cheeks.

"Two things. Let's change what you just said. If your dad had kept his gun locked up so you never got your hands on it, he'd still be alive. *He* made the mistake, not you." Man, he hoped this was sinking in.

Jake stared at him, seemingly mesmerized, eyes red, wet and swollen.

"The other possibility is, it happened, and your dad lived with the consequences. They would have been bad. Probably he'd have lost his job. From what your mom says, he was pretty devastated by the way his parents and brothers and sisters turned their backs on him. But he still had you and your mom. Again, *he* made a choice. You didn't make it for him. If you could have, if he'd asked you, you would have begged him to stay around, wouldn't you?"

Jake's teeth chattered, but he nodded.

"You are not to blame, Jake. Not for any of it. I know it's hard to convince yourself, but I'm also sure your mother has told you the same thing."

He kept nodding, as if he couldn't stop.

"That's because it's true. Not because she wants to protect you from the knowledge that you did something bad. You didn't. The mistake was your father's. Only his. Do you hear me?"

Tears ran freely down Jake's lean face, so like his father's. "I wish—" he licked away tears "—he hadn't."

"Yeah." Damn. Ethan grabbed the hem of his T-shirt and wiped his own eyes and face. "I wish he hadn't, too."

Except then he'd never have met Laura and Jake, or, if he had, the circumstances would have been completely different. If he'd felt that jolt of attraction, of recognition, the first time Laura smiled at him, he'd have had to pretend to himself he hadn't. He would never have had the hope of making these two his family.

But seeing the depth of misery on this boy's face, he knew if he could wipe out that one horrifically stupid thing Matt Vennetti had done, he would. Of course he would. He'd give Jake back his father, Laura back her husband, Matt the life and job he'd loved.

He knew something else: if Matt had truly loved his wife and son, he'd want them to get past this. He'd want someone to take care of them, love them. He'd be pissed as hell at his family, not to mention at himself.

Ethan blinked, realizing suddenly that some of the moisture he was feeling wasn't tears. He looked up, and his face was bathed with cool drizzle.

He wrapped a long arm around Jake's neck, gave him a quick, hard hug, and said, "I think we just ran out of luck. What say we go in? I'll run interference with your mom if you want to go take a shower and change into dry clothes."

"Oh." Exposing a skinny, pale torso, the kid imitated him and used his shirt to scrub his face. "Yeah. Okay. I don't want Mom to see me."

"I figured." Ethan smiled ruefully as they started for the front door. "I didn't mean this to get so heavy. But I want you to think about what I said, okay? I'm telling you the truth. None of it was your fault."

"Except for sneaking out and unlocking your glove compartment so I could see your gun," Jake said as if by rote.

"*Hold* my gun. *Seeing* implies no touching."

Jake made a face at him. "Yeah, yeah."

Ethan laughed and lightly cuffed him at the exact

moment he heard the sliding door open. "Uh-oh. Better run."

Looking alarmed, Jake fled.

LAURA GOT ONE good glimpse of her son's distraught, tearstained face before he rushed past her and into his bedroom. That look was enough to rouse the mama bear in her.

She advanced toward Ethan, not caring that her hair was probably hanging in wet strings and she'd splattered paint on her face. "What did you say to him?" she hissed, in a voice she hoped Jake wouldn't hear through his bedroom door.

The lingering laughter on Ethan's face vanished; his expression shut down faster than she'd known to be possible. After a minute, he said, "Nice assumption."

"You were laughing at him."

He stared at her for the longest time, something moving through his eyes she didn't understand.

And then he shook his head, his lip curling. "I'm outta here." Just like that, he turned and headed toward the front door.

"What do you mean, you're *out* of here?" On a burst of alarm—*oh, no, what did I do?*—Laura chased after him.

"You heard me." He paused with the door opened and looked at her one more time. "Tell Jake he can call me anytime. Assuming you wouldn't rather he not see me or talk to me." His laugh felt as if it was stripping skin from her flesh. "And to think I wondered why Matt's friends in the department weren't there for you."

And then he was gone, the door closing sharply in her face.

Frozen in shock, Laura gaped at it.

"What did you *do*?" her son cried, behind her.

Her teeth wanted to chatter. She clenched them, hearing the deep-throated engine start out on the street, the sound receding a moment later. Not fast—Ethan was too safety-conscious, too self-controlled, to speed no matter how angry he was.

Jake barreled into her, knocking her aside. "Get out of my way! I have to talk to him!" His voice was thick with tears.

"He's gone," Laura heard herself say in a stunned voice.

He wrenched open the door nonetheless to look out at the street, then spun to fix her with an agitated, accusing stare. "Why would you do that?"

She felt remote, as if she were dying but still had a need to understand what was happening.

"I saw your face. You've been sobbing. He had to have said something."

"He said none of it was my fault!" Jake yelled. "That it was Dad's! And I cried, okay? Because I always think it was *me*, that I killed Marco and Dad, too. Only I could tell Ethan meant what he said, that he really thinks it wasn't me."

A sound escaped her throat. It might have been a whimper.

"And now he's gone and he won't come back and it's *your* fault!" Anger and bewilderment apparent, he turned and ran for his room again. When the door slammed, she flinched.

She retreated a step, and when she felt the wall at her back, she slid down it until she was sitting, knees drawn up, arms wrapping them. As small as she could become. As small as she felt inside.

Despair poured through her, and she didn't even try to block it. Her mind stayed blank for a very long time.

When thoughts finally started edging into it, she could only catch sidelong peeks at them before they whisked out of sight.

Even as she fell in love with him, a gentle, patient, strong man, she had also held him responsible for everything she associated with guns: hideous violence, terror, gut-wrenching grief she hadn't thought she'd survive.

Her stunned self thought, *I knew he wouldn't say anything hurtful to Jake. I did. So why—?*

Because even as he'd become her refuge, even though she had no reason to think he'd ever actually shot anyone, he also represented everything she had rejected. Men who carried guns. Who might *someday* use them. Who tempted Jake to become something she feared.

He'd found Jake at the gun show and cared enough

to bring him home and talk to her. But he'd been at the gun show in the first place.

*I never asked him why.*

Out of consideration for her, he never again carried a weapon into her house—but she knew it was there just outside in his vehicle, available for him to put it back on his hip the minute he left her house. She was always conscious of its existence.

*He's like Matt.*

But her conscious self knew he wasn't. They did the same job. That's where the resemblance ended.

*You* think *that's where it ends*, whispered the voice in her head that represented all her fears.

She saw that last expression on his face, shock, disbelief, hurt and bone-deep anger, and knew how bad she'd blown it. And she couldn't even lie to herself and believe she'd said one hateful thing in a burst of fear for Jake. No. She'd spent the week working herself up to being convinced Ethan wasn't good for Jake.

*Or me.*

When the truth was, despite all Jake was going through right now, Ethan might be his salvation. No one but Laura had ever been as good to him, and there were things she, a woman and his mother, couldn't be to a boy on the cusp of adolescence. Ethan had been exactly what Jake needed, at a time he needed him most.

*And I just drove him away.*

The most pathetic part of all was the knowledge

that followed: she was curled in a fetal position on the floor not because she'd driven away the man who could be her son's salvation, but because she'd driven away the man *she* needed. *The man I'm falling in love with.*

Except…he scared her, too, and she'd spent too long attuned to the frightened part of her who could not survive the same kind of agony again. Who thought it was better to hide than to open herself up to life and the risk and possibility of loss that implied.

She listened to the silence in the house and thought drearily, *I ought to go talk to Jake*, but didn't have it in herself, not yet.

And then she thought, *It's not Jake I need to talk to*, but wondered if Ethan would even open his door to her.

ETHAN DID, BUT only because she'd called and begged.

Goddammit, he didn't want to see her right now. Not yet, if ever again. He was too raw, more devastated than he'd been by the time he and Erin split up.

He snorted at the thought, pacing the limited confines of his living room. It wasn't like what Laura said should have come as a shock. He'd known she was pulling back, seen accusation in her eyes. *He* was synonymous with all the evil guns represented to her, and, goddamn it, he would never apologize to anyone for what he did for a living.

"Shit," he said aloud, knowing she'd be there any

minute and wishing he hadn't answered when she called and asked timidly if she could come over to talk to him.

He'd succumbed because he so hated hearing that timidity, the diminishment of a voice that was usually confident. He'd have felt like an asshole if he'd said, "Sorry, don't want to talk to you." So he'd reluctantly given her his address and said he'd be there. Now he was on edge, his nerves sensitized as he waited.

The knock, when it came, was timid, too.

Ethan groaned, scrubbed a hand through his hair and went to let her in.

She'd showered and changed clothes since he saw her, although at the sight of flecks of paint in her hair he felt a flicker of something that would have been amusement and tenderness if he hadn't been so mad and hurt.

She'd missed a spot of white paint just below her ear, too.

Jaw tight, he stepped back. Her gaze skated over his face, and then she sidled past him.

Ethan closed the door and faced her, arms crossed and, he suspected, expression hard.

Laura rushed into her speech. "'I'm sorry' may not be good enough, but I have to say it anyway."

He shook his head. "It's not even the point. The truth is you've painted me with the same brush as your husband. I get it. I hoped we could get past that, but we can't. I'm especially sorry for Jake's sake—"

"Please!" she cried, her eyes huge and luminous. "Please listen."

Ethan huffed out a breath. Why was she putting them through this?

Wringing her hands, she took whatever sound had come out for assent. "I was getting past it. I was." She swallowed. "Until…I got scared. That's all. Do you know what it was like, hearing that gunshot and running into the house thinking it's got to be okay because nobody screamed or is crying or anything, only that was because Marco was dead and *couldn't* scream and Jake was catatonic?"

Oh, hell. Yes. He'd seen enough trauma in his years on the job to be able to imagine that scene all too vividly. The dead little boy, and the shocked one standing over him, his hands sagging as he held on to a huge heavy weapon that he hadn't understood.

Ethan took a step closer to her.

"And then—" She faltered, bit her lip. "And then Matt."

In her brief pause, all Ethan's anger evaporated.

"I was so angry, so hurt, so lost." All the pain she'd felt was in a voice that was too soft, as if she had rolled over to expose her underbelly. "How could I do it all by myself? Only I did." She let out something like a sob, although her eyes remained dry. "I thought we were all right, except that day you showed up with Jake, I had to face the fact that we weren't. That I'd failed."

"Laura." Her name was all he could force through a throat that had closed.

"You gave me hope. Not just for Jake's sake. For mine. I have trusted you. I have. Except…getting past my fears is *hard*." Tears that still hadn't fallen filled her voice. "You can't know what it's like. I need you…I need you to understand that sometimes my doubts get to me. I haven't seen Jake's face look like that since he was a little boy, and everything rushed over me. And…and…"

"Damn it, Laura." He took the last step needed to close the distance between them, and gathered her into his arms. For a long moment, she stayed stiff. "You don't have to do this," he said hoarsely. "I do understand. You don't have to grovel. I got my feelings hurt, and I lashed out. *I* was the jackass."

"No." She tipped her head back and searched his face with desperate eyes. "No, it was me."

He gave a ragged laugh. "You sound like Jake."

"He told me you said none of it was his fault. He could tell you meant it." She sounded shaken. "I think…he almost believes it's true, because you said it."

"Does that bother you? Because you've said the same thing and he didn't believe you?"

"Of course not! Do you know what a miracle it would be if he could really, deep down, convince himself he wasn't to blame for any of it?"

He gently squeezed her nape, and felt her body start to soften. This close, he could see every shadow in eyes darkened to navy right now, every quiver of her mouth.

"Do you know he thinks it's his fault Matt killed himself?" he asked.

Her throat worked convulsively. "Yes. At least, I guessed. I didn't want to destroy Matt in his eyes. You know? A boy ought to be able to believe his father was strong, but what Matt did—"

"Was inexcusable." Ethan knew he sounded harsh and didn't like seeing the shock on her face, but this had to be said as many times as necessary, to her *and* Jake. "You were right to be angry. When life got hard, he opted out. He abandoned the two of you in the worst possible way. That doesn't mean he wasn't a great guy in a lot of ways, and that Jake shouldn't be encouraged to remember what was good about his father. And maybe this wasn't my call, but I think it's a hell of a lot better for Jake to understand that his father screwed up big-time— *and* let him down big-time—than for him to blame himself."

For a minute he thought she'd argue. Her eyes revealed everything she felt, and, at that moment, it was too much.

But finally she said, "Yes," and tucked her head under his chin, letting herself lean against him, as if she'd lost the strength to stand independently. Maybe only for a minute—but right now, she needed him.

Ethan laid his cheek on her head and closed his

eyes, but there was something else he had to know before this went any further.

He drew back a little, until she raised her head enough to meet his eyes.

"Laura, is that why you're here?" His voice was a little rough, a little deeper than usual. "Because you've decided maybe I'm good for Jake after all?"

"Well…partly. I mean, of course—" Color stained her cheeks, and for a moment her gaze fell. But then she was courageous enough to let him see everything. "No. I'm here because of me."

Ethan made a ragged sound and kissed her.

# CHAPTER ELEVEN

FOR AN INSTANT she was passive, feeling a rush of gratitude as much as anything. He'd forgiven her. She could hardly believe it. But the urgency of his touch was like a swig of whiskey chasing a sip of cool water. Heat licked through her, liquid fire. She rose on tiptoe and flung her arms around Ethan's neck, parting her lips to let him in.

He groaned and lifted her, turning in a slow circle as he took her mouth with devastating gentleness. His tongue stroked and teased and asked.

She answered wordlessly: *yes, yes, yes*. It was like a fever, snatching her between one breath and the next. Fear that she'd lost him transformed into passion. She'd never felt this astonishing need to rub against a man, to touch him, to try to climb under his skin. Self-consciousness, any sense of shame, were lost as she plastered herself as close as she could get, whimpered and rocked.

He wrenched his mouth away. "Laura."

She cried out in protest.

"Laura, can you stay?"

Stay? She struggled to understand. All night? It was only afternoon. Of course not. *Oh.*

"I left Jake at my sister's."

His arms tightened convulsively around you. "I want you."

"Yes" was all she could manage.

He hustled her to his bedroom. All she really saw was the enormous bed. King-size, she realized, but of course a man his height needed the length. It had been untidily made, she saw, as in a duvet yanked up to partially cover the pillows.

The bed made what they were about to do real, cooling her fever ever so slightly. She had a cramp of unease. Did she even remember how to make love?

But suddenly she didn't care. He knew. She wanted him so desperately. Maybe remembering wouldn't help anyway. Making love with Ethan wouldn't be the same as anything she'd done before.

She bit her lip and turned her head to see that he was watching her. Holding himself completely still, waiting for her.

"Cold feet?" His voice was husky, the tension in his body language telling her he thought she'd chickened out.

Didn't he know she was way too far gone for that? Needy and aching, she skimmed her fingertips along his rough jaw. "Nerves, but no second thoughts."

He snatched her up and fell with her onto the bed. She thought she heard a "Thank God" on the way down, but didn't process it. How could she, when, his weight only partially caught on his elbows, he pressed her into the depths of the duvet and mattress? His big hands framed her face and he took her mouth in biting kisses, as if he was as starving for her as she was for him.

Now his hips were rocking, and he'd positioned himself where it felt the best. Her thighs separated and she pushed up in an instinctive effort to take him inside her. She slid her hands under his shirt, too, and explored his broad back. Muscles bunched beneath her hands, and she traced the pads of muscle that bordered his spine. His skin was smooth and hot, and she kneaded as she went, wringing some groans from him.

At last he rolled, even as she tried to hold on to him until she saw him sit up and yank his shirt over his head. The next second, he had hers off as fast.

His eyes went darker. "So pretty," he said hoarsely. He touched the simple front clasp of her bra with one fingertip, making her shiver with anticipation, and then slid that finger between her breasts instead. Teasing. Then he laid both hands over her breasts and gently lifted and squeezed, before making a rough sound as if *he'd* lost patience and opening her bra so that her breasts spilled out.

She hardly saw him move, it was so fast. He closed his mouth over one breast and suckled, giving her a stab of astonishing pleasure as she looked helplessly at his dark head. She lifted a hand and slipped her fingers into his hair, the coarse silk sliding between her fingers as she pressed his head closer.

He moved to the other breast, circling her nipple with his tongue, nipping lightly, sucking in a way that had her hips rising and falling.

"Please. I want— Ooh," she moaned.

He looked up, eyes almost black, his mouth damp and a little swollen. "Do you know how beautiful you are? I've wanted you since the minute I set eyes on you."

"Me, too," she whispered, and then remembered the first glimpse, when she'd been so scared for Jake, when the big gun riding at Ethan's hip had loomed so frighteningly. "Maybe the second time."

He laughed, and unbuttoned and unzipped her jeans. He made a sound of appreciation at the skimpy peach-colored panties he found beneath, but peeled them off with the jeans. She'd already lost one shoe; the other dropped when he reached her feet. She was left wearing socks and a bra that was spread wantonly open. His gaze drifted over her, the heat in his eyes erasing her momentary self-consciousness.

"Your skin is so white." His big hand spanned her rib cage as he explored. "So soft."

Laura looked her fill, too, at a powerful chest dusted with brown hair that arrowed down to the waist of his jeans. She touched him, too, but he backed off so that he could take off her socks. The way he encompassed each foot in turn in his hands made her toes curl in pleasure that grew in power as he moved up her legs, squeezing, stroking, until he reached her ultrasensitive inner thighs and she heard herself making small sounds that ought to embarrass her but somehow didn't.

And then, oh, finally, he was touching her where she needed to be touched. She responded helplessly, but she wanted—

"Not by myself," she begged. "Take your pants off."

"Yeah." His voice was almost unrecognizable, his face taut. "God." He pushed himself off the bed and shucked his jeans and gray knit boxers, staying bent for a moment.

Shoes, she thought, hearing a thump, then a softer one.

But he had something in his hand when he stood. Her eyes widened. "Oh, thank goodness. I didn't think—" She forgot the condom as she took in the sight of *him*, tall, built long but powerful, his erection…impressive.

His movements were jerky as he ripped the packet open and sheathed himself before coming down beside her, tugging her half atop him and kissing her. Her momentary alarm vanished, lost in the exquisite sensations his mouth and roving hands brought. He was almost…leisurely now, as if he wanted to savor instead of taking greedily.

She was the one who got greedy and straddled

him, rising above him and trying awkwardly to cant her hips so that he'd fit inside her.

Ethan said something, she didn't know what, and flipped her, pushing inside by the time her back came down on the bed. It was almost uncomfortable, just for a minute, but so good, too. She told him, breathlessly, and he said, "Yes." That was all, but his face was cast in lines of torment and lust and tenderness as he began to move. Deep, slow, then faster, harder.

He set a rhythm that felt so perfectly *right*, her body tightened, tightened until she didn't think she could bear it—and then imploded. Holding on tight, she called his name, felt the vibration of a groan and then he went rigid as he buried himself deep one last time, throbbing inside her.

He came down with some of his weight on one shoulder, but she reveled in the feel of him, heavy on top of her. The hammer of his heartbeat, the musky scent of man, the connection. *Never move*, she begged silently, keeping her arms tight around him.

HE SAID THE right things. He thought he had anyway. Laura looked grateful, which Ethan hated.

They had made love a second time then showered together. She'd set off to pick up Jake, and he had met them at the house, after which he took them out to dinner.

They'd all been subdued, presumably each for

a different reason. Ethan suspected Jake was embarrassed about his breakdown. He was a boy; he'd likely absorbed the macho message that boys don't cry. Then there was the aftermath: Ethan had no idea what he and Laura had said to each other, either after he'd stomped out or when she picked him up to bring him home.

Laura…well, he wasn't sure what she was thinking, either. She'd gone back to being shy with him. Could she be embarrassed by her passionate response to him? God, he hoped not. Knowing she wanted him desperately enough to shed her inhibitions was a major ego boost. He'd never had sex that good. He wanted to keep having it.

How they'd manage, given that she had a kid, he had no idea. It wouldn't be happening as often as he'd like, that was for sure. Not unless—

But he wasn't ready to go there. And that was what had him staying quiet, a little wary. Because understanding and forgiveness was one thing, confidence another. He wanted to think Laura could overcome her fears enough to truly accept who he was and what he did for a living, but he wasn't sure he believed it would happen. She had a lot to overcome. He'd try to be patient. But the way he'd felt when she turned on him… He didn't know how many times he could come back from that.

He'd also discovered something about himself that shouldn't have been a surprise, but still was. On the job, he took the risks he had to. He'd never had a problem with it. Off the job—a high adrenaline lifestyle wasn't for him. He was competitive, or he wouldn't have been the athlete he had been; he still enjoyed being active. But he didn't jump out of airplanes or do any kind of extreme sports, and relationships fraught with tension weren't for him. Passionate highs, he could go for; passionate fights or icy silences, no. That last year with Erin had been miserable beyond belief. Every day, he'd had to brace himself before he went home, never knowing what her mood would be, what new accusations she'd throw at him, whether she'd be sulking, or vivacious and expecting him to respond as if yesterday she hadn't been sulking.

Maybe his parents had had some tough times they'd hidden from him and his sister. He couldn't be sure. But what he remembered was his mother happy when Dad came in the door, kissing him first thing, giving him time to unwind if he needed it. When things had gone bad at work, Ethan would hear them talking quietly. He used to get embarrassed at how often he'd walked in on them cuddling, or Mom sitting on Dad's lap.

Dad had listened to her, too. Now that he could compare them to other couples he knew, he saw that they had a remarkably balanced relationship. They were partners, there for each other, happiest when they were together.

And, damn it, that was what he wanted. He wanted it with Laura, but he didn't like this new tension he felt. First time around, he'd jumped in without checking to see how deep the water was, and he'd gone under; this time, he'd inch his way in.

No hurry to do the meet-the-parents or sister and brother-in-law thing. Jake complicated their relationship enough. It was pretty obvious Laura *hadn't* told him she and Ethan had started anything, and that was fine, Ethan decided. Better, maybe.

Through dinner, Jake kept watching them as if he did sense undercurrents, but Ethan couldn't imagine that, at his age, the boy could read sexual cues. Laura's lips did still look a little puffy, and one cheek had been abraded by his beard. Ethan winced at that sight. Note to self: shave next time.

Ethan had suggested pizza again so they'd have the distraction of arcade games first, and a relatively noisy environment while they ate. He got Jake talking some about his classes, and then told a couple of stories making fun of himself from his first year on patrol. Laura told them about the store's efforts to head off credit card fraud, and about how incredibly comfy the new line of mattresses were.

She gave her son a laughing glance. "I swear, if not for the burden of being a mother, I'd have locked myself in after closing and spent the night on that bed."

"You would not!"

"Why not?" she teased. "I had a great bed, a faux fur throw, amazing pillows, a lamp and a book in my purse. What more could I want?"

Ethan was laughing by this time. "Dinner?"

"I could have ordered in."

"Your customers might have been a little disconcerted to find crumbs on the bed when they tried it out."

"Yeah!" Jake chimed in.

"I didn't stay, did I?" She made a face. "Usually I don't covet what we sell that much, but the bed…"

Huh. He'd have to go try it out, Ethan thought. Maybe down the line…

No. Slow and easy, remember? And, hey, his mattress had worked out just fine this afternoon. He suppressed a grin at the memory, and then saw Jake eyeing him suspiciously.

*Yeah, kid, if only you knew,* he thought in amusement.

Now Laura was giving him a minatory look, as if she'd read his mind. Her fault for raising the subject of beds.

On the drive back to their house, Jake said suddenly, "Are you coming in when we get home?"

Ethan glanced into the rearview mirror. "Probably not. We've had a good time, haven't we?"

"Oh." The boy went silent.

With tomorrow being Sunday, Ethan wanted to suggest they do something together, but it would be smarter to back off a little. He couldn't expect Laura to make the next move, though; he kind of thought it was now his turn. Still, he wanted to see how the wind blew.

"My sister and her family are in town this week-end," he said, which was true. When he'd gone over—was it just this morning?—he'd half intended to invite Laura and Jake to Sunday dinner at his parents' tomorrow. He felt the tug of temptation now, but resisted it. "You two have plans?"

"Boring stuff," Laura said brightly. "Grocery shopping, laundry, housecleaning, bills. And home-work, right, Jake?"

From the backseat came an "Oh, yippee."

Her laugh sounded a little forced.

*Want to ditch all that and come meet my family?*

It hovered on the tip of his tongue, but he needed to feel a lot more sure of her than he was before going there.

He was both relieved and sorry to be coming up on their house. He signaled and pulled into the driveway behind her car.

"Thanks for dinner, Ethan," Laura said, promptly opening her door. "I think I'm falling behind on the meal count. I owe you a few."

She didn't say, *Especially since you didn't stay for lunch today.* She didn't have to.

"Ask and I'm your man." Poor phrasing, and it came out sounding hoarse, but he meant it.

She'd hopped out, but now looked back in at him, her hand on the door. "Monday?" she said tenta-tively, hope on her face.

He couldn't imagine she loved cooking after a long day at work, but that didn't keep him from an immediate, "If you mean it, we're on. Unless," he began to add, but she finished for him.

"Something comes up." She rolled her eyes, but humorously, and there was no edge in her voice. "I understand. I'm usually home by five-thirty. Anytime after that."

They said their goodbyes, and he didn't back out until they had disappeared inside and he saw lights come on.

"So, TELL ME about your week." Randall leaned back in his chair, lifting one leg and clasping his hands around the knee. Jake wasn't stupid. He knew what the guy was trying to say with his body. *We're friends, just talking.*

Uh-huh. Sure. Slouched low on the sofa, Jake stared at his feet. "I didn't shoot anybody," he said disagreeably.

"I think I'd have heard about it if you had. Okay. Let's try this. Tell me one bad thing about your week, one good."

"It rained all week so I couldn't do anything outside." Which was a bummer when it was practically June. What if it rained all summer?

The therapist chuckled. "I'll give you that. I'm a runner. I had to use a treadmill all week."

Jake was interested enough to lift his head. This guy wasn't big, like Ethan; he wasn't much taller than Mom, in fact, but he looked strong in that skinny way runners did.

"Do you do marathons or anything like that?" he asked, surprising himself with his curiosity.

"I ran the half marathon here in Portland last year. I'm training now for a full marathon. I'm even thinking I'd like to run the Boston Marathon one of these years."

"Sweet," Jake said, impressed. He couldn't imagine running for *hours* without stopping for rests.

"So. Good thing," Randall reminded him.

"Um...Ethan took Mom and me to this place called the Portland Rock Gym."

Randall nodded. "I've been. It's fun, isn't it?"

"It was awesome! Even Mom tried it. She was good," Jake admitted, somewhat grudgingly. She'd been totally fearless, which he hadn't expected. "Ethan was great. And he's certified to belay, so we didn't have to have anyone else help us."

"And, hey, indoors!"

Jake grinned. "Yeah. I liked it so much, Mom's thinking about signing me up for one of their summer camps. Except..." He made a face. "They're kind of expensive."

"You think she'll be able to swing it?"

"I don't know. 'Cuz I want to do a basketball camp and a baseball camp, too."

"What do you do during the summer if you're not at some kind of sports camp?"

Jake shrugged. "Go hang out with my cousins. But that's boring."

They kept talking. Randall didn't ask about guns

or anything like that. Jake didn't see what the point was, but, well, he was kind of getting to like Randall. He was better than that guy Mom had made him see when he was a little kid, after... Well, *after*.

Mom looked so hopeful when Randall walked him out, Jake stared at her in amazement. What did she think was going to happen? He'd get fixed in one hour? Like an oil change on the car? Roll him in, the guy goes to work, drive on out, clean oil, new filter?

Jake didn't *feel* fixed.

Except, this had been a good week. He'd actually kind of lied to Randall. The climbing wall was awesome, but what he kept thinking about was the way Ethan had talked to him Saturday. The steel on his face and in his voice when he said, *I'm telling you the truth. None of it was your fault.*

What happened when Marco died had blurred for Jake, because he'd been such a little kid. He didn't remember that much from when he was five. Except he could still close his eyes and see Marco, mostly after he'd fallen. The blood and— He shivered and blanked that out. But he knew he hadn't meant to pull the trigger. He wasn't even sure he exactly *had*. The gun had been lots heavier than he'd thought, and as he was climbing down from the counter he'd kind of started to drop it because his hands weren't big enough, and then there'd been a crack of thunder and Marco—

Dad always said not to touch his gun. That was

the part that he hated to remember, because he had disobeyed. Everything bad happened because he'd wanted to show Marco Dad's gun.

But what Ethan said was burned into his brain.

*Your dad carried a Glock that didn't even have a safety. It didn't allow for an "oh, oops," for you to learn a lesson. He didn't mean anything bad to happen, either, but he was the adult. A law enforcement officer, no less. He screwed up.*

Jake had loved his father. It was getting harder to picture his face, but sometimes he could still close his eyes and see Dad laughing, or feel his hands steadying Jake's stance as he swung a plastic bat or settled the too-big motorcycle helmet on his head. If it was all Dad's fault...did that mean Dad was really a bad person?

Except, Jake believed the other thing Ethan had said, too, about how it was okay to still love Dad because he *wasn't* bad, he was really a good man. One who made a terrible mistake.

Two terrible mistakes.

*If he was really a good man, he wouldn't have left Mom and me.*

Sometimes Jake burned with anger when he thought about Dad deciding to check out, never mind what would happen to his kid.

The other thing was he *wanted* to blame his father. Because then he didn't have to believe it was all his fault because he'd done something Dad said not to do.

And did that make *him* a bad person?

Only then he'd remember how strong Ethan had felt with his arms around him, and that last half headlock, half hug before they went inside. And he could tell Ethan wasn't faking.

*Maybe Dad really did screw up, and then he couldn't face his own mistake and what it meant. If that's the way it was...* Walking out to the car beside Mom after the counseling session, Jake's knees got weak, the relief was so humongous.

*Not my fault.*

*But he was my dad.*

Once they were in the car, Mom waited before starting it until Jake had fastened his seat belt, then said, "Ethan called while I was waiting for you. He thinks he can get away Saturday so we can do something if you'd like."

He felt a burst of pleasure, but he also looked at her sort of suspiciously. She hadn't asked how the session with Randall had gone, in that bright voice like she usually did. Instead, she sounded...hopeful. As if Ethan coming into their lives had done something to her, too.

He didn't like that when he tried to picture Dad now, he sometimes saw Ethan.

*Who would never have left us.*

Even thinking that made Jake feel guilty, which tangled him up inside again, except...he kept having this weird, floaty feeling, as though he was one of those birthday balloons, bobbing toward the ceiling.

*Not my fault.*

But not his fault meant it *was* Dad's fault. And if Jake didn't keep believing in his father, who would? And then he felt sick again, and then…

*Not my fault* popped into his head again, and he didn't even know his mother was talking.


"THERE'S THE OCEAN," Jake exclaimed, from the backseat of Ethan's Yukon.

Laura smiled at the excitement that made him sound a lot younger than he had lately. She had to admit, there was something about the sight of the vast Pacific and the long, pale beach that had anticipation bubbling in her, too. It had been ages since she and Jake had done anything like this. Maybe for a vacation, she'd find herself thinking, but those came only once a year, and Seaside was only an hour and a half drive from Portland. Perfectly possible for a day trip.

Naturally, it was Ethan who'd suggested this. Ethan, who'd driven with the rock-solid competence with which he did everything while keeping Jake and her both laughing.

He'd insisted they get going early and make a full day of it. "We can stay for dinner, too. Watch the sun go down."

It was the first of June, which almost qualified as

summer. Going to the beach made it official. *And* it was sunny.

He parked not far from the Promenade, the oceanfront boardwalk that distinguished Seaside from other Oregon Coast towns. Salty air filled Laura's nostrils the minute they got out, a breeze making the morning a little chilly. So, okay, only sort of summer, she decided, pulling her sweatshirt on as Jake did the same.

"Can we go to the beach first?" he begged.

Pocketing his keys, Ethan grinned at him. "I was thinking we should do some shopping. Browse some boutiques. What do you say?"

Jake blew a loud raspberry.

Laughing, Ethan said, "Okay, no shopping. What say we wander the Promenade for a while, though? Once we go to the beach, we'll be sandy and maybe wet. I seem to remember some bumper cars. Then have lunch, *then* hit the beach."

Jake loved the idea of bumper cars. Ethan raised an eyebrow at Laura, who said, "That sounds like a plan to me."

From that point, they wandered. Even Jake was awestruck by the setting and the people. Joggers and cyclists and in-line skaters wove in and out among the strolling pedestrians. Good smells came from restaurants, and window displays in the dreaded boutiques caught even his gaze. They agreed to buy a bag of taffy, but wait until they were back from the beach. Ethan whipped them all at some arcade games, but reluctantly watched while Jake and Laura drove bumper cars.

"Pretty sure I'm too big to fit," he said ruefully, his expression reminding her of a boy's when he was denied a treat.

They played miniature golf—Jake turned out to have the magic touch with a putter—and finally had a lunch of hot dogs and chili.

The wind was sufficient that Ethan announced his intention to buy a kite. Laura found a place on the Promenade to sit and watch the waves roll in while man and boy disappeared on their quest, returning triumphant.

They all took off their sandals and left them with a bunch of others, and found an empty enough stretch of sand for Jake to run with the kite until it caught enough air to take flight. Ethan let the string unreel, calling encouragement until the purple and gold dragon soared upward.

When it dipped and started a sharp dive, Laura groaned, but this time Ethan took off running, doing something with the string, and the kite rose again.

She felt happiness so acute, it almost hurt. Did Ethan have any idea how much difference he was making to Jake? Or her?

The *her* part frightened her a little, if she was truthful. What she felt was so huge, it sometimes swelled inside her chest until she didn't think she could contain it. What if Ethan was too good to be true? She wasn't that special. What did he see in her? What if all he felt was some kind of obligation? Poor, sad widow and boy, left all alone. He took seriously the protect and defend part of his job. He must know they needed him.

Shading her eyes against the sun as she watched Ethan let Jake hold the reel and patiently coach him on how to control the kite's dips and spirals, Laura thought, *That's not all it is.*

Of course it wasn't. He must constantly encounter women and children who sparked his protective instincts. He didn't spend the day at the ocean with them. Make love to the women, make time for the children.

And she'd seen how much she hurt him with her doubt.

For all that this had been one of the best weeks of her life, she knew she had ground to make up. Since she had left his apartment after they made love last weekend, he'd been all about having fun. The three of them together. He hadn't once even suggested lunch, the way they'd done the previous week. Out of desperation, she had Wednesday night when he called, but he said he couldn't. Which was maybe true, and maybe not. That week, he'd only kissed her a couple of times, but lightly when she stepped out on the porch with him when he was leaving. So, okay, Jake was home. But Laura knew that wasn't the only reason he was holding back.

He didn't trust her, of course. And she couldn't blame him.

She wanted to believe she could prove to him that he could, but every so often she had a bad moment. She'd had one this morning.

After beating Jake to Ethan's SUV and calling, "I get the front seat!" she'd hopped in and found herself looking at the glove compartment. Outside, Jake protested and Ethan laughed, but she hardly heard them, because...there it was, right in front of her. Surreptitiously, she reached out and tried opening it, but it was locked. Oh, God. Was his gun in there? She wanted desperately to believe he hadn't brought it today, but suspected he had. Matt had never gone anywhere without his.

"You never know when shit will happen" had been his defense. And she understood why anyone in law enforcement would come to believe that. But...could she live with it always there, somewhere close?

Her heart said yes...but she felt a hesitation first, a still moment shadowed by horror.

Ethan would never be as careless as Matt was— but Jake had managed to get his hands on Ethan's gun, too. Because it was *there*, and Jake knew it.

*He's in counseling. And...look how happy he is. How happy I am.*

If she chickened out, she'd be letting fear cheat her and Jake. At a moment like this, seeing them reeling in the kite as they came toward her, faces lit with matching grins, she couldn't imagine being dumb enough to do that.

"I want to get my feet wet," she declared when they were close enough.

Ethan lifted a hand to shade his eyes as he looked out at the ocean. "Did you see the surfers? If we were here for another day…"

"Yeah!" Jake agreed.

Laura rolled her eyes and laughed. "Wet suit or not…*brrr*." She mimicked a shiver.

Ethan slung a casual arm across her shoulders, leaving Jake to pick up the kite that had finally settled onto the sand. "We'll get you on a surfboard sooner or later," he murmured, his mouth close enough to her ear to make her shiver for real. With Jake's back momentarily to them, he nuzzled her neck. "Damn. Don't suppose he'd like an overnight with his cousins?"

Laura grimaced. "They're away for the weekend. Besides…you know it'll be late by the time we get home."

"Huh." He straightened when Jake turned toward her, but kept his voice soft, just for her. "Lunch Monday?"

The heat in his eyes told her food wasn't what he had in mind. A different kind of heat pooled low in her belly. "Yes," she said hastily, and hoped Jake would think her cheeks were flushed from the wind.

## CHAPTER TWELVE

ETHAN GOT OUT of his Yukon, slammed the door and stood for a moment taking in the chaotic scene. Strobe-like flashes from fire trucks and police cars lit the dark night and streams of water arced toward the burning house. Firefighters, suited up and unidentifiable from any distance, dragged hoses and called instructions and cautions. Shocked neighbors wearing pajamas and hastily donned coats huddled together in small groups to stare. A flash bulb momentarily shocked his retina. Press…? He couldn't tell, but then saw the flash go off again. No, someone was photographing the audience, not the action.

Inevitably, he locked on the swastika, bigger than ever, on a still intact side of the wood-framed house.

He let out a vicious string of curses.

A familiar voice said, "I was afraid you didn't know some of those words. Clean-living guy that you are."

Ethan shared a few more words he knew with Detective Sam Clayton. Then both men sobered.

"You just get here?" Ethan asked.

"Beat you by ten minutes." Knowing where

Ethan was going with this, he added, "Whole family got out. Dad ran back in for the cat, which scratched the shit out of him and took off like a rocket."

Brave man.

After exchanging a few more words with Sam, Ethan set out to find the home owners, who had been squeezed into the backseat of a squad car. Mom held a girl who was maybe seven or eight, Dad, a boy a couple of years younger. All four were staring at their house, utterly riveted, their expressions shell-shocked.

He opened the door on the sidewalk side and squatted to be eye level with them. He regretted exposing them to a more powerful dose of the pungent scent of wet, charred wood, but knew the closed car door wouldn't have protected them from it entirely anyway. And he needed to get answers while events were fresh in their minds.

"I'm Detective Ethan Winter," he told them, displaying his badge and keeping his voice gentle. "You're the Friedlichs?"

Almost to the end of the *F*s, he couldn't help thinking. Skimming the phone book, he'd noticed a Fromel who lived not much over half a mile away, and he guessed there might be a few others. He remembered a kid from high school named Joel Funk. Damn, Ethan hoped Joel and his family, if he had one, didn't live in the area.

There were a lot of disturbing aspects to this case, and among them was the fact that, so far as he had yet determined, the first attack had been on the Eckstein home. Why not the Adelmans, the Bernsteins, the Cornfelds—maybe that didn't sound distinctively Jewish enough, so, okay, the Cherniks? No Davidson, not Dorfman, no Dushkin. Why start in the *E*s?

And who was the next slated victim? The Garfunkels? Or would the anti-Semitic slimeball jump to some letter he liked better than *G*?

And, damn it, why go in alphabetical order? Just because he was running his finger down names in the phone book?

Now Ethan questioned the Friedlichs, Michael and Sarah, and learned that Michael was always an exceptionally heavy sleeper and that tonight Sarah had taken some cold medication that had really knocked her out, too. It was little Rachel who had roused her whole family.

Ethan smiled at her and said, "Lucky somebody was alert," and saw her dimple with a smile before she hid her face against her mom's shoulder.

"I'd already taken the medicine when Michael said, 'What if that vandal comes after us next?'" Sarah said, her voice hollow. "But it seemed so unlikely." Her dark eyes looked past Ethan's shoulder to the ruin of her house.

He glanced over his shoulder, glad to see the fire had been knocked down, although the damage this time was extensive. This fire, he was especially enraged to have noted, appeared to have been set right below the bedroom wing.

Alphabetical order. Escalation.

He ground his teeth, intercepted a couple of alarmed stares and managed to hide his fury.

"What woke you up?" he asked the girl, who whispered, "I heard a crackling sound and I could see orange out the window."

Her brother had been asleep when she woke him. She was the closest thing to a witness, and she hadn't seen anything but fire.

A paramedic had already checked them out and determined that none of them had suffered smoke inhalation or burns. He offered to find them a ride to a nearby hotel, and they accepted. Whether anybody would sleep was another question, but he could tell the parents wanted their children away from there. Her instinct a common one, on the way out Mom had managed to grab her purse with her cell phone in it, the number of which she gave him.

When he thanked them and stood, his place was taken by a fire chief he knew. He was giving them his phone number so they could talk in the morning when Ethan walked away.

Clayton had already organized several of the uniformed officers present to question neighbors. Turned out it had been one of the firefighters from the first company who had immediately started snapping pictures of the spectators. Along with several local television trucks, Lieutenant Pomeroy arrived, dressed in heavy-soled boots to go in, but the minute he saw Ethan he shook his head.

"You know it's going to be a while before I can get close."

Ethan nodded. "You responsible for someone taking pictures?"

Pomeroy grunted agreement. "You know how often arsonists hang around."

Ethan did—but his gut feeling was that the fire wasn't the point for this perpetrator. He'd started with common vandalism, gone for shock value—the mannequin—then seemingly sought around for something even flashier. More destructive.

Fires were easy to set; they were newsworthy, they spread panic. This guy wanted attention, that was obvious, but did he get a rush from watching flames leap into the night? Ethan couldn't even say why he was so sure that wasn't the case.

He said, "I need to know if this one got out of hand because it had more time to spread or whether there was more accelerant or multiple points of origin."

Pomeroy gave him a sharp look. "You think our guy wanted this one to be bigger."

"Don't you?"

"He's getting more grandiose as he goes."

"Just because he's having fun? Or—" and this was what Ethan feared "—because he's working himself up to something?"

"Nice thought." One Ethan had expressed to him

before. Pomeroy sighed. "I can tell you that the first company to get here thinks the fire was set on the exterior of the structure, like the previous ones. Doors were intact and locked. A few windows had blown, but likely because of the heat."

Both men turned when Sam Clayton strode up, but from his head shake they knew he had no good news.

"Closest we've got to a witness is an old lady who lives a block thataway—" he nodded up the street "—and saw a car gunning by. Trouble is she hadn't put on her glasses yet."

They all grimaced.

"No idea how many people were in the car. Or make or model." He spread his hands. "It was really booking, though, she says."

"That's it?" Ethan growled in frustration.

"As usual, it was the sirens that woke most people. A few of the closest neighbors heard the fire or smelled smoke. Three called 911. But they're sure they didn't see anyone outside until the firefighters arrived."

"Wonderful."

Ethan left not that much later. Investigating the fire scene itself was Lieutenant Pomeroy's job, not his. Tomorrow morning, he'd want to expand the questioning of neighbors—not all of them had rushed outside to watch the fire, especially folks with younger kids. And, as with the past fire, the kids could be useful witnesses.

He had more questions for the Friedlichs, too, once they'd calmed down and had time to think. He was growing more attached to the theory that all of this was nothing but stage dressing for the main event. And, if that was the case—what if the Friedlichs *were* the main event? No question they could have died tonight. This fire had rapidly grown out of control. If the girl hadn't woken up when she did, they'd have been in trouble.

But he didn't really believe this family was the target. How many people would know David and apparently his son were heavy sleepers? According to them, Sarah usually awakened at the slightest sound. If not for the cold medication, she'd have hustled them all out, called 911 and the fire would have been knocked back without doing anywhere near the damage it had.

But he was going to be very surprised if there weren't at least two and maybe three points of origin, a significant escalation from even the last fire. So he needed to find out whether there was anyone who really hated one of the Friedlichs.

And if tonight hadn't been the main event...he had a bad feeling it was coming soon, and people would die.

"How do you know Ethan will even show up?" Jake complained. "He didn't come last night, like he said he would. But he has to eat, even if he's working, right?"

Laura lifted the pan lid to stir the goulash. "Not necessarily. Or if he does, he may grab something at a drive-through he can eat quick. It's his job, Jake. He doesn't always work nine to five."

She'd have minded his cancellation last night more if she hadn't seen him Monday. *Seen.* What a lovely euphemism for having fabulous sex that had left her smiling for the rest of the day. Not that she hadn't been disappointed, too, when he'd called to cancel yesterday, even though she'd expected it after watching the morning news.

News footage had showed first the flames leaping into the night sky, then the charred shell of a home that remained come morning. When the camera had panned from the crudely spray-painted swastika to a stunned-looking family that included two elementary-age kids being helped into a patrol car, Laura had felt both sick and angry. She'd known Ethan was there somewhere, although this time the reporter had cornered a fire investigator instead.

Of course Ethan wasn't free by five thirty to hang out with her and Jake.

"I guess not," her son mumbled. "Did Dad do that, too?"

"Yep." She wiped her hands on the kitchen towel and went to kiss his cheek. "It's the nature of the beast."

So was carrying a gun, she thought more bleakly, bemused because she knew which one of those flaws—if she could call it that—bothered most women more.

"There's something I've been meaning to talk to you about," she said. "This seems like the time."

He froze.

"Ethan and I are…" Oh, Lord—she should have prepared a speech. "Well, dating. We've had lunch several times and…I didn't want to say anything to you in case nothing came of it, but…" *Oh, spit it out.* "It sounds silly when you're our ages, but I guess you could call him my boyfriend."

He stared. "Ethan likes *you*?"

"You don't have to make it sound so unlikely."

He shrugged awkwardly. "I didn't mean it that way. I just—"

"Never expected your mother to date again?" she said lightly.

Her son scrunched up his face. "I mean, does he kiss you and stuff?"

Definitely *and stuff.* Laura grinned at him. "Yep. Someday you'll understand."

He didn't say anything for long enough that she began to worry. She started setting the table even though she usually had him do it, keeping an eye on him the whole while, waiting for…what? Hurt feelings?

Finally he burst out, "Are you guys going to get married?"

After setting down a cork-backed tile in the middle of the table, she straightened and made sure to meet his eyes. "I don't know. It's a little soon to say. I really like him, but…I guess I still have some qualms about the gun thing. You know how I feel about that."

He nodded.

"And I haven't dated at all since your dad died, so this is a big step for me." She hesitated. "Would you mind?"

After a minute he shook his head, but he wasn't looking at her, either. And then he asked, "So… what if you break up?"

Of course that was what really worried him. She couldn't blame him.

"We've talked about that. Ethan says he'll be there for you no matter what. Honestly, that was another one of my qualms. Ethan's good for you. I don't want to mess that up. But he swears he won't let it, and…" She hesitated.

"He means what he says," her son said with certainty.

She smiled at him. "That's what I think, too."

"I hear him!" Jake said suddenly, and took off like a shot for the front door.

As she heard him wrench it open, Laura turned on the burner to heat water for noodles, and realized she felt light as air. Her own words echoed in her head. *He means what he says.*

She truly believed that.

The fact that she did shouldn't have been a surprise, but still somehow was. She had become so guarded, trust wasn't a natural response for her.

Her phone rang, making her jump.

Dinnertime, she thought in exasperation. Probably a sales call.

But she recognized the phone number that showed on the screen, even though she had deleted the names of the people who went with it from her contacts list.

Bruno and Palma Vennetti.

Which was calling? But she knew. Papa Vennetti did nothing without Mama's permission. He barely spoke.

*Ignore it.*

But sharp anger had her picking up the phone. "Hello."

"Laura?" Mama's voice was unusually hesitant. "This is—"

"I know who it is."

This pause gave her a savage sense of satisfaction.

"Emiliana said you wouldn't talk to her."

"I did talk to her. Long enough to make it clear that I have no interest in hearing from anyone in the family again."

The front door opened and closed again. Jake's excited voice played counterpoint to Ethan's bass rumble. Laura headed for the sliding door to the deck. This wasn't a conversation she wanted to have with Jake in earshot.

"If you were a churchgoer the way you pretended

to be," Mama Vennetti chided her, "you would understand forgiveness."

"Oh, that's funny." Laura slipped outside, only distantly aware of the drizzle, and slid the door closed behind her. When she looked back, Ethan raised an eyebrow. She pointed to the phone and he nodded. "Gee, how long did it take you to forgive a five-year-old boy? Or am I jumping to conclusions? Maybe you haven't."

"I have called to tell you how deeply I regret my own behavior," Mama said as if she hadn't heard a word Laura said. "We made the mistake of letting Matteo think we didn't love him—"

Laura interrupted with a snort. "You mean, you abandoned him. Your own son. And your grandson, too."

"Marco was also our grandson."

"Yes." She turned her back on the house and gazed at the backyard without seeing anything but the past. Acid ate at her stomach. "Do you know how much *we* loved Marco? He spent more time at our house than at yours. He was…he was—" Her voice broke. "His death left us all bereft. It scarred us all. That does not excuse what you did to Matt and Jake. Jake lives with the belief that he is responsible for his father's death, too. But you and I both know that isn't true, don't we? If you had said, 'Matteo, this was an awful thing, but we love you,' he'd still be alive. I hope you ask God's forgiveness. He may be better at it than either of us is." Breathing hard, she ended the call, and then stayed where she was, shaking.

*Oh, God*, she thought. *Did I ever say anything like that? I didn't leave him, but...*

The door slid open behind her. Not Jake. Please not Jake. She couldn't make herself turn.

The long arms that closed around her were Ethan's. He pulled her back against him and rested his cheek against her head.

"Something's wrong."

"I think I'm a hateful person," she whispered, and turned to wrap her arms around his torso and press her face against his broad chest. He must have felt her tremors, because his hands moved soothingly up and down her back.

Resting against him, drawing strength from him, she finally grew calm enough to say, "That was Matt's mother."

"Mama." After a minute, he said, "The family rolled out the big gun, then," and she gave a choked laugh.

"Yes. Although the family had nothing to do with it. Mama makes the decisions."

"She's the general."

"The Pentagon's loss," she mumbled into his shirt, then lifted her head. "What did you do with Jake?"

He smiled slightly. "Persuaded him to dive for cover."

She laughed again, her body starting to relax

until she got to remembering. "I was really awful, but she deserved it, too. Do you know what she said?"

He shook his head, his eyes so kind she could have wept.

"That she regretted letting Matt think they didn't love him. Think! Can you imagine?" Outrage tightened her throat anew.

"Implying that of course they did love him? And he should have known it?" His grunt satisfied her vengeful side.

"The conversation didn't get off to a great start when she chewed me out for my lack of the Christian virtue of forgiveness."

"Hypocrisy in action," he murmured.

"Yes, except—" Laura searched his face. "She's right. *Should* I forgive them?" *Have I forgiven Matt, even now?*

Tiny creases deepened on his forehead. "I don't know, Laura. Maybe you'll be ready someday but this is too soon. Maybe they don't deserve forgiveness. As crummy as what they did to Matt is, I'm even more pissed that they couldn't see how alone you and Jake were after losing him."

She bumped her forehead lightly against that solid chest. "By then...I'd probably have told them where to stuff any apologies."

He bent to kiss her head. When she lifted her face to his, his mouth moved softly over her temple, her cheek, her mouth. "Warning me not to piss you off?" he murmured.

He had a gift for making her laugh even as she closed her eyes and savored the gentle touch of his lips. He wasn't asking anything of her, just...giving.

"I told Jake," she said.

"Mmm." He nibbled on her lower lip. "Told him what?"

"About this." She turned her head to try to capture his mouth. "That we're dating."

"Dating?" he teased, his voice rich with amusement.

"I also said you're my boyfriend, and that sounds even sillier, so don't smirk at me," she said tartly even as she repressed her own smile. "And that was *your* suggestion, if you may recall."

"Huh." His smile grew to an open grin. "So it was."

"Did he say anything to you?"

"Just now? No, but I thought he was looking at me funny."

"That's because you kiss me and stuff. And he can't figure out why you'd want to."

He squeezed her ass with one big hand. "Oh, he'll understand sooner than he thinks. Give him another year."

Laura made a face at him. "Gee, good to know."

"I'm trying to remember when a guy starts having wet dreams."

"Eww!" She pushed him away. "I don't want to know. Ever! Is that clear?"

Laughing helplessly, he held up both hands in acknowledgment and surrender. Only then the smile slid away, leaving tenderness. "You okay now?"

"Yes." She gasped. "Oh, no! The water's boiling."

As she reached to open the door, she felt him right behind her.

"Maybe I could sneak back in tonight after he's gone to bed."

"Dream on," she told him, then turned to narrow her eyes. "And not a word about what kind of dream."

He laughed so hard she shut the door in his face.

THE NEXT TWO weeks were good. So good, Ethan was suspicious. Jake hadn't once begged to have a chance to shoot at the range. He hadn't thrown a temper tantrum, at least not one Laura had mentioned. Maybe the counseling was helping, Ethan found himself thinking, or could be they were in the eye of the storm.

He was happy with how things were going with Laura, too. Which didn't mean he was ready for this.

Now parked outside the counseling center where she took Jake, he frowned as he looked at the building. He didn't want to be there. It felt like a commitment he'd sworn he wouldn't make yet.

Dr. Randall Lang had requested the favor of his

presence. So, okay, Ethan could understand that; apparently, Jake talked about him a lot. Well, of course he did—Ethan saw Jake at least three days a week, sometimes more.

This, though—this felt like something bigger than the therapist wanting to meet Jake's mother's boyfriend. Were non-family members usually included? It wasn't as if he lived with them.

Although he was beginning to wish he did. His apartment felt increasingly bare and lonely. When he wasn't having dinner with Laura and Jake, he'd taken to mostly grabbing a meal out. Cooking just for himself exacerbated the feeling of loneliness. In restaurants, well, at least there were other people around or he ate with fellow cops.

Shaking his head, he got out, locked up and started across the parking lot. He deliberately distracted himself by thinking about his morning.

Pomeroy and Clayton had thrown up their hands and agreed to a plan Ethan had cooked up. Beginning tomorrow, the three of them would spend a few hours every night keeping watch on a potential next victim of the swastika arsonist. He was uneasy waiting even that long; this had been a long break between attacks. But Pomeroy had had to fly to Seattle and wouldn't be back until late afternoon tomorrow, and Clayton had a personal commitment. Ethan had had no choice but to concede that tomorrow night would be good.

Neither Pomeroy nor Sam Clayton totally bought

into his theory, but when they looked at a map with pins stuck in to indicate where incidents had occurred, they could all see the pattern. Ethan strongly suspected they'd find the perpetrator lived smack-dab in the middle, were they to draw a circle taking in every attack.

What they'd done was search for people with Jewish names who lived within that circle—and a few blocks outside it—and chose the next three that struck them as likeliest. They eliminated some who were in apartments or town houses, unlikely targets. Two houses were brick, tough to set on fire without breaking in. Of course, the attack might take a different form if one of those people was the point of all this…but Ethan was betting not. He thought the fires were going to keep getting bigger, and that their guy had started this whole thing because he knew whoever it was he really hated would be vulnerable to fire.

The three had pretty well drawn straws. Every incident had taken place between one and three in the morning. Midnight to three, they planned to be out there. Another bonus was, if dispatch called, they'd be the first to arrive on any new scene. Pomeroy was taking the Fromels, Clayton the Gartenhaus family, and Ethan the Gelfmans, who by chance lived only ten blocks from Laura and Jake.

And, yeah, pretty close to the middle of the imaginary circle.

One of the things he'd done that morning was

research the Gelfman family. What he'd learned had his radar humming. Michael Gelfman had lost his wife to cancer close to ten years ago. He'd remarried three years ago, this time to a Gentile woman who already had a child, a boy who was now seventeen. In the past year, young Austin March had been arrested twice—once for assaulting a teacher, the other time for a fight with another boy that ramped up when Austin pulled a knife.

Gelfman's stepson was an angry kid likely to have made enemies. He could well be the ultimate intended victim. But the stepfather struck Ethan as target material, too; there had been two potential domestic violence calls to the address since Gelfman married Austin's mother. In both cases, responding officers hadn't been satisfied but had had to leave, unable to confirm anything criminal had happened.

A troubled household interested Ethan a great deal in this context.

With a grunt, he put the Gelfmans out of his mind and strode into the counseling center without letting himself hesitate. Laura and Jake were already seated in the waiting room. At the sight of him, both their faces shone with relief and pleasure. They wanted him there. He wanted to be there for them. Of course it was right that he be part of this. Whatever had had him jumpy settled.

"Hey," he said, kissing Laura on the cheek when she stood to greet him. "I was afraid I was late."

"No, this is perfect." She smiled at him. "Thank you for coming. I know getting away during the afternoon can be a problem for you."

"Nothing that exciting was happening today."

True enough; except for the meeting—and Pomeroy had come to him and Clayton rather than the other way around—Ethan had spent his day thus far glued to his computer and phone. That summed up a lot of his days, come to think of it. Mostly he gathered information. Thrills and chills were rare. His mother, experienced wife of a law enforcement officer, had breathed a sigh of relief when he left patrol for the detective gig.

Jake had barely started to say something when they all heard his name and their heads turned.

The guy smiling at them was about Ethan's age, good-looking. With those wire-rimmed glasses, almost geeky, but clearly athletic, too.

"Detective Winter," he said, holding out his hand as soon as they got close enough. "Thank you for coming."

They shook. "No problem."

Dr. Lang led them down a short hall to his office, and then sat in one of the chairs. Ethan, Laura and Jake settled together on a comfortably worn sofa. Ethan laid his right arm along the back, behind Jake's shoulders, his fingers just touching Laura's shoulder. He knew what message he was sending to the good doctor and decided he didn't care.

"If I understand correctly," Dr. Lang started

things off by saying, "you knew Jake's father but had met Laura only at the funeral until fairly recently."

"That's right." He explained again that he and Matt had worked together early in both their careers, then had taken different directions and in fact had been separated geographically, as well, ending up working out of different precincts. "I attended Matt's funeral out of respect and…" his pause was infinitesimal "…a memory of friendship. Otherwise, I hadn't set eyes on Laura or Jake until I spotted him at the gun show."

No, he said, he wasn't married and had no children, only a two-year-old nephew so far, who lived with Ethan's sister and her husband in the Seattle area. He liked teenagers, and had done some volunteering, teaching personal safety and hunter safety classes, talking in schools and the like.

"Jake reminds me of his dad and maybe a little bit of myself at that age," he said, and saw shy pleasure on the boy's face. He couldn't tell what Laura was thinking.

"How so?" Dr. Lang asked.

"He looks a great deal like his father. Have you seen a picture of him?" Turned out he hadn't, but Laura promptly produced one from her wallet.

Ethan wasn't sure he liked the idea she still carried a photo of her dead husband. He knew that was unreasonable. It might be as much to reassure Jake as anything. He couldn't help feeling an uncomfortable jolt of jealousy, though.

Dr. Lang studied the picture, then Jake. "Can't argue about the looks. Your dad was a handsome man."

Ethan dredged his memory for qualities in the guy he'd liked: a happy-go-lucky attitude, a genuine liking for people that won him a positive response, a love of jokes and pranks that made him popular at the station. Apparently those qualities had gone along with carelessness and the unfailingly optimistic belief that nothing bad would ever happen, and he guessed Laura was thinking the same but hoped Jake wasn't.

"Jake's more serious," he said, thinking it through, "but he has reason to be. I get the feeling he was really well-liked until his current troubles, and he will be again." He squeezed Jake's shoulder. "He's fun to hang out with."

He explained that he'd been sports-mad at Jake's age, too, and physically restless, needing to use his body hard so he could focus when it was time to study or sit in class. "I guess I identify partly because the year I turned twelve was a tough one for me." Why hadn't that occurred to him until now? He had no idea. "My father is a US marshal," he said. The therapist nodded his understanding. "Dad was working on something complicated." He knew what now, but wasn't going to explain. "He was gone a lot, and my mother was scared. Neither of them would tell me what he was doing, so I was scared, too. I got into some trouble at school that year."

"Really?" Jake looked at him. "You didn't tell me that. What did you do?"

"Mostly it's what I didn't do. My work. Plus, I had a teacher I really disliked—math," he said as an aside. "He made fun of a couple of students who couldn't fight back. I did it for them." He grimaced, making sure Jake saw the expression. "Wasn't smart enough to take it to the principal."

"What happened?" Jake sounded fascinated.

"I was lucky the same way you are. My mother stood by me. Dad finished that assignment and I grew up a little."

Conversation became, he was sure by design, more general, with them all talking about what they'd done the past week. Hearing Jake chattering about Ethan this and Ethan that, he almost winced. No wonder Dr. Lang had wanted to meet him, he thought ruefully.

Walking out at the end with Laura, Jake bouncing around them like an excited puppy, he wondered who he'd been kidding. Taking it slow? Yeah, that was something you could do dating a woman who didn't have a kid. But he'd long since crossed a line where Jake was concerned. With Laura, he could try protecting himself, but with the boy...*I'm all in*, he thought. If Laura ever decided to cut him out of Jake's life, that would be bad.

Out in the parking lot, a decision he hadn't even known he was debating made, he stopped Jake with a hand on his shoulder even as he looked at Laura.

"Hey," he said. "How would you feel about Sunday dinner at my parents'?"

# CHAPTER THIRTEEN

MEETING THE PARENTS was scary.

Laura hadn't been in this position for a very, very long time. Of course, she wasn't 100 percent sure Ethan had told his parents he was dating her. Maybe he'd talked only about Jake. But the warmth in his voice told her he was close to them, so she suspected they knew exactly how he felt about her. Maybe more about how he felt than *she* did.

In the midst of an attack of nerves during the drive, she discovered she was a little intimidated by his father's profession, too. So, okay, what he did probably wasn't all that different from Ethan's or Matt's job, but…she kept thinking, *He's a fed.* And that sounded big and bad.

And finally, the original plan had been for Ethan to pick them up, but he'd called not that long before she'd expected him and said in a terse voice, "Any chance we can meet there? Something came up."

She had assured him that was fine, taken the address and plotted her route online. But now she wondered if this hadn't been some sort of test. What if his parents had demanded he set it up? She pictured them saying, *Let's find out now whether she can take the stresses.*

And yes, that was dumb—she knew Ethan wouldn't do that to her. But the very thought had stiffened her spine. She'd show them all what she was made of.

Jake was really quiet during the drive, too. When she pulled up in front of the house, which she loved on sight, he said, "I don't see Ethan's truck."

"No, it looks like we beat him here," she said with fake good cheer. "That's okay. We knew something was holding him up."

The eternal *something* that any police officer's spouse had to learn to live with.

Not letting herself dawdle, she got out and then reached in the back for the pie his mother had agreed to let her contribute. Jake was waiting on the sidewalk by the time she reached it.

"Look at that arch," he whispered. "It doesn't go into the house."

"No, it leads into the garden." The house, two-story, brick and likely dating to the 1920s, had a fairy-tale feel, with a particularly pointy roof, small-paned windows, some of which had arched tops that echoed the one extending to the side of the house, and a green-painted front door also with rounded top. To make it all more perfect, one of Ethan's parents loved roses. Many were in glorious bloom in a profusion of shades from creamy white through pale pink to deep rose and even purple. The long canes of a climber clambered over the brick arch, what had to be an old-time rambler scrambled over the detached garage, and a huge rugosa bush filled the space between the front windows. The glimpse she got into the side yard looked magical, too, and the rich scent filled the air.

"And I was feeling good because I finally got around to painting the deck at our place," she grumbled under her breath.

"What?" her son asked.

"Nothing."

She rang the doorbell, and then waited in trepidation.

The door opened, and a woman beamed at them. "You must be Laura. And Jake. Come in, come in!" She peered past them. "Still no Ethan?"

"No. I hope he can get away so you aren't stuck with us on our own."

His mother laughed. "You should hope. Without him here to defend you, I can grill you!"

Wide-eyed, Jake inched a little closer to Laura.

Ethan's mother was even taller than Laura, and thin. Short hair that must have been blond was being allowed to go white. She had laugh lines on her face that made her instantly likeable.

Seeing Jake's move, Mrs. Winter laughed. "Just kidding. Grilling suspects is my husband's specialty, not mine. I'm Selena Winter." As she and Laura shook hands, she smiled over her shoulder at the man who was joining them. "Speaking of my husband…Joe Winter."

He looked startlingly like his son—or maybe it was the other way around. Strands of silver in hair a little darker than Ethan's and deep wrinkles beside his eyes betrayed his age, but he was still a big, obviously fit, handsome man.

"Ethan said you played college basketball, too," she said.

His grin looked much like his son's, too. "Whipped him on the court until he turned, oh, about eighteen."

His wife snorted. "Try fifteen or sixteen."

He clasped a hand over his heart. "Now you're just being mean."

They all laughed.

"Tell you what, Jake," Joe Winter said. "How about we grab a ball and shoot some baskets until Ethan gets here? The women don't need us in the kitchen and who wants to sit around?"

Selena almost caught him with her elbow, but he knew her well enough to dodge at the right time. Laughing, he steered Jake away. Jake looked shy, but went with only one backward look at his mother.

"Brave boy," said Ethan's mother.

"Thank you." Laura was still feeling a little shy herself.

Dinner, she discovered, was a pot roast. She put together a salad while her hostess finished dropping biscuit dough on a cookie sheet and, after removing the cast-iron pan that held the pot roast from the oven, popped the biscuits in to bake.

"If Ethan's late, I'll reheat his dinner," she promised, but then cocked her head. "I do believe I recognize that engine."

Laura did, too. Something relaxed inside her.

Selena glanced at her. "Ethan told us some of what Jake is going through and why. I hope you don't mind."

"No. As long as you don't say anything to him. I imagine, given your husband's profession, you're better able to understand than most people."

Selena took the biscuits from the oven. "Did Ethan tell you I was a high school guidance counselor?"

"No," Laura said in astonishment. "Seriously?"

"Oh, yeah. Ethan and his sister really loved it when they were in high school."

Laura giggled. "I can imagine."

"He had to listen to me at home, Ethan said." Selena was almost straight-faced. "But that was enough." The two women laughed, and she added, "Fortunately, there were two of us on staff. Ethan got assigned to the other counselor."

"Whose advice you reinforced the minute he walked in the door at home."

"Truthfully, I never really needed to." Her expression softened. "He's always been self-directed and...determined." She rolled her eyes. "His sister, now..."

Laura chuckled. "He told me she was hell on wheels at a certain age."

"Pretty well every other year. Honestly. They talk about the terrible twos, and I'd read four-year-olds can be difficult…"

"I was horrible at thirteen."

"Yes, but six? Eight? Ten was okay, but eleven…" She shook her head. "I'm sure this sounds unmaternal, but it's such a pleasure watching her take a turn as a mother."

Both women were laughing again when Ethan walked into the kitchen. Laura saw his quiet satisfaction before he hugged his mother, then kissed Laura's cheek. So, no secrets here about their relationship. And that expression on his face…got to her.

Jake appeared. "They've got a really great basketball court here," he declared with obvious enthusiasm. "Ethan's dad painted a free-throw line and everything."

"I thought the seam in our driveway was about the right distance."

"It's, like, a foot off," her son grumbled. "So I'll get used to shooting from it, and then at the gym my shots won't be right."

"If you know the seam is a foot off, you can adjust where you shoot from," Laura pointed out.

"What's a little paint in the driveway?" Joe Winter said, sotto voce.

His wife gave him a scolding look.

Conversation stayed light at the table. It turned out that Selena was the gardener. She offered to share when she divided her fall blooming perennials, if Laura had room for any, and suggested a tour of the yard after dessert.

Nobody brought up the subject of what had delayed Ethan, and she didn't see any strain on his face. His dad did grimace when he rose from the table to pour the coffee.

"Damn knee," he muttered.

Ethan raised an eyebrow. He waited until his father had disappeared into the kitchen before leveling a look at his mother. "I thought the knee replacement did wonders. Made him a new man. How many times have I heard him say that?"

"Macho idiot," Selena said fondly. "The new knee did wonders. Unfortunately, he needs another one, and he's resisting. He is not a good invalid. He *hated* the week he spent in the nursing home after the surgery."

"Yeah, I can see why." Ethan's forehead was creased. "His boss isn't leaning on him?"

She blew out an impatient breath. "Who knows? I suspect he saves his groans for home and they think he's hunky dory."

"Damn it, he's smarter than that!" Ethan glanced at Jake. "Uh…darn it."

Jake cackled. "I've heard you swear before!"

Ethan bent toward him and said in a stage whisper, "Don't tell your mom."

Jake thought that was funny, too.

Laura tried to tell Ethan's mother that *yard* was a better word for what surrounded her house than *garden*, but nonetheless agreed to accept any and all offerings for the new bed she intended to dig out around her now-spiffy deck. Not wanting to raise expectations Ethan didn't have, she managed to evade a suggestion the two women get together for lunch, however.

Ethan left at the same time they did, waiting while she opened her car door to again kiss Laura lightly, and then laughing when Jake gagged.

"Kissing girls is fun."

"Mom's not a *girl*," her son said, sounding revolted.

"Yeah, but, see, I'm not a boy, either." Ethan grinned at her son. "So I like to kiss *women*. Happens as you grow up."

"Not to me," Jake said with confidence.

"Hmm." Ethan glanced at Laura. "Do you have a recorder running? We're going to want to play that back."

"I have an excellent memory," she assured him.

Jake rolled his eyes and got into the car.

"See 'ya," Ethan said. "Lunch Monday?" His voice had grown huskier.

"Yes, please." Her primness was ruined by the sultry note that surprised even her. "And dinner Tuesday or Wednesday?"

His eyes flared. "How about *and*?"

Oh, dear God. Was he hinting he wanted to be there every night? She knew that was what she wanted, too, but…she needed time. He knew that.

Somehow, she found a smile. "If you come too often," she joked, "you'll discover what we *really* eat for dinner most nights."

"Macaroni and cheese out of a box?" He bent to kiss her cheek again, nuzzling just the slightest bit. His last words were soft. "Bring it on."

And then, shaken, she found herself behind the wheel, waving at Ethan's parents, who until this minute she hadn't realized were still standing on the front porch, and at Ethan, too, who flipped a hand and strolled toward his SUV as though nothing of note had occurred.

Starting the engine gave her a chance to regain her composure. Not until she pulled away from the curb did she glance at Jake.

"Have fun?"

He shrugged, but not in that new, sulky way he'd developed. "Ethan's dad is nice. He said I could call him Joe."

"Mr. Winter is probably still more polite." She didn't add, *If you meet him again.* "I liked his mom, too," she said. "Guess there's a reason Ethan is a great guy."

"Uh-huh." Jake sounded abstracted. "Do you miss your mom and dad?"

"Yes," she said, surprised at the direction he was taking the conversation. "I wish you remembered

them." They'd been killed in a head-on collision
with a drunk driver when Jake was three.

"Sometimes I think I do," he said doubtfully.

"You might. Most people do have a few memories as far back as two or three years old."

He looked straight ahead. "I think...she might
have been hugging me. She had on this apron with
a black cat on the front. At least...I know Aunt Jenn
has that apron now. So maybe I'm mixed up."

"Mom loved that apron. She wore it a lot. She
made the world's best apple pie."

"And Grandad took me fishing, didn't he?"

"He did." She smiled at him. She had no idea
whether he actually remembered that; she talked
often about her parents, and when he was younger
Jake had loved going through photo albums with
her. It was nice to think he might hold on to real
memories of his grandparents, though.

"I kind of wish I still had my other grandparents,"
he said suddenly. "I mean, I know they don't like
me, but...you know."

She hurt for him terribly. "It's not that they don't
like you. It was..." As always, she had to struggle to
explain the unexplainable. "Such a shock, I guess.
And they felt torn between Marco's family and us."

"So they chose Marco's family," he said matter-
of-factly.

Yes. That was what they'd done. If a choice had
to be made, she even understood that one. Marco's father, Rinaldo, had been devastated, as had

his mother, Donna. Where could be safer for their young son to play than at his cousin's house, with Jake's father a police officer? *She* had had to make the excruciating phone call telling them their son was dead. Matt had been completely unable to.

*How did I not know until then that he was a weak man?* she wondered, not for the first time. If he hadn't bailed on her so shockingly and finally, would their marriage have survived? Or…if he'd assumed the burden of living with what he'd done, might he have grown into a stronger man she could have loved again?

She shook off the useless speculation, the hamster wheel of what-ifs.

"You haven't said. Do you see your cousins at school? Has either of them talked to you, um, recently?" She knew he'd hear what she didn't say: *since they quit bad-mouthing you.*

"Nick did." Tino's oldest was a year ahead of Jake, a seventh-grader. "He sort of said he was sorry. And that he kind of remembered me. 'Cuz we played together."

"Yes." Thank God she was pulling into her driveway, because her vision had suddenly blurred. "You and Nick and Marco."

"Uh-huh." He cleared his throat. "He looks like me."

She tried to smile despite the tears. "Handsome." Her son ducked when she ran her fingers through his dark hair. "I've seen him staring at me a few times. Like…" His voice trailed off.

"He's curious."

"I guess." He sneaked a look at her, his eyes red. "I thought maybe, after Uncle Tino said he was sorry, that, I don't know…" Once again he stumbled to a halt.

"They'd want to see you?" Her voice was thick. "I think, um, they do."

Now he looked at her, his face a study in bewilderment. "How do you know?"

"Your aunt Emily called. One of your dad's sisters," she prompted, since it had been such a long time since they'd really talked about the Vennetti side of his family. At his nod, she made herself continue. "Then, just the other day, your grandmother called, too."

"Did they…want to talk to me?"

"We didn't get that far. I was so angry, I told them not to call again."

His Adam's apple bobbed, but he didn't say anything.

"I should have talked to you. It wasn't my decision to make, not entirely anyway." Laura bit her lip hard enough to hurt as she waited for his response.

"That's okay," he mumbled. "I mean, they didn't want to see me then, so why should I want to see them now?"

"That's how I felt about it."

But he was saying what he thought she wanted

to hear, not what was in his heart. Ethan had said something once, that she didn't exactly remember, suggesting that it could be meaningful to Jake to be included again in his father's family. To see their regret and acceptance. And no, he was unlikely to ever feel for them—at least for the older generations—what he would have if they hadn't turned their backs, but could he build lasting relationships with his cousins? There were half a dozen who were within a year or two of him.

Even if she couldn't forgive…could she pretend to? For Jake's sake? Or, if not, at least give them access to him?

"Let's both think about this," she said to Jake's bent head. "Your aunt Emily was a really nice woman. We were friends."

His head came up, his eyes suddenly fierce. "But not good enough," he said with a sharpness that echoed her anger.

"No. But going against the rest of the family would have been hard. Your Grandma Vennetti…"

"Dad called her a bully once." Jake looked as startled at the recollection as Laura felt. "I don't remember what she did, but he was mad."

"Well…everyone does walk on eggshells around her. But being a strong woman isn't a bad thing. What *is* bad is that no one ever stood up to her."

"Not even Dad." His tone was strange.

"He called it respect," she said softly. The two of them had quarreled over his insistence that when

Mama summoned them for any occasion, however inconvenient, they went. "He fought her more than anyone else in the family, you know." This was a better memory. "She was mad that we didn't give you an Italian name. And she wasn't happy about him going to college. He could make good money being a carpenter like Tino, she said. Or what about a plumber?" Unconsciously she mimicked Mama's cadence. "Your father ignored her, because he knew what he wanted to do."

"Did any of the others *want* to go to college?"

"I don't actually know." She made a face. "I hope no one will try to stop the cousins in your generation."

"*I'm* going to college," he declared.

Laura smiled at him. "You better." She unlatched his seat belt and then hers. "What say we go in the house? The neighbors are probably all wondering what we're doing just sitting here."

Opening his door, he asked, "Do you think they really wonder?"

Laura chuckled. "Maybe Mr. Wooten. You know how he's always peering out between the blinds."

"Maybe he'll call the police." Jake sounded newly enthusiastic. "'Cuz he'll think we're scared to go in. Like we saw someone through the window."

"Right. Maybe we should wave at Mr. Wooten, just to be on the safe side."

"Yeah!" Jake turned and did, and Laura stifled

a giggle when she saw the blinds in their elderly neighbor's front window quiver.

MAN, HE HATED stakeouts. Ethan always forgot what a low threshold for boredom he had. He hadn't been kidding when he said that about needing intense physical activity to allow him to settle down to a quiet activity or to concentrate when he had to.

A grin tugged at his mouth. Yeah, okay, he'd had some pretty intense physical activity today. Way too brief, though. He'd be embarrassed at his lack of endurance if Laura wasn't as impatient as he was. They invariably shed clothes the minute his apartment door closed behind them, and often didn't make it as far as the bed. He'd be developing a real fondness for his sofa, except he'd discovered the fabric was unacceptably rough on a bare ass. Laura had decided it was *his* turn to be on the bottom, and he'd found out why. Maybe he'd consider buying some new furniture… Except *she* had a great sofa.

Ethan contemplated that sofa briefly, but knew damn well not much if anything would ever happen on it. If Jake wasn't home, there was the possibility that he'd come home unexpectedly. Even if they were married…yeah, the sofa thing wasn't happening.

And yes, increasingly he was thinking that word.

He had a passing memory of walking into his father's home office one time when he was something like thirteen or fourteen and finding Mom sitting on the desk with her blouse open and Dad's hand inside her bra. Even as he grinned again, alone there in the dark, Ethan remembered his horror. Some things a guy didn't want to see his parents doing. Not at *any* age.

He was reaching for his insulated coffee mug when a flicker of movement caught in the corner of his eye had him going absolutely still. For a moment, he didn't see anything. Maybe it was a cat or—

A teenage boy. There he was, swinging down from his second-story bedroom via a tree limb. Had to be Austin March. Ethan touched his watch to check the time. 2:36 a.m. Mom and stepfather would not be happy to know the kid was sneaking out in the middle of the night.

Appearing beneath a streetlight, he didn't seem to be carrying anything. He broke into a trot, though, and Ethan didn't even try to resist his curiosity. Maybe it was the wrong call…but he wanted to know where the kid was going.

He let him get far enough away that Ethan was able to open his door and close it quietly. Then, seeing his chance when Austin disappeared around a corner, Ethan broke into a run, too. He stuck to front lawns as much as possible so Austin didn't hear running footsteps behind him.

It wasn't a long pursuit, only seven blocks before Austin faded into the darkness between two houses. Ethan did the same, moving as soundlessly as possible.

A low voice came to him. "Yo. I'm here."

"You're late."

Damn, Ethan wanted to see the speaker, but the darkness was near impenetrable.

"The dickhead stayed up late watching TV…" The rest became indecipherable. He heard the soft sound of a sliding door. Damn it, they'd gone inside.

A light came on, but he could barely see it leaking around and through some blinds. Probably only a lamp. This kid—and something about the voice as well as the subterfuge convinced him it *was* a kid—wouldn't want his parents to know he welcomed visitors at this time of night, either.

Pondering his options, Ethan eased behind a rhododendron.

Maybe the two had girls here. Maybe they'd stolen a six-pack or a bottle of whiskey and planned to get drunk. Or high, if they'd gotten their hands on something else. All…well, okay, *innocent* wasn't quite the right word, but normal behavior for teenage boys.

He could go back to the Gelfman house, keep watch the way he was supposed to, make note when Austin got home. Or he could wait, hope to find out what these two intended.

He squatted down, back against a fence post to

get more comfortable. Two boys, right age. Right neighborhood. Right time of night.

No, he wasn't going anywhere.

FORTUNATELY, JAKE WASN'T any more talkative in the morning than Laura was. He'd slept through the night when he was six weeks old, and by a year old slept until eight or later. Not a morning person herself, Laura had been incredibly grateful, even if it was occasionally exasperating trying to get him up for school.

She was especially slow starting this morning. Sleep had been elusive with her brooding over her anger at the Vennettis and the question of whether Mama was right.

Matt had been impossible to separate from his family. It was why the isolation from them, when it came, had devastated him so entirely. Even so, she suspected it would pain him to think of Jake growing up not even knowing aunts and uncles, cousins and grandparents. *Matt* would have forgiven them.

She thought.

She finished her cereal and inhaled her coffee, not surprised when Jake finished his own bowl of cereal and made a couple of slices of toast to top it off.

"Do you mind buying lunch today?" she asked, watching as he spread jam lavishly on the toast.

"It's something gross." After a pause, he said grudgingly, "I can make my own."

"Thank you."

He sat down across from her, but instead of immediately gobbling his food, looked at her with his face set in an unfamiliar way. "So, I've been thinking about Dad's family. Like you said I should. And I don't want to talk to them."

Coming out of the blue like this, it took a minute to sink in. *Apparently*, she wasn't the only one who'd been brooding.

She nodded. "Why don't you talk to Ethan about it? He might have more perspective than you and I do."

"But *he* doesn't get to say, right?" The spark of resentment was unmistakable.

"No, of course not. Jake, I won't make you do anything you don't want to."

"Then why should I talk to him about it? I told you. I don't want anything to do with them." He shoved about half a slice of toast in his mouth.

Not in the mood to chide him for his table manners, Laura pretended she didn't see.

This was her fault. The poison of her anger had spread to him. Did that have something to do with his fascination with guns?

That worry was even more wrenching than her fear that his obsession had to do with him accidentally shooting Marco.

But he wasn't suicidal. Was he?

Sick now, she was grateful that Ethan would be coming over for dinner. Barring the ever-possible "something happening," of course. *Don't let something happen today*, she begged. *We need him.*

She dropped Jake off at school as she often did, since it wasn't far out of her way to work. She stayed at the curb longer than she should have, watching as he trudged toward the entrance, his book bag slung over one shoulder. Her heart wrung at the sight of him seeming so alone, even though common sense said it was chance none of his friends were arriving at the same time.

She couldn't let herself call Ethan during the day, any more than she would have called Matt midshift to remind him to pick up some milk on his way home. In an emergency, yes. Otherwise, no.

She was tired and letting it get to her, that's all. Jake wanting to talk about his father's family was a *good* sign, suggesting he trusted her. It might be seeing Dr. Lang that had gotten him thinking about the past. After the first visit, she hadn't asked what he and Randall talked about. She'd been reassured in the one session by how comfortable Jake seemed with Randall and with Ethan there, too.

It would probably be surprising if he *didn't* have some mixed feelings about Ethan, she reflected, as she unlocked the back door of the store and let herself in. Since she was, as usual, the first to arrive, the silence as she began turning on lights let her follow her train of thought.

There was no question Ethan had stepped in as a father figure for Jake, who was probably battling guilt at not staying completely loyal to Matt's memory. Or he might still resent the fact that Ethan had nabbed him at the gun show and therefore been responsible for getting him into trouble, leading to her taking away his precious magazines and gun catalogs and making him go back into counseling.

And then there was the fact that it was Ethan who had decided he couldn't finish the hunter safety class while also refusing to give him a chance to shoot at the range.

And honestly...she'd expected some fireworks when she told him she and Ethan were dating. He had to wonder, didn't he, whether Ethan hadn't used him to get close to her?

Instead, he'd been mostly agreeable these past couple of weeks. Once, early on, he'd asked, "You still have my magazines, right?" She'd agreed she had kept her word. She asked if he'd talked to Randall about them, and he'd done the turtle thing and said, "Not really."

Oh, God, she thought now—she needed to check tonight to be sure those damn magazines *were* still untouched. And, yes, look under his mattress. No, he was smarter than that—search his room, then.

Standing stock-still in the middle of the vast, eerily empty and silent store, she breathed deep and waited for the panic to subside.

*Oh, Ethan. Please be able to make it tonight.*

## CHAPTER FOURTEEN

LEANING BACK AGAINST the kitchen counter, Ethan braced himself with his feet apart and drew Laura to stand between his thighs. He cupped the back of her head, breathed her in and said in a voice not pitched to be heard beyond the two of them, "Got to tell you, fond as I am of your son, I'm really starting to crave time with just you."

They had this moment only because Jake's friend Ron had called and he'd taken the phone while he went to change into sweats and athletic shoes because Ethan was taking him to the indoor climbing gym again.

"Lunch…" she began, but he groaned.

"I can't for the rest of the week. I didn't tell you I'm doing a surveillance gig at night. Means I'm not hitting the sack until something like 3:00 a.m., if I'm lucky. I guess I could call lunch breakfast…"

She smiled weakly. "If we actually ate."

He flashed a grin and bent his head to kiss her neck. "Doesn't seem like we've had much time just to talk."

Laura nodded her agreement, even as her knees

grew weak and she tipped her head to give him better access to her neck and throat.

"I've been worried about Jake—"

Frustration showed on his face when he lifted his head. "I know you are, but that's what I'm trying to say. There's an us, too. A you and a me."

She stiffened slightly. "I'm a mother."

His hands slid down to her upper arms and he gave her a small shake. "I know," he said, his voice softening. "But even a mother is entitled to a life outside her kid's."

On something like a whimper, Laura leaned against him and wrapped her arms around his waist. "I want one," she whispered. "It's just…"

"You've spent six years entirely devoted to Jake and his needs. Letting go at all isn't easy, is it?"

She shook her head but didn't say anything. How could she relax her vigilance until she was absolutely positive Jake had truly healed?

She couldn't.

But…Ethan was also right that she desperately wanted something more for herself. Inevitably, Jake would draw away from her in the next few years. Already he didn't confide in her the way he had when he was younger. He'd be a teenager before she knew it. What's more, he was a boy, and she hadn't even had a brother to give her any insight into what it was like growing up male. When he was younger, it hadn't mattered as much, but from here on out…

"Maybe we could go on a date," Ethan said suddenly, in a low growl. "Out to dinner. Just us. To a movie, if you want. Or a play, or concert."

She rubbed her cheek against him, feeling the softness of his T-shirt against her cheek, and the hard muscles beneath. "Yes. Please. I want you for Jake, but I want you for *me*, too. I do."

"Okay." He sighed, his embrace slackening. "I hear him coming."

Oh, Lord, she hadn't. Fine mother she was.

She straightened and took a step back just in time. Jake burst into the kitchen.

"Are you ready to go—?" His lip curled at the sight of Ethan and his mother standing so close together. Ethan's hands still rested on her waist. "Are you *cuddling*?"

"Something like that," Ethan said with a smile. "I'm trying to talk your mom into going out with me for a nice dinner."

"Without me?" He sounded outraged.

"Yep." Ethan's eyebrows quirked. "You and I are going somewhere without her, aren't we?"

"Well, yeah," Jake said, his indignation subsiding. "Except you asked her if she wanted to come."

"So I did." Ethan kissed her cheek and looked at Jake. "Let's get going. We have walls to climb."

"Yay!"

They left in a rush, making Laura wish for a moment that she *was* going with them. She'd had the feeling, though, that Jake could use some time with Ethan, and, honestly, she was so tired, the idea of climbing hadn't been all that appealing tonight.

A book and a hot bath with fragrant oil sounded like bliss to her right now.

But first, she was going to search her son's bedroom.

JAKE DIDN'T KNOW WHY, but on the way home he said, "Did Mom tell you one of my aunts and my grandma Vennetti called?"

"She did." Ethan braked for a red light. "Both calls upset her."

"She asked if I want to talk to them. She said she shouldn't have decided without asking me."

"I'd agree with that." At a stop, Ethan turned in his seat to look at Jake. "How do you feel about it?"

He shrugged, still gazing straight ahead. "I told her I don't want to. After...you know, I never saw anyone from Dad's side of the family until Nick and Gianna started at my school this year." He felt and sounded belligerent. "They didn't care about me, so why should I care about them?"

"I don't blame you for feeling that way," Ethan said after a minute. Jake liked how he always seemed to pause to think about what you'd just said, instead of jumping in with *his* opinion without really listening first, the way most adults did.

"Mom said I should talk to you. I guess she thought you'd argue with me."

Ethan laughed. "Not sure that's a compliment."

Jake smiled a little. "I think she sort of wanted to argue with me, but she sort of didn't, too."

"So she passed the buck? I think you're right. She was really angry that anyone from your dad's family would call now after ignoring the two of you all these years." He grunted. "Your grandmother insisted that your mom had to learn to be forgiving. I gather your mother blew her top. She pointed out that's kind of like the pan calling the kettle black, but probably not that nicely."

Jake nodded. "So—*are* you going to argue?"

"Argue? No." With the light green, Ethan pressed on the accelerator. "I do think it's possible that you'll eventually regret not having any contact with such a big part of your family. Your dad was really close to them, you know."

"You mean, until they decided he wasn't worth spit."

"It was hard for them." Ethan's tone was mild, as if he wanted Jake to know he wasn't pushing him to feel any different, just commenting. "When you really hurt, it can make you want to lash out. I doubt Marco's mom and dad were in any shape to understand that you and your mom and dad hurt, too."

Jake's fingers bit into his thighs. He didn't like thinking about back then, or about Marco. But lately…he hadn't been able to help himself.

"But what about Grandma and Grandad? And… and my other aunts and uncles and cousins? Didn't they love us at all?" It was a cry from his heart, even though he knew that was a dumb thing even to say.

"Yeah." Ethan's voice was husky. He reached over and squeezed the back of Jake's neck. "They did. They were just torn, and they all thought Marco's parents had been hurt the most, so they took their side."

"But…" He had to swallow what felt like a big lump in his throat. "After Dad died…"

"Remember they were especially angry at your father."

"And me."

"Yeah, they were. They forgot how young you were." Ethan was quiet for a minute. They were between streetlights, and Jake couldn't make out his face. "Until your mother reminded them."

"That's why Uncle Tino cried." Jake couldn't even imagine that. Mostly what he remembered was Uncle Tino slugging Dad.

"It is."

"Now they feel bad, so I'm supposed to say it's okay they didn't even come to Dad's funeral?"

Ethan put the turn signal on. They were only a block from home.

"No, I wouldn't say that. It isn't okay. Maybe you should see them just so you have a chance to say exactly that. I'll bet there have been a million times you've wished you could."

Jake twisted his mouth. Sometimes he did imag-

ine what he'd say if they showed up on the doorstep
to beg his forgiveness.

"As I reminded your mom, you have a bunch of
cousins near your age. None of what happened was
their fault."

"Except Nick and Gianna," he mumbled.

"Maybe except them," Ethan agreed. "Although
all they knew was what their father had told them.
It sounds like maybe they're ashamed of themselves
now."

Jake shrugged, remembering Nick's awkward,
sort-of apology.

"It might be cool to have more cousins. Find out
more about your dad's side of the family. Hear stories from when he was a kid." Ethan pulled into the
driveway and put the gearshift into Park although
he left the engine running. "This really isn't something you have to decide now, though. They want
to make it all better right now, or maybe convince
themselves it's all better, but it's not their call. It's
yours. Maybe in a year you'll feel different. Three
years, ten years. Even as an adult, you could look
up some of those cousins. So don't stress yourself
too much about it, okay?"

Jake nodded. He felt better hearing that. Because,
well, sometimes his friends talked about stuff they
did with their grandparents—Evan's had taken him
to Mexico for a week, *without* his parents—and
Jake felt funny, knowing he had grandparents who
pretended he didn't exist. Plus, it had been weird,

seeing how much he and Nick looked alike. It might be almost like having a brother.

But he also didn't want to forgive any of them. Almost as bad as remembering what happened with the gun was this time afterward when Jake had heard a weird sound and gone to look into his parents' bedroom. Dad had been sitting on the bed, bent over with his elbows on his knees and his hands covering his face. Sobs shook his whole body. Tears had dripped from between his fingers. It scared Jake so bad, he ran back to his room and cried, too.

Thinking about it still scared Jake more than about anything because... He didn't know. Daddy was big and strong and he wasn't *supposed* to break down sobbing! Only he did, and then he killed himself, and Jake almost hated him because he left Mom and him, and didn't he *know* how much they needed him?

Usually he felt guilty and maybe a little bit scared all over again when he thought, *Ethan would never have done that.* But this time...this time he thought defiantly, *I hope Mom does marry Ethan so he can be my dad.*

"You okay?" Ethan asked, and Jake nodded.

"I guess I should go in. 'Cuz I didn't tell Mom, but I have a little bit of homework to do."

Ethan just laughed. "If you'd told her, she might not have let you go, and I had fun. But you'd better get on with it so she doesn't find out. So scoot."

Jake opened his door but turned back. "Are you really coming to dinner tomorrow night, too?"

"I'm planning to. Do you mind?"

Jake shook his head, suddenly feeling a little shy. "It's cool."

"Good." Ethan was smiling when Jake slid out, said good-night and slammed the door.

WEDNESDAY GOT OFF to a damn good start as far as Ethan was concerned. Asleep by four, he woke up at eleven feeling fine. So fine, he called Laura and asked if she'd like to take a lunch break. He even had time to gobble a bowl of cereal before he picked her up and they came back to his apartment for sex that seemed to get better every time, even though, how could it?

Laura giggled when he said something like that. He loved looking at her face at moments like this. Even though her mouth was puffy from him devouring it and she had some whisker burn on her jaw and, uh, he ought to point out the hickey he seemed to have given her—she might have been years younger than she often appeared. Her eyes were a clearer blue than usual, as if a cloud had passed, leaving only sunlight. He wondered how often in the past six years she'd looked as carefree as she did right now.

They even had time for him to make a sandwich for her, and for them to talk for a few minutes. He told her a little bit about his conversation with Jake, not giving away the parts he thought were confidences, but letting her know Jake had asked his opinion.

"No idea what he'll decide," he concluded, "but I told him there's no hurry, either. He can look Matt's family up tomorrow, next year, in ten years. I think that took some of the pressure off."

"And he doesn't need any more pressure right now." She made a face. "Are we talking about my son again, and when we're actually having time without him?"

Ethan grinned. "Couldn't help myself. Slap me next time."

She slid off the breakfast stool to kiss his jaw, all she could reach. "Or I can distract you some other way."

"You can, but not now, unless you want to take an extra long lunch break." Which sounded good to him, even though he ought to be heading to work himself. He did, after all, have other investigations in the works besides the swastika creep. Among other things, he had a court appearance on Monday, for which he needed to do some review.

She sighed. "No, I have an appointment at one thirty. In fact, we should get going."

That hour—okay, hour and a half—with her eased some of his worry that she'd latched on to him mainly for Jake's benefit.

Dinner was good, too. When he and Jake played one-on-one, he could tell Jake had been continuing to put in time out there. Over dinner, he was a likeable, friendly kid who didn't seem capable of the anger Ethan had seen him display.

It would be nice to think what he saw was reality, but given his job, he knew better. Even a kid Jake's age could hide a hell of a lot.

Yes, but was he? Ethan's instinct said no. He thought Jake was actually working through some stuff and coming out the other side.

Ethan's middle-of-the-night stakeout was mind-stultifying boring. The kid didn't even slip out of the house to hang out with a buddy, as he had the one night. A couple of cars passed, neither slowing. A light came on upstairs in a house two doors down and across the street, then went off a couple of minutes later. Someone who'd gotten up to take a piss or pop a couple of aspirin, Ethan diagnosed. The Gelfman house, however, stayed completely dark. No kid stole out his window to go a-wandering.

Driving home, Ethan called Sam first.

"Nothing was stirring, not even a mouse," Sam intoned.

David Pomeroy sounded tired and grumpy. "We fire guys aren't as quick to pull a weapon as you boys and girls who wear a different badge. I came real close tonight to blasting the biggest goddamn dog I've ever seen, though. Could've sworn it was a man, crouched to get through the hedge the Fromels have seen fit to grow around their front yard. Have I said how much I hate hedges?"

He had, but Ethan didn't remind him.

"I'd been getting sleepy, so I got out, found a decent spot to watch from in a dark corner of the yard, and then the hedge rustles. This dark shape comes through. I snap on my flashlight and call, 'Police, freeze or I'll shoot,' only it keeps coming and its eyes are glowing a maniacal green. The thing had to be, shit, I don't know, a Great Dane or wolfhound, except it looked more like a bear."

Ethan grinned despite his own exhaustion. "Sounds like a Newfoundland."

"And he was friendly! He licked me. I couldn't get rid of him! The whole time I'm hustling back to my vehicle, he's trotting along trying to lean on me. Pleased as punch someone else is up and about in the middle of the night. I'm thinking, crap, someone's going to wake up any minute. They'll call the cops. I get in, and the damn dog puts his front feet on the door and stares in the window at me, tongue lolling. What do you want to bet he scratched the paint?"

"Might have been a she. Love at first sight."

Pomeroy had something obscene to say about that and rang off.

Thursday night was much the same, minus the dog tale. Ethan could feel his confederates' enthusiasm slipping. Both had vowed to keep watch through the weekend, at least, before they revisited the plan.

LAURA STARED, AGHAST, when she opened the door to let Ethan in Friday evening. "Oh, no! What happened to you?"

"That bad, huh?" He gingerly touched his swollen, discolored cheekbone. "Took a punch." He'd jumped in during a melee at the station. Nothing to do with him, but one of the two officers trying to control a belligerent drunk had gone down, and they'd needed a hand. He told Laura about the incident.

"Punching a police officer is a dumb thing to do. Even if you're drunk, you should know better." She rose on tiptoe and gave his cheek a featherlight kiss. "A black eye, too."

His smile was slightly more crooked than usual. "How about some concealer?"

"I kind of doubt it would cut it for you." She led the way to the kitchen. "As it happens, I don't own any. What you see is what you get."

"And I like getting you a whole lot," he said huskily.

"Shush," she said, laughing. "Although Jake must not have heard the doorbell."

"How could he not?"

"Earbuds, what else?" Although she'd picked up a spoon, she didn't object when he drew her into his arms. "You're right," she murmured, just before his mouth found hers. "Let's not call him until dinner is on the table."

The interlude was all too brief, but nonetheless

satisfying. Jake was always too eager for Ethan's arrival to remain oblivious for long. He popped into the kitchen saying, "How come Ethan's not— You are here!" Then his mouth dropped open. "What *happened*?"

Ethan explained that a man hadn't taken well to being arrested. "He was off-the-charts drunk," he added.

"So now he's in trouble for attacking a police officer?" Jake asked, wide-eyed.

"Probably. It wasn't my arrest. I kind of hope they didn't put my name in the report," he said wryly. "Last thing I need is one more court appearance on my schedule. Once the idiot was behind bars, I went looking for an ice pack."

Ethan won her gratitude after that by successfully diverting Jake with graphic descriptions of several similar injuries he'd received on the basketball court—apparently, a well-applied elbow could do a lot of damage. Jake reminisced about the egg-sized lump that had popped out on his head when he fell off his bike a couple of years ago.

"This friend and me, we found a piece of plywood and set up a ramp." He was smart enough to give Laura a cautious glance. She hadn't been very happy about the ramp.

There it was, she thought ruefully, the boy versus girl thing. She didn't think of herself as timid, but she'd never had the slightest desire to launch herself into the air on a bike.

Ethan, though, was nodding as if he completely understood. She rolled her eyes, and he laughed at her.

"My friends and I were into skateboards. No skateboard park in those days. We laid a piece of plywood to cover some cement steps. The sidewalk sloped there, see. If you got up some speed and made the turn just right, you'd shoot up the ramp and catch some serious air." Noting her evil eye, he cleared his throat. "Not that I'm recommending it. I actually broke my arm that time. My mother was not happy."

Jake sneaked another look at *his* mother. "I bet."

"She pointed out that I could have broken my head instead."

"But didn't you wear a helmet?"

"Uh…"

"You *didn't*!" Jake sounded both shocked and intrigued.

Ethan sobered. "No, and I'm here to tell you to wear the thing. Having a cast on my arm for a month put a serious crimp in my athletic schedule. Took a while for my muscles to regain their strength, too. Getting a major concussion, that would be a lot worse."

"Assuming you didn't do permanent brain damage," Laura said tartly.

"Assuming," he agreed.

When it was time for him to go, she stepped out on the front porch with him and closed the door to give them another moment of near privacy. "Are you still doing the stakeout?"

He grunted. "I'm not excited about it tonight."

"You hurt."

"A headache." His big hand cradled her face. "I'll take some more ibuprofen. Won't kill me."

She winced. "Just…be careful."

"Chances are, nothing will happen."

"But you think it will, sooner or later."

"'Hope' is more accurate. Otherwise, we'll keep trailing two steps behind. I don't like this one, Laura. The guy is working up to killing someone. I want to stop him first."

She nodded. "I know. I understand."

"Good." His voice was soft, velvety. His kiss started that way and became urgent.

This was one of the rare times when Laura could wish she was childless. Not that Ethan would be able to stay anyway, she reminded herself. The chill she felt as he left wasn't from the night air. She wrapped her arms around herself for warmth, watching when he backed out of the driveway, then drove away. As a detective, his job was less dangerous than Matt's had been as a patrol officer. Ethan had survived years on patrol himself unscathed. But…she couldn't forget that he carried a gun for a reason.

ETHAN WOULDN'T CALL what he had a premonition. More common sense, or just the voice of experience. The long, long interval since the last fire worried him, given the fact that the crimes had been escalating. Usually impatience went with that. He had an itch between his shoulder blades he couldn't scratch.

Whatever his reasoning, he thought tonight was the night.

Not all the incidents had taken place on weekend nights, but four of the six had. The intervals had varied, from a couple of weeks to less than a week.

So…tonight, maybe tomorrow night.

He hadn't been in place long when he saw movement in the dark yard. He narrowed his eyes, not sure he hadn't imagined it. But…yep, the kid was dropping from the tree. Once again he had nothing in his hands. He might be going anywhere. Friday night, party time, although Ethan would've expected him to head out way earlier.

He heard the sound of an approaching car, although he didn't see headlights. Austin March reached the sidewalk and trotted away, ignoring Ethan's SUV parked at the curb across the street.

He waited a minute, and then opened the door. He'd disabled the dome light, and now left the door cracked open. He'd be returning in a hurry if Austin hopped into his buddy's car and a vehicle pursuit was necessary.

The friend was parked midblock, probably on purpose since the street lamps were close to the corners. But, lurking in a front yard landscaped with shrubs, Ethan saw enough.

Having looked up the address where Austin visited on his last nighttime jaunt, Ethan already knew the friend was eighteen-year-old Tyler Smith, who might or might not graduate from high school in June depending on whether he pulled his grades up enough. Like Austin, he'd been in trouble with the law, although in his case the offenses related to drugs.

Tyler wore his hair in a Mohawk, and he was opening the trunk of his car. The boys went into a huddle behind the trunk lid.

Ethan pulled out his phone and typed a text message to Pomeroy and Clayton.

Looks like a go. March and friend met up. Keep watch.

But the boys didn't close the trunk and get in the car. Instead, they appeared on the sidewalk carrying…shit. Gas cans. Austin had a bag slung over his shoulder, too. And they were skulking back toward Austin's house, which meant they'd pass within a few feet of Ethan.

He gave thought to stopping them *now*, but, while carrying gas cans, matches and red spray paint would be plenty suggestive, it wasn't as good as catching them in the act. So he quit breathing and averted his face as the two passed.

"You sure they're asleep?" one of the two whispered. Had to be Tyler.

If there was an answer, he didn't hear it.

He was unsurprised, but also stunned in a way he never quite got over, no matter what atrocities he saw. That the kid wanted to kill his stepfather, Ethan got. He had a suspicion Gelfman was abusive. But, unless part of young Austin's plan was a heroic rescue of his mother, he was planning to burn her alive, too.

That took a degree of anger combined with cold-bloodedness that he didn't want to understand. Not ever.

He stayed where he was long enough to type another text.

Gelfman house is target. Need backup.

Send.

FUNNY, HOW THINGS played out. And what a man thought about at a time like this, watching a teenage boy spray paint a swastika on the front of his own house. Probably not because he was anti-Semitic, but instead as cover for a murder.

He could hear Jake Vennetti's question.

*So...if you were, like, staking out a house and*

*they showed up and started, you know, painting the swastika and throwing rocks and maybe setting a fire, you wouldn't pull your gun?*

He already had. The Glock was heavy and reassuring in Ethan's hand. Damn, this was the biggest swastika yet, the sharp turns jagged. Austin didn't seem to mind the drips that Ethan had no doubt would look like blood in a better light. The can made a faint hissing sound that wouldn't be heard any farther away than Ethan stood, in the deeper shadows beside a huge lilac bush on the property line. It was no longer in bloom, but something nearby was, the fragrance light but intoxicating. Tonight it seemed wrong.

Ethan was able to hold off because Tyler, too, only stood by watching, the gas cans at his feet. Once the gas was first splashed onto the house walls, there'd be no choice but to step out of cover.

Where the hell were Pomeroy and Clayton? He didn't see any indication either of the boys was armed, but he couldn't be sure they weren't, either.

Yes, he'd explained to Jake, he would pull his weapon, because he could use it as a threat to achieve an outcome that didn't include violence.

Now, though, he felt a prickle down his spine. These weren't vandals; they were killers in the making. If he told them to freeze and put their hands up, would they really do it?

His gut said no.

*I'd be prepared to defend myself, but otherwise I wouldn't shoot anyone*, he had told Jake.

*Feeling cocky, were you?* he mocked himself.

The hissing stopped. Austin March threw the can aside and bent over, unscrewing the lid on one of the much larger red cans. His friend did the same to the other. The unmistakable smell of gasoline mixed with the innocent scent of flowers in bloom.

Both boys headed toward the corner of the house, each with a can in hand.

*Wouldn't want to spoil the artwork.*

Ethan followed.

Tyler was using some muscle to splash gas as high on the wall as he could get it. Austin was out of sight, likely on the other side of the house.

Ethan ran, circling around to the back. Instinct told him Austin was the bigger danger. When he reached the backyard, sure enough, the kid was flinging gasoline on the walls with abandon.

Ethan braced his feet and steadied the Glock. "Police! Put that can down and your hands in the air!"

Austin threw the can aside, flicked something— a lighter, goddammit—and fire leaped into the air. Then he tore around the house, yelling, "Run!"

He heard himself say, *No, I wouldn't shoot someone in the back to keep him from getting away.* And, yeah, something about how vandalism wasn't a death penalty crime, and neither was arson.

*Unless it's done to commit murder.*

He peered cautiously around the corner of the house to make sure they *were* running.

*Crack.* A bullet nicked the wood inches from where his head had been.

*Son of a bitch.* The kid had a gun. One of the kids had a gun.

He heard distant feet slapping on the sidewalk. So Tyler *was* running. Probably imagined if he got away, no one but Austin could identify him.

"Police!" Ethan yelled again. "Put down the gun. Don't be an idiot. You shoot a cop, and you're facing the death penalty."

Austin's reply was laced with obscenities. At last, a light came on upstairs. A muffled voice called something. And a vehicle he recognized was approaching fast, although without siren. It would pull to the curb not twenty feet from where the teenage gunman hid in the shrubbery. Damn. No time to call or text and warn Pomeroy off. One shot through the windshield...

Ethan threw himself on his belly around the corner. Austin March's gun barked. Splinters stung his cheek, but this time he could see the kid.

Coldly, just the way he did at the range, he pulled the trigger. Once. Twice.

The boy went down, and Ethan raced across the yard to him just as headlights swept over the yard and the car screeched to a halt at the curb.

A handgun lay inches from Austin's hand. Ethan kicked it away, holstered his Glock and crouched, praying he hadn't just killed a seventeen-year-old boy.

# CHAPTER FIFTEEN

WEEKENDS, LAURA ALWAYS aimed for something more inspiring for breakfast than cereal. She'd heard Jake stirring when she got out of the shower, so she felt safe in starting breakfast.

Scrambled eggs, she decided. Maybe waffles tomorrow morning. She turned on the small TV on the counter to the news and took out eggs, milk, margarine and ricotta, tuning out the all-too-familiar commercial for home owners' insurance that was playing.

While the pan heated, she started cracking eggs, thinking about the fact that Wednesday was Jake's last day of school. She'd signed him up for a baseball camp that started a week from Monday, but she hadn't yet made any other decisions. It was time she decided how much else she could afford. He was bound to get bored if he spent most of the summer hanging out with his younger cousins.

The news came back on. "A violent scene in a quiet Portland neighborhood last night," one of the commentators said, shaking his head gravely. "Police caught the swastika arsonists in the act last night, arresting one while gunning down the second. Jeff, you were at the home where the shooting took place. Tell us more."

Gunning down? Oh, dear God. *Please not Ethan.*

Laura quit so much as breathing, her gaze riveted to the TV. She'd just broken an egg, but hardly felt the cold yolk and white slithering over her fingers.

The reporter stood across the street from a scene much like the previous ones. A fire engine partially blocked the swastika lavishly painted on a two-story wood-frame house. Police cars were parked askew on the street.

"Don, this home reportedly belongs to a family named Gelfman. As you can see, the Gelfmans were targeted by the two young men who have come to be known as the swastika arsonists. The police have not yet released their names, but have said one is eighteen years old and the other seventeen. The eighteen-year-old is now under arrest. The seventeen-year-old is at the hospital in critical condition, currently undergoing surgery."

He talked about a police stakeout and how the officer watching the Gelfman home had confronted the boys.

"As viewers likely know, Detective Ethan Winter of the Portland Police Bureau unit dedicated to cases involving bias crimes has been the lead on this investigation. He was also the officer who staked out this home last night." The reporter turned to gesture grandly. This time the camera scanned another side of the house, charred and obviously wet. "One of the two young men was armed with more than spray paint, gasoline and a lighter. He shot at Detective Winter, who returned fire before backup could arrive." The TV now showed an aid car with lights flashing pulling away from the house. "We're told that this is not Detective Winter's first shooting as an officer of the law. Five years ago, he shot and killed a man during a convenience store holdup. His actions at the time were of course investigated…"

As the reporter kept talking, the camera turned on a huddle of police and fire officials. Enveloped by shock, Laura didn't hear the rest. She was aware only of Ethan, the tallest man present. He glanced toward the camera, his expression grim, the black eye and bruising giving him a disreputable look.

The news returned to the studio.

"We'll keep you updated as we learn more," the anchor said, just as Jake entered the kitchen. Laura all but lunged for the TV to turn it off. Heart drumming, all she could think was, *Thank heavens Jake didn't see that.*

Except…unless she sequestered him, he would later, wouldn't he? There'd be another report this evening. And what if the boy died? Even his friends might be talking about this. The one who'd been shot—the boy *Ethan* shot—might attend high school locally.

He'd killed someone before? Why hadn't he said?

Because he knew how she'd feel about it.

"I'm making scrambled eggs," she heard herself say. "Why don't you get some toast going?"

"Sure."

Halfway through the meal, Jake said, "I wish Ethan was coming over today. Can I call him?"

"No!"

He stared at her. "But…why not?"

*I can't protect him from everything.*

"Ethan was involved in something last night," she said carefully. "I'm sure he'll be tied up all day."

"How do you know? Did he already call? Or text or something?"

Laura took a deep breath and set down her fork. Her appetite was nonexistent anyway.

"He was on the news. You know about his investigation into whoever has been spray-painting the swastikas and starting fires?"

Her son's head bobbed.

She told him about the stakeout Ethan had been conducting, and how according to the news he'd caught two teenagers in the act last night.

"That's good, isn't it?"

A flash of memory hit Laura broadside: him asking Ethan the same thing, then saying, *That's why people want guns, isn't it?*

*Don't overreact.*

"It's good that he stopped them before anyone died in a fire they set," she said carefully. "But according to the news, he shot one of the two, a seventeen-year-old boy. Now *he* may die."

"He said police officers only shoot when they're being attacked or…or they have to—to save someone else. Remember?"

She did. But…a *boy*? Wouldn't there have been another way?

"Yes. But there's no point in our speculating about it. He won't be free to tell us about it—there's always some kind of investigation when a police officer fires his weapon."

"Did Dad ever?"

"Somebody shot at him during a traffic stop once and he returned fire. Even though he only shot out the tires, he was still placed on administrative leave while it was determined whether he was justified in firing his gun."

"Oh. You never said." Jake's forehead crinkled. "But if somebody was shooting at him…"

"He wasn't in any trouble. It's routine."

He looked down at his half-finished breakfast. "I hope Ethan comes over *soon*."

Laura didn't. She wanted not to hear from him until she knew more. Why he'd shot someone. Whether the boy survived. Why, when most police officers never shot to kill, he'd done so twice already in his career.

As she pretended to eat, all she could see was Marco and Matt, both dead from bullets to the head.

*I can't deal with this.*

She loved him.

She quite desperately did not want to see him until she'd had time to calm down, to think.

The doorbell rang.

HE COULD TELL Laura had heard, and wasn't taking it well. Ethan didn't even know why he'd come over. No, of course he did—he'd been fool enough to hope.

"Ethan." Even her voice was stiff. "I didn't expect you."

"You saw the news," he said resignedly.

She didn't step back to invite him in. "I thought you'd be stuck in interviews forever."

He glanced at his watch. "The shooting happened eight hours ago. I have been interviewed. Repeatedly. I'm on my way home to sack out. I wanted to talk to you before—" He shrugged. "Too late."

"Before what?" she asked, looking wary. Then her mouth formed a horrified O. "He died? Is that boy dead?"

He should be tired enough to be numb, but wasn't. Instead—damn. This felt a lot like he'd taken a bullet to the chest.

"No, Laura, he's not dead. I'm not either, but thanks for noticing."

"What?" Her shock showed. "I saw you on the news, so I knew—"

His temper exploded and he leaned in. From her

expression, he thought his teeth must be bared. "Yeah? What did you know, Laura? Tell me. In case I missed something."

"Why are you talking to me like this?"

Did she think he'd *buy* this bewildered act?

*"What did you know?"*

"That…you shot a seventeen-year-old boy." Her chin came up. "That you shot and killed someone else a few years ago. Why didn't you tell me, Ethan?"

"Because of course that defines who I am." He half laughed, shook his head and backed away. "Why would I, when you're so damn sure that pulling the trigger is never justified. You know what? I'm done," he said flatly, turned and walked away.

She called after him, but he didn't care. Didn't even slow down. He jumped in his Yukon and sped away from the curb, his hands gripping the steering wheel so hard it creaked. He was a block away from her house when he made himself pull over. He wasn't in any shape to drive.

Ethan closed his eyes, rested his head back and willed his muscles to relax.

*Breathe.*

He just needed to get back to his place.

Right. Because his apartment was so homey.

No, he realized, he'd go to the one place he knew he'd be received with open arms and no prejudgment.

Home.

HE THOUGHT ABOUT KNOCKING, but his mother looked so astonished every time he did that, he used his key to let himself in the house.

"Ethan?" he heard immediately. "Is that you?" His mother appeared from the kitchen, her eyes worried. "Oh, honey! I'm so sorry." She rushed to him and pulled him into a tight embrace.

This was what he'd needed from Laura. *What I'll never get from her*, he realized bleakly.

His father was close behind his mother. He put his arms around both of them. For maybe a minute, the three stood there, Ethan soaking up comfort and hoping he could hold on to it later, when he was on his own.

Then they broke apart, but his mom grabbed his hand and tugged him toward the kitchen. "We hoped you'd stop by. Thank God you're all right. Except for your face."

"Tough one," his father said. "And just a kid."

"Unfortunately, also a sociopath."

While his mother made him breakfast without even asking, he told his parents why he was sporting the black eye, then about the night's events. He caught himself lightly touching the tiny scabs on his already bruised cheek and temple where splinters had struck him. He was damn lucky one hadn't gotten his eye.

"We wanted to be home just in case, but I thought you'd go to Laura," his mother said as she set a plate of pancakes in front of him, her free hand squeezing his shoulder. He knew she needed to touch him to reassure herself. *You're here. You're all right.* He'd always be her little boy.

"I did," he said flatly and, looking up, met his father's eyes.

"What did she say?" Dad asked in a hard voice.

"Not so much what she said as what she didn't." He picked up his fork. "'Come in' was conspicuously missing."

"What?" Back at the stove, his mom spun to face him. "I don't believe it."

"Believe it," he told her wearily. "I told you. She hates guns, and for good reason. The fact that I carry one has always been an issue between us. I never told her I'd used it to kill before. My fault. Of course reporters had that little fact at their fingertips. And this kid…he's not that much older than Jake." He shrugged and began to eat.

"But…" His mother sounded bewildered.

"I shouldn't have started anything with her. Now I'm ending it. I'm only sorry I brought her to meet you. I let myself feel optimistic."

Her "Oh, Ethan" was drenched with sympathy. Dad just looked pissed.

His phone rang. Laura's number, he saw, and silenced it.

Now Mom looked troubled. "She's not Erin, you know."

He ignored her. "Once I turn in all the reports, I'm on leave." He looked pointedly at his father. "If you'd gotten the second knee taken care of, I'd ask if you could take a few days off and maybe wanted to head into the mountains with me. As it is…" He shrugged.

His father's eyes narrowed. "Your mother has been talking. The damn knee is fine!"

"Uh-huh."

"It is!"

His phone buzzed, letting him know the caller had left a message. Ethan kept eating.

Neither parent raised the subject of Laura Vennetti again, for which he was grateful. Right now, he didn't want to think about her. As wounded as he felt, deleting her message without listening seemed like a plan to him.

JAKE WAS HOVERING in the living room when Laura got home. Without ever quite looking at him, she felt him studying her face. In case he didn't already get it, she shook her head and walked past him.

This was the third time today she'd gone to Ethan's apartment. Third time was supposed to be the charm, right? The first time…well, maybe he hadn't gone straight home. Early afternoon, she tried again. She never left Jake alone in the evening, but she'd made an exception for one last try.

"He might not have been home," Jake said to her back, sounding tentative.

She knew better. This last time, she'd have sworn she *felt* him on the other side of the door, willing her to leave. He certainly hadn't returned her phone call.

Strike three and you're out was way more apropos than third time's a charm, it occurred to her.

"Mom? Aren't you going to talk to me?"

She drew on her last reserves to say, "Later. Right now...I need to be alone for a few minutes."

"But...why? You're scaring me," he said in a rush.

Laura slowed, stopped and finally turned. Jake's eyes widened in horror.

"Mom?"

Oh, no. She lifted a hand to her face to find it wet. She was crying and hadn't even known it. "I'm sorry," she whispered. "I—" *Have no idea what I was going to say.*

"He's not coming over again, is he?"

"Probably not. Oh." She swiped at her face. "Maybe for you." He'd promised, hadn't he? And he was a man who kept his promises.

"It's my fault," Jake cried.

"What?" Laura stared at him. "What are you talking about? This is all *my* fault. Mine. You...you heard me this morning. I was awful!" She hadn't known until she closed the door that Jake had heard every word.

Face twisted with distress, he shook his head. "But that's because you hate guns, and you do because of *me*. Because I ruined everything, and because I've been making more trouble now. Some-

times I think I should do like Dad did!" He raced
forward, his shoulder striking hers as he tried to
pass her in the hall.

Somehow she got a hold on him and wrapped
him tight in her arms. Her own tears, her own des-
olation were forgotten.

"No! Oh, no, Jake. Don't *ever* say that! Do you
hear me?" She shook him, still without letting go.

He was crying so hard he couldn't answer. Her
own face crumpled and she laid her cheek against
his, mingling their tears. Some instinct had her
rocking, as if he was still a baby she believed she
could keep safe forever more.

Now she knew better. *But...I can still try.*

"It was never your fault," she finally squeezed
out in a thick voice. "Never. Never." She kept saying the one word and he kept crying.

It seemed like an eternity until his shoulders
quit shaking and he only rested against her. Laura
smoothed a hand up and down his back. "I love you.
Don't ever say anything like that. I can't imagine—"
Her voice broke, and he looked up.

"I didn't mean it. I won't, Mom. That's not what
I wanted—" His turn to stop.

"Wanted?"

"I mean, with the gun. Like, when I sneaked out
so I could look at Ethan's."

She tried to smile, and hated to think what it
looked like with her eyes red and swollen and snot

probably running along with the tears. "You know what he'd say."

His mouth twisted. Not quite a smile, but he was trying, too. "That I wasn't just looking."

She hugged him, hard. "We need to sit down and talk. Um…after I blow my nose."

He grabbed the hem of his T-shirt, and she narrowed her eyes in automatic warning. His grin, however weak, heartened her. He'd been teasing.

They split up, Laura going to her bathroom to blow her nose and splash cold water onto her face. After patting it dry, she peered at herself in the mirror and made a horrible grimace. Oh, well—Jake didn't care what she looked like.

His eyes were still red, but otherwise he'd made a better recovery than she had. "Are you hungry?" Laura asked. "Never mind. Dumb question."

He always was. And…thinking and talking about dinner anchored her, made it possible to pretend he hadn't said what he had. No, no. This was just another evening.

"How about if I just stick a pizza in the oven?" Frozen pizza was one of her fallback meals when she was too tired to cook. Usually she at least managed a vegetable, but tonight that felt like too much effort.

After turning on the oven to preheat, she grabbed them each a cola and they sat down at the kitchen table. The time to quit pretending had come. The desperate need to convince him that the burden of guilt wasn't his to bear mingled with her own feeling of emotional vulnerability. With Ethan, she'd had the chance of a lifetime and thrown it away. But she couldn't—wouldn't—let Jake pay for her mistakes.

First and most important…"Will you tell me why you're so obsessed with handguns?"

He gave a one-shoulder shrug and scrunched up his face. "I…don't really know. I never thought about killing myself, though! Not once."

"Okay." Funnily enough, she believed him. Laura reached across the table and squeezed his hand. "I'd never forgive you if you did, you know."

This grin was a little stronger than the last. "Yeah." Then it blinked out. "Did… I mean, were you mad at Dad, too?"

It wasn't hard to cast her mind back. "Yes. Sometimes I still am."

"Because he killed himself."

"Yes. And because he left the other gun out in the first place." She took a breath. Always in the past, she'd soft-pedaled Matt's culpability, thinking she was protecting Jake. Now, she wondered if she hadn't left a vacuum he'd filled in his own way. "Do you remember how often I chewed him out when he tossed that damn gun on top of the refrigerator?"

He nodded, and then shook his head. "Kind of."

"Over and over. He'd put it in the safe, but I could see him rolling his eyes, too. He just wouldn't take me seriously."

"That's why he felt so bad."

"Because I'd asked and asked and he'd ignored me? I don't know," she said honestly. "He'd have felt as awful even if that had been the first time he'd been careless. With the consequences so terrible..."

Jake bowed his head. "Me getting it."

"Marco dying." She waited until he lifted his head and met her eyes again. "Because your father had a five-year-old son who was fascinated with his gun because Daddy carried one. Because that's what little boys do given half a chance. Because *he* did something incredibly stupid."

"Did you still want, you know, to be married to him?"

The question was remarkably perceptive for a boy his age. Her first reaction was, *No. No, I almost hated him for what he did.* But that wasn't the whole truth, either.

"I don't know," she admitted. "I...hadn't let myself think like that yet. We were all devastated. When his family turned their backs...I couldn't."

His gaze was unexpectedly searching. She hoped he didn't see deep enough to discover... What? But she knew: the rage and pain that had felt very much like hate.

Had Matt known? For the first time, she let herself fully face it, and still didn't know the answer. But she suddenly understood something she hadn't before, not completely. She'd thought a million times, *If only I'd been able to forgive him, maybe...*

But, dear Lord, what if it really had been *her* silent condemnation, the cold shoulder she'd turned to him in bed, the words of comfort she could never bring herself to speak to him, that in the end had led to the despair that drove him to kill himself?

*I've wanted to blame his parents. His brothers and sisters. Everyone but me.*

It was too late for forgiveness to mean anything to him, but it wasn't too late to forgive Matt's family, who hadn't felt anything she didn't, too. And to think she'd consoled herself that *she* hadn't deserted him when really she had in every meaningful sense except for continuing to live in the same house with him.

She realized she was sitting there with her mouth hanging open, whatever she'd meant to say unspoken. Jake stared at her, anxiety making him look simultaneously older than his age, and younger. Frightened again. And, dear God help her, so much like his father.

"Mom?"

"I'm sorry." Oh, crap, she was crying again. "I just…I wish…maybe that I could go back and have a do-over."

"Like…like have locked up Dad's gun?"

"Well…of course," she said, jolted. Yes, if she could do something over, that should be it. "I was actually thinking that I should have held your dad and told him I knew he didn't mean anybody ever to be hurt. That I still loved him."

"You didn't?" Jake's voice cracked.

Filled with sorrow, she shook her head.

"So...so you think it was your fault he killed himself," he said slowly.

Why she kept trying to smile when the timing was inappropriate, she had no idea. It was a woman's failing, a need to soften harsh truths. "I suppose I do."

They sat in silence for a moment, her remembering the blinding rage she'd felt when Matt's sister Emiliana had called and then when Mama Vennetti did the same. *Maybe*, she thought wretchedly, *I can't forgive them unless I can also forgive myself. And...I don't know if that will ever happen. If I deserve forgiveness.*

So it turned out she understood the concept of forgiveness after all. *Sorry, Mama.* It was only the execution that was lacking.

What was it Mama had said? That they'd made the mistake of letting Matteo think they didn't love him?

*I made that mistake, too.* And hers had been the greater sin. Mama had had to think about her other children, especially Rinaldo, grieving for his child. For her other grandson, the one dead because of Matt's carelessness. *But the two people I was supposed to love most in the world were Jake and Matt. And I failed Matt.*

"I did the same thing this morning," she heard herself say, stricken. "To Ethan. He needed me—"

*To love him, not to judge him.* Nothing she could say to Jake.

"Uh-uh. It was different," Jake startled her by saying. "Dad did something bad. But I'll bet Ethan didn't."

"Do anything wrong?"

"Yeah!" He stared at her almost defiantly. "You should have trusted him."

He might as well have whacked her a good one. "Yes," she said in a small voice. "I should have."

"He wouldn't shoot anyone who wasn't trying to kill him. Or maybe someone else."

"No. He wouldn't." Her certainty filled her with a glorious sense of peace that was almost immediately tainted by shame. Of course Jake was right. She knew Ethan better than that. His kindness, his patience, the *care* he took in everything he did. "I'll bet the minute he disarmed that boy, he went right to work trying to save his life."

"That's what I think, too." Jake lifted a hopeful gaze to hers. "So will you tell him you're sorry?"

She gave a tremulous smile. "I...already did. I left him a message earlier. If I get the chance, I'll say it again. But, well, you know that saying, too little, too late? I'm afraid that applies here."

He frowned. "You mean, he won't forgive you?"

"Or...he won't be able to feel the same about me. When you need someone and they let you down..." She shrugged, not letting him see how painfully those words resonated. *I really didn't learn my lesson.* "But I meant it when I said I was sure he'd be around to see you."

Jake nodded unhappily.

The oven timer chimed and she pushed herself to her feet to take out the pizza she had no appetite to eat.

After slicing it and carrying it and plates to the table, she looked at her son. "I'll tell you what this makes me realize."

"What?"

"It's time we let your grandmother and your aunt say they're sorry. It doesn't mean we have to accept their invitations and let them envelop us in family again—that part is entirely up to you—but refusing even to listen, that's wrong." Unchristian, she thought wryly. Oh, how she hated ever to admit Mama Vennetti was right.

Her son pondered what she'd said, and then finally nodded. "If you can do it, I can, too."

Now she smiled at him and meant it. "We're tough."

"Grandma Vennetti was an awful good cook," he reflected. "I bet *she* never made Dad eat anything like this when *he* was growing up." Then he took an enthusiastic bite of pizza.

Even as Laura laughed, her heart ached. Because Ethan should have been here.

ETHAN LAY IN bed staring at the ceiling. Light shifted across it whenever a car passed down below, despite

the closed blinds. He should be sleepy. It had been…
he had to count, but his exhausted mind balked.
Something like thirty hours since he'd last slept.
*Hell*, he thought, *at least I can sleep in tomorrow.*
The only thing on his schedule was Sunday dinner at his parents'. Maybe after that he should take
off—it was too early in the season for backpacking
in the mountains, but he could do something over
on the coast. But that made him think of Seaside,
and he winced.

Okay, go stay with his sister. Play uncle. The kid
would probably be glad to stay home from day care
a few days. They could do the aquarium, the Wood-
land Park Zoo, eat fish-and-chips at Spud's. Carla
probably had friends she'd happily introduce him
to. He could take a woman out. Maybe one would
even invite him home with her. Some mindless sex
might wipe out the memory of sex that…hadn't
been mindless.

He swore, grabbed the spare pillow and slapped
it down over his face.

No, he didn't want mindless sex.

*She's not Erin, you know.*

Of course he knew that. Erin had turned out to
be shallow. She hadn't liked his job because it in-
terfered with their social life. He groaned. No, even
Erin wasn't that shallow. She'd resented his job because she thought he too often chose it over her. She
was threatened by it. Maybe he'd even have felt the
same, if she had been often unavailable because she

was consumed by her work that she loved. Hell, they'd both been young.

No matter what, Laura's issues ran a whole lot deeper. He'd known that.

Dragging the pillow off his face again, he went back to staring at the shifting light on the ceiling.

*When I went by her place this morning, was I testing her?*

Did it matter? Whether he'd set her up consciously or not, she'd failed. Big red *F*. Circled.

Because she didn't immediately throw her arms around him the way his mother had?

Wasn't that enough? he asked himself.

Had he really given her a chance? What if he'd said, Can I come in, Laura? If he'd told her what happened. Why he pulled the trigger. About his frantic attempt to stem the bleeding despite the knowledge that this kid had intended to burn down his house with his mother and stepfather in it.

What had she really said that was so wrong? Memories swirled like a kaleidoscope. Her horror at the idea the boy might have died. *I saw you on the news, so I knew—* Him being an asshole. *What did you know, Laura?* Her shock. The way she'd clung to the door frame, as if her legs were giving out. He wondered if her fingernails had left gouges. The anguish in her voice as she called after him. *Why didn't you tell me, Ethan?*

*Why didn't I?*

Because he'd been afraid. Because he hadn't trusted her to see past her fears.

Which she hadn't.

Ethan swore and punched the pillow.

No, he hadn't given her a chance, because he was so damn sure she'd let him down when he did. Big tough cop, couldn't take a *real* risk.

He still wondered if he had the guts to take that risk, let himself get hurt and trust the woman he loved would learn to trust *him*.

The safe thing was to let it go. Let her go. Figure out how to keep his promise and spend some time with Jake without seeing Jake's mother.

Rigid, he lay staring at that damn ceiling until his eyes burned.

# CHAPTER SIXTEEN

WHEN THE DOORBELL rang the next morning right after breakfast, Jake catapulted out of his seat and raced for the front door. It had to be Ethan, it *had* to be.

He flung open the door, and he'd been right. "Ethan!"

His hero gave him a funny half smile. "Hey."

"Jake?" Mom called, sounding alarmed. "Is someone here?"

He ignored her. "You look awful." The black eye and bruises were changing color, to purples and reds and yellows.

Ethan grimaced. "I noticed. Uh…I came hoping we could go for a walk, or maybe take the basketball to the school."

All of Jake's excitement crashed. "You're not here to see Mom?"

"She left me a message last night asking me to talk to you," he said gently, his expression giving nothing away. "I want to make sure you know we'll stay friends no matter what."

"But…"

His gaze lifted, and Jake could tell it was Mom Ethan was looking at, but he said, "What do you say?"

"Um, sure. If it's okay with Mom."

She had stopped on the other side of the living room, almost in the hall. "Thank you for coming, Ethan," she said, superpolite, as if he was someone she didn't know very well. A father of one of Jake's friends, maybe. "Of course you can go, Jake." Then...then she turned and went into the kitchen.

Jake felt really bad. He didn't want to be friends, he wanted— *I want him to be my dad*, he admitted silently, now that it was too late. Mom wasn't even going to try.

He fetched his basketball, and they drove to the school. Kids were playing on both the hoops. Ethan said, "Can we just walk around the field?"

Jake nodded. He stared down at his feet as they started out, him rolling the ball between his hands. Ethan didn't say anything until they'd walked almost the whole length. Finally he let out a gust of breath.

"I never told you or your mom that I'd shot and killed someone before."

Jake stopped. "How come?"

"I suppose I knew what your mother would think about it." He ran a hand over his head, messing up his hair. "But it wasn't fair to you. I could have said I know what it feels like."

"Except it was different for you," Jake mumbled.

"I mean, you probably *had* to shoot the guy, instead of it being a big dumb, awful mistake."

"It's true that the shooting I was involved in wasn't a mistake," Ethan agreed, letting the *big* and *dumb* part go, "but knowing you caused someone else's death haunts you no matter what. It *should* haunt you. You should ask yourself whether you could have done something differently, what effect the decision you made is going to have on other people. It's tough for an adult, and has to be way worse for a kid."

Jake toed the grass.

"Friday night—" Ethan half turned away, yanked at his hair some more, then turned back. "I kept thinking about that conversation you and I had. Would I pull my weapon in that situation? Would they put up their hands?"

Jake couldn't help looking up at that. "They didn't, did they?"

"No. One of them took off. The other one had a gun of his own."

"Did he try to shoot you?"

"He did. I still wouldn't have shot him, except that I'd called for backup and a fellow officer was about to pull to the curb not very far from where that kid was hiding with a gun. There was no way to warn Lieutenant Pomeroy, and I couldn't take a chance the boy would shoot him through the windshield or when he got out. Lieutenant Pomeroy is a fire investigator, not a cop. He started his career as a firefighter. He carries a gun now, but he isn't as well trained in using it and his instincts aren't the same as a cop's, which puts him in even greater danger."

"Mom said you wouldn't have shot anyone if you didn't have to."

The expression on Ethan's face shocked Jake. He didn't even totally know what he was seeing, but he looked away because... It was like something he wasn't meant to see.

"She said that?" Ethan asked hoarsely.

Jake nodded. "She said the minute the guy went down you'd probably raced over and tried to save his life."

"I did." Still hoarse.

Jake sneaked a look. "Is he dead?"

"No, it looks like he'll live to stand trial. He's not eighteen, but I have no doubt he'll be tried as an adult."

"For setting fires?"

"And attempted murder. We have reason to think the vandalism and fires were just a screen so when he got to burning down his own house, no one would think he had anything to do with it."

"He was trying to kill his own *family*?" Jake's voice squeaked at the end.

Ethan put his big hand on Jake's shoulder and squeezed in that way he had. "Stepfather for sure, maybe his mother, too. We'll probably never know for sure. Right now, he's not talking. His friend has said some things, but my suspicion is he was being used and is starting to realize that."

"Wow."

"No shit." Ethan gave a half-assed grin. "Don't tell your mom I said that."

"I won't."

They turned left and paralleled the chain link fence across the back of the field where Jake and his friends played soccer and baseball for PE and at recess.

"Did you hear what I said to your mother yesterday morning?"

Jake nodded. "She kept going to try to talk to you and say she didn't mean whatever you thought she'd done."

"I know. I wasn't in the mood to listen."

"She hurt your feelings."

"Yeah." He let out a long breath again. "The thing is, Jake…I think she hates what I do for a living. At least the part that involves carrying and using weapons. I hope I never have to shoot anyone again, but I can't promise her I won't. Mine's a dangerous job."

"She cried," Jake said abruptly, hoping Mom wouldn't kill him for telling Ethan. "She never cries."

When he looked, he saw that Ethan had quit walking again. He'd bent his head, closed his eyes and was pinching the bridge of his nose. "Damn," he said softly.

"I thought it was my fault." Jake talked fast,

knowing he had to get this out. "Like always. Because if it weren't for me, she wouldn't be so freaked by guns. You know? And Marco wouldn't be dead, and Dad wouldn't be, and…" It occurred to him that Ethan and Mom never would have met then, which had him stumbling to a stop. "At least you two wouldn't have had the fight," he concluded.

"Jake, you know that's not true," Ethan said, frowning. "You've got to let go of thinking everything is on you."

"I said maybe I should do what Dad did," he said defiantly, seeing shock in Ethan's eyes. "Mom flipped out." He scrunched up his face. "I told her I didn't mean it. And I didn't. I don't! I think… I want to make everything different. You know? Like, if I can know what I'm doing with a gun like Dad's, then I wouldn't pull the trigger by accident and…I know I can't go back! Except I wish I could," he finished more softly.

Ethan studied him for a long time. "That makes sense," he said. "You need to feel competent with a gun in your hands. You know you can't change what happened, but at least you'd know it never will again."

It sounded kind of dumb, but… "I guess."

Ethan nodded. "Okay. I'll talk to your mom. See if she'll give us permission to start going to the range."

A couple of weeks ago, he'd have been really

excited, but now he only felt cautious and…he didn't know. "You mean that?"

Ethan gripped his shoulder again briefly. "I usually mean what I say."

"But you must lie to people when you're investigating them."

Ethan's grin lightened the mood. "Damn straight."

"You swore again."

"Maybe she'll wash my mouth out with soap. She ever do that to you?"

"No!" Jake stared at him. "Did your mom?"

He laughed. "No, but she threatened a few times."

"She's really nice," he said awkwardly. "Your mom, I mean. And your dad was cool, too."

"I'm lucky," Ethan agreed. They were approaching the paved area behind the school, and the basketball court was still occupied. "What do you say we head back to your house?"

"Yeah, sure."

Would he just leave? But they were almost to his SUV when Ethan looked at Jake. "I have a favor to ask of you. Once we get home, uh, could you give me a few minutes alone with your mom?"

*Yes!* But instead of pumping his fist like he wanted, Jake shrugged as if to say, no big deal, and said a simple, "Okay."

LEAVING JAKE PRACTICING LAYUPS, Ethan rang the doorbell. He could have had Jake let him in, but… man, she might not be willing to talk to him. Waiting, he was more nervous than if he was serving a warrant on someone he knew was more likely to open fire than negotiate.

The door opened and Laura appeared, surprise on her face when she saw him. "I didn't hear your car." She peered past him. "You can just come in if you need to use the bathroom, you know."

"I don't need the bathroom." He swallowed to try to relieve his throat. "I'm hoping you'll be willing to talk to me."

For all that she'd endured, until now he had never thought the word *fragile* in relation to her. He hated that he was to blame. But she nodded, turned and walked to the same chair she'd chosen the first time he stepped foot in her living room. Accepting her need for some space, he took a seat on the sofa. Same end. Déjà vu.

As he tried to find the right words, she beat him into speech.

"Let me say something first. Whatever you thought yesterday was wrong. Hearing about what happened upset me, but I never for a second thought you'd shot that boy because— I don't know. You wanted to hurt him. I know you did what you had to, and hated doing it. I know you better than to think anything else. And I wish—" Her lips pinched, but she never looked away from him. "I'd just told you I was sorry and asked how you were."

He felt lower than a slug, digesting nature's refuse. "You don't owe me an apology, Laura. I owe you one. I realized last night I came here *expecting* you to be judging me." He had to say this. "Almost… challenging you to turn me away."

She stayed straight and dignified, but he would never forget the expression in her eyes when she said, "You wanted an excuse to end things."

Ethan shook his head. "I think I've been afraid all along that you wouldn't be able to deal with what I do for a living."

Understanding replaced some of the pain he'd seen. "Because your wife couldn't."

He scrubbed a hand over his face. "I suppose. And because damn near every other cop I know has been divorced at least once."

"And I lived up to your expectation." She gave a sad excuse for a smile. "Or should I say down?"

"No. I jumped to conclusions."

"You did." There was the dignity again. She was not going to break and cry.

Or…maybe she didn't feel enough for him to justify tears? *Hell*, he thought. There he went again. He knew she did. Hard to miss real torment on someone's face.

He shook his head. "The one thing you asked of me was patience, Laura. We both knew you had a lot to deal with. So me, what do I think but that you shouldn't suffer a single doubt when you hear on the news that I shot someone. Not just someone, a teenage boy not much older than your son. The one who has suffered for years because of an incident with a handgun." He shook his head. "Oh, yeah, and I have no doubt it was reported that I'd shot and killed before, and never told you."

She nodded. "That…bothered me."

"I didn't tell you because I thought if I did you wouldn't give me a chance. I apologized to Jake for that, too. I could and should have told him. I felt some of the same things he did. My honesty could have helped him. Instead I left him standing alone, feeling like he's the only person in the world who's ever had to deal with seeing what he saw, with knowing he was responsible."

"Ethan—" Sympathy quick on her face, she leaned forward. "You had no obligation to us—"

"Sure I did. I fell for you the first time I set eyes on you. No," he corrected himself. "The second time. At the funeral…I guess I didn't really see you."

She nodded. Now—damn it, now her eyes shimmered with the tears she wouldn't shed when she thought he was rejecting her.

"And when I realized everybody else had abandoned the two of you, I made up my mind to be there for Jake if you'd let me. I owed it to both of you to say, I'm someone you can talk to, and here's why. He needed to know part of my…sense of commitment to him had to do with my own history. The department requires counseling for an officer who kills someone. I had my parents, too. All he had was you, and you were traumatized, too."

"Were you married when it happened?"

He shook his head. "Already divorced."

She swiped at her eyes, probably thinking he wouldn't notice. Ethan wanted real bad to move to the coffee table or even the sofa so he could touch her, but he didn't know if he'd be welcome. And, damn it— He gave a hunted look toward the front window. Every so often, he caught a fleeting glimpse of Jake when he moved far enough from the hoop. Ethan wished Laura had invited him into the kitchen in the first place, even though he knew why she hadn't. Kitchens were for people you trusted.

"I didn't even give you a chance yesterday, not on your doorstep and not when you came by my place later."

"Three times."

"Three?" he said, stupefied, only then remembering that Jake had suggested she'd tried to find him more than once.

She sniffed and nodded.

"I guess I was only there the last time."

"I could *feel* you. I imagined you glowering at the door, willing me to go away."

"Truthfully, I think I was sulking." He offered a crooked smile. "Feeling wronged. It wasn't until I'd gone to bed and couldn't sleep that it hit me maybe I was the one who'd done wrong."

"No!" she cried with sudden passion, her eyes the deepest blue he'd ever seen. "You had a right to expect me to…to give you some trust."

"But, see, I hadn't trusted you." He moved his shoulders. "Laura? Can I come over there and at least hold your hands?"

Her tears overflowed, but she was laughing, too.

He didn't circle the coffee table; he stepped over it. She rose to meet him, her arms going around his neck as his closed around her. He was shaking, he realized in shock, and she soothed him by stroking the nape of his neck even as she grabbed hold tight with her other arm. The feel of her fingers sliding into his hair had him shuddering.

He'd hardened the moment he felt her body against his, but the relief pouring through him felt even better.

His lips moved against her hair. "Will you give me another chance, Laura?"

She pulled back enough to look up at him with desperate eyes. "I never thought you'd give *me* another chance."

"I'm not that stupid. Just…a little slow sometimes."

She burrowed against him. "The past day has been horrible."

"Yeah. I needed you."

She stiffened. "And I let you down."

"Don't even think that. I should have said I missed you."

He heard a sniffle. "I suppose Jake is dying to come in and see what we're doing."

"Probably." He felt a trickle of amusement, but that's all. Mostly—damn. He wanted to get Laura alone so he could convince himself she was really his.

"Um." She withdrew slightly and tipped her head back. "Will you stay for lunch?"

More déjà vu. How many times had she asked him that? But this time…

"Actually," he said, "I was hoping you and Jake would come with me to Mom and Dad's again. Sunday dinner is kind of a big deal for us." He hesitated barely a moment. "It's always just family."

Her stunned expression told him she understood what he was saying. Since Erin, Laura was the only woman he'd taken to meet his parents, far less to Sunday dinner.

"If…if you—"

He laid a finger over her lips before she could say, *If you mean it.* "You know I do."

Tears welled in her eyes again. "Oh, Ethan."

He bent his head—and caught a flash of movement with his peripheral vision. "Jake's coming," he growled.

She moaned, then laughed, and finally rose on tiptoe to kiss him on the lips just as Jake burst into the house.

LAURA LIFTED HER head from Ethan's naked chest. "Your mom lectured me today."

After the midafternoon Sunday dinner spread at his parents, she'd managed to off-load her son on her sister for the night. Jake had packed and then hopped out of Ethan's SUV with nary a protest, which confirmed her belief that he was as gone on Ethan as she was, if in a different way. She and Ethan had come back to her house rather than his apartment after he mentioned how empty his refrigerator and cupboards were.

"And we might want a late-night snack," he'd said hopefully. "Breakfast, too."

Now, in response to the idea of his mother chewing her out, he jackknifed to reach a near-sitting position, disturbing her very comfortable sprawl half atop his big body. *"What?"*

Grateful for his outrage, she nonetheless pushed until he subsided. "It wasn't like that. She just… talked about her lifetime of being married to a man in law enforcement." *Warned me not to hurt her son again.* Warned nicely, which Laura had appreciated. "Shared some lessons learned."

"Lessons?" He was definitely wary.

"How she copes when she thinks your dad is involved in a dangerous operation."

"How does she?" Now Ethan sounded interested.

"Stays really, really busy. Takes her anxiety out in physical activity. That's why she became a gardener, you know. Digging big holes and slashing and burning are therapeutic."

"No, actually I didn't know."

Laura was quiet for a minute. "She talked a lot about trust, too."

He started to swear, but she shushed him.

"All kinds of trust. She said if you and I are to have a relationship, I need to put my trust not only in your judgment and your integrity, but in your competence. I have to believe you'll stay safe because you're good at what you do."

His broad chest rumbled with unhappiness. "Did you remind her you were already married to a cop?"

"I don't think she needed a reminder. I actually suspect that was part of the reason for the talk. Because she knows I lost faith in Matt's judgment." She mulled that over. "Not his integrity or necessarily his competence on the job. But his judgment..."

"Yeah." Ethan lifted his head high enough to kiss her again. "Don't know how you could help it."

"It was actually really sweet of your mother. She sounded...fierce. It must have been nice, growing up knowing your mom was always on your side."

"Didn't you?" he asked, in that tender way he had.

"I suppose." Laura didn't even know why she sounded doubtful. "Of course my mother loved me. But I was a good little girl, and I don't know what would have happened if I hadn't been. That's all."

He flashed a wicked grin that creased his darkly

stubbled cheek. "Are you suggesting I wasn't always a good little boy?"

Laura giggled. "Were you?"

"No." Now, *he* took a moment to reflect. "Maybe it was because of Dad's profession I always felt a pressure to be...I don't know, strong, brave."

"Manly," she teased.

"Yeah, well, that came naturally."

Laughter turned into a long kiss that could have led to more serious activity, except there were still things she wanted to know.

So she rose onto her elbow, needing to see his face. "You're not in trouble for the shooting, are you? You didn't say."

Now he shook his head. "Discharging a weapon means an investigation, that's all. And a brief vacation, whether you want it or not. I did what I had to do, Laura."

Was that a warning? She rubbed her cheek against the wiry but still surprisingly soft hair covering powerful muscles. "I really never doubted that. Just now, I was going to get mad if someone was seriously questioning you."

His chest vibrated with a laugh and she felt his relaxation. "Okay."

"The boy..." She studied him. "Are you not supposed to talk about stuff like this?"

"Did Matt?" he asked, eyes keen.

"Oh, when something funny happened." She shrugged a little. "Bad stuff, he'd take to his cop buddies. Sometimes that stung. I guess it's normal, though."

"Yeah, it is. We think no one outside the profession will understand. Maybe we're afraid of admitting we were scared shitless, or went off into the weeds beside the road to puke, or cried later. So we get together and crack macabre jokes, and we all know what's really underlying the laughter."

"You didn't talk to your wife, either?"

He had such beautiful eyes, the green predominating when he was serious like now. "I tried a few times. I upset her. I guess it was easier for both of us if I didn't."

Laura struggled for how to say this. Maybe she was making a big assumption from the few things he'd said, like *I fell for you* and *It's always just family*. But if they were to have a future, she needed it to be different than her marriage.

"I can keep things you tell me to myself, if that worries you."

"No." His hand slid up and down her back, somehow reassuring. "I know you would."

She never looked away. "If you're, well, serious about me at all—"

"You know I am," he interrupted.

Laura nodded. "Then I'd like it if you would talk to me. Tell me when you're hurt or scared or mad. Let me in. Matt left me feeling sort of sidelined. He went to his mother, his brothers, his cop buddies, but not me. And I can't help wondering if this isn't one of the reasons for the high divorce rate among cops. Maybe some women—or men—can't handle it. But maybe a lot of them could have, if they'd been given the chance."

Ethan searched her face as deeply as she searched his, and then his mouth curved, just the least little bit. He cupped her jaw and cheek in one of his large hands, his thumb skating over her lips. "Like my mother always has," he said huskily.

It was hard to think when he looked at her like that. "Does your dad talk to her?"

"Yeah." He cleared his throat. "Yeah, he does."

Laura nodded.

"I always wanted what my parents have."

"*I* want what your parents have." She knew her smile was tremulous but couldn't help it. "He looks at her sometimes as if…"

When she trailed off, Ethan finished. "As if they were newly married instead of nearing their fortieth anniversary. Yeah. I've noticed." He grinned, but his eyes were heavy-lidded. "In fact, they have a habit of embarrassing me regularly."

"That sounds like fun," she murmured.

"Jake doesn't know what he's getting into," he said huskily, and tugged her higher.

This kiss was unbelievably tender and so sensual her body melted like candle wax.

She felt his arousal, but to her astonishment, he eased out of the kiss, rubbed his cheek against hers and then tucked her into place on his shoulder again.

"The minute I realized that kid was set on burning his own house, I knew," he said, his voice hoarse.

Astonished, Laura realized he was going to do exactly what she'd asked from him. Talk to her.

He went on, "I kept getting flashbacks of me telling Jake how I might pull my gun just to scare these kids into giving up. And there I am thinking, it's not happening. I overheard the friend asking if he was sure his mother and stepfather were asleep."

He dealt with things like this every day. Laura thought of other investigations he'd mentioned in passing, his understanding and patience and lack of ego, and now it was her heart that melted.

"You really think he wanted to kill them?"

"I know so." He'd gone rigid. "He thought the house would go up and no one would ever suspect. Because we stopped it, we have him cold. Before he went outside to meet his buddy, he got the gas can from his own garage and poured gasoline up and down the stairs inside and splashed it all the way to the wall where he was lighting a fire outside when I confronted him."

Laura heard her jaw crack as her mouth opened in shock. "He'd set it up so the fire would leap to the stairs and trap them."

"That's what he did."

"Oh, dear God."

"That says it all."

"And you feel bad because you shot him?"

Ethan grunted. "See, here's the thing. I got some really bad undertones. Austin hated his stepfather with a cold ferocity. If he wasn't molested, he was sure as hell terrorized. I could see on the mother's face that she knew why and had taken her husband's side."

"Oh," Laura said softly.

"Doesn't excuse what he did. But..." He shook his head, stared at the ceiling and talked. Talked until he was hoarse. About the expression on the boy's face as Ethan worked frantically to stop the bleeding. About the other time he'd shot to kill, what it was like looking into someone's eyes when death arrived.

She hugged him and she stroked him and she thought he couldn't have given her a greater gift, odd though this one was. And she knew.

*I love this man.*

*He loves me.*

Too soon for the words, maybe. *But...I hardly need them*, she thought, dazed.

And eventually they did make love for the second time that night, emotion shimmering between them. His fingertips spoke as they traveled from one pleasure point to another. She conveyed everything in her heart with her lips. And their bodies, once joined, moved with a harmony that transcended any words.

*I mean what I say,* he'd told Jake today, and she'd seen awed acceptance on her son's face.

When Ethan made love like this, he meant that, too.

Afterward, holding him, the swell of love she felt was both painful and liberating. *Tomorrow*, she thought, *I'll call Mama. I can forgive even myself.*

"Hungry yet?" she murmured, and Ethan's body shook with laughter.

"Yeah. Damn it, I am."

As they reluctantly parted, she sighed. "I suppose we ought to put some clothes on."

"Oh, come on. The nosy old guy across the street has to be asleep by now."

"Don't bet on it," she said darkly, and Ethan laughed again, bent and found something he tossed to her. His shirt.

So that was what she wore when they raided the refrigerator. He'd put on his jeans, but his chest remained bare, as did her legs. The thought crossed her mind that in theory she was supposed to get up in…seven hours to go to work, but, hey, when was the last time she'd taken a personal day?

Between one bite and the next, Ethan looked at her. "I'm not going to want to go to bed tomorrow night without you."

"No."

He gave a small nod as if satisfied, seeing she'd

understood. They needed to build trust, but…maybe it wouldn't take all that long.

Oh, she hoped not.

# EPILOGUE

*DÉJÀ VU,* LAURA THOUGHT, standing on the sidewalk in front of Tino Vennetti's house. The only difference from the last time she'd been there was that Jake was with her and Ethan this time, too. Jake didn't actually seem any more eager than she was to move. Ethan played much the same role he had that day long ago. With a reassuring hand on each of their shoulders, he waited patiently for them to be ready for what awaited.

Jake and Tino's oldest, Nick, had been cautiously working their way toward something approaching friendship. He'd come over to Laura and Jake's house a couple of times to shoot baskets out front. Even though she'd known what to expect, the sight of a boy who looked so much like her own son had blown her away. She'd had the heart-clenching thought that Marco would have looked like them, too, had he lived.

Today, she and Jake had agreed to come to Sunday dinner at Tino's house. Palma and Bruno Vennetti—aka Mama and Papa—were to be there, as well, although they were spared a get-together with the entire family. Laura wasn't quite ready for that.

Truthfully, she didn't feel prepared for even this. Being nice to Mama and Papa…it boggled the mind, but she was grimly determined. Jake… well, she wasn't 100 percent sure what Jake felt about this meeting, except that he'd agreed to it.

Her one proviso had been the addition of Ethan to the guest list.

My *fiancé*, she'd said, loving the sound of the word. He'd asked her to marry him Labor Day weekend, on a trip to the Columbia Gorge to windsurf. In the know, Jake had made himself scarce when Ethan and she strolled to a cliff top above the broad, powerful Columbia River as the sun was setting. Taking her completely by surprise, he'd held her hand and actually gone down on one knee to pop the question.

The wedding was going to be simple, and soon. No later than the middle of October, they'd agreed. Ethan was already moving his stuff into her house and living with her and Jake.

The upcoming wedding—this was the middle of September already—was one of the reasons she'd accepted this invitation. Her relationship with the Vennetti family felt unresolved, and with the issue of whether she could forgive them tied up with her need to forgive herself, she'd decided it was time.

The curtain behind the front window twitched.

"Mom?" Jake sounded nervous verging on panic.

From somewhere, she found a smile. "Let's do it."

"Do we *have* to?"

Her smile became more natural. "Come on, what's the worst thing that can happen?"

"Uncle Tino can punch you. And then Ethan would punch *him*."

Ethan chuckled. "I think we're past the stage where punches are likely to be thrown. But your mom's right. The worst that can happen is a little blood, maybe a broken tooth, a black eye or two…" He shrugged, grinning when she gave him a look.

"The worst is, your grandmother will say something nasty to me, I'll say something even nastier back, and we'll stomp out," Laura said. "And if that happens, so what?"

Jake thought about it. "Yeah," he decided. "So what?"

They marched up the walkway as a family. Halfway to the house, Laura saw the front door open. It was Tino who stepped out to greet them, his arm slung over Nick's shoulder.

"Thank you for coming," he said. "Nick's been looking forward to this."

Nick rolled his eyes in typical, adolescent boy fashion. Laura hid a grin.

"Thanks for inviting us," she said, mounting the steps. "Tino, you haven't officially met Ethan Winter."

"Detective." Tino held out a hand; the two men shook.

Shame on her, she liked the way Ethan dominated any other man physically. In this case...the thought was disconcerting because Tino was an older version of Matt. But she let the brief pang of guilt go. She was learning to be easier on herself.

Tino swept them inside. Jake stuck close to his mom and Ethan as they entered the living room, where an older couple rose from their seats on the sofa.

Both stared at Jake with a stunned intensity. Jake's shoulder bumped hers as he edged closer yet. Laura wanted to say, *You could have watched him grow up*, but kept her mouth shut. She was oddly disturbed to see how much both had aged. More than they should have in the intervening six and a half years since she'd seen them, she thought. They'd become old. Maybe losing a son and a grandson did that to you.

"Palma." She nodded. "Bruno. This is my son, Jake, and my fiancé, Detective Ethan Winter."

Their gazes moved in unison to first her face, then Ethan's.

"Mr. and Mrs. Vennetti," he said in his easy way. "Make it Ethan, please."

Jake squared his shoulders. "You're my grand-parents."

"Yes," Mama said. "Your cousins call us Grand-mama and Grandpapa."

He nodded but made no commitment. Laura was proud of the poise he was showing. He'd grown up a lot these past four or five months, since Ethan had corralled him at the gun show. He was still in coun-seling, but about a month ago he'd told her with much the same composure that she could throw away his collection of gun magazines. Then he'd grinned wickedly.

"I mean, recycle them."

Now, Mama asked, "Will you sit with us? Tell us about yourself? What you like and don't like?"

He politely agreed, but chose a chair that left some space between him and these strangers who wanted to pretend they hadn't turned their backs on him, his father and his mother.

*That's not charitable*, Laura reminded herself. They'd been angry and grieving. Marco's father, also their son, had needed them to stand for his loss.

Trusting that her surprisingly grown-up son could handle the situation, Laura took the scal-loped potatoes she'd brought to the kitchen, glad when Ethan chose to stay with Jake. He'd be sure everything was okay before he left Jake on his own. Nick and Tino stayed behind, too, she noticed.

Tino's wife, Renata, and she had become more comfortable with each other when they made arrangements for the two boys to get together. Even with none of the rest of the extended family there, the kitchen was noisy and chaotic. Tino and Renata had six children, most of whom seemed to be chasing each other through the house.

"What a crowd," she exclaimed. "I don't know how you do it."

Renata laughed. "The big ones help with the little ones. Don't tell Mama," she lowered her voice, "but we think we're done with our family. Enough is enough."

Rebellion in the ranks. "Not a word," Laura said with a smile. "Is there anything I can do to help with dinner?"

Renata accepted her offer, and along with the two oldest of her daughters worked to get dinner on the table.

"They're beauties, Gianna and Maddalena," Laura told her in a quiet moment, when they'd been left alone in the kitchen.

"Yes, I think they get that from Tino's side. Me, I was never that pretty. But have you seen pictures of Mama when she was young?"

"I'd forgotten, but she was beautiful, wasn't she?"

"Your Ethan, he's a handsome man," Renata added in an undertone, just as one of her daughters burst back into the kitchen with a question.

Eventually the whole family gathered at the long mahogany table in the dining room. Mama, of course, took pride of place at one end, while

Tino, the man of the house, sat at the other. Laura saw the flicker of amusement in Ethan's eyes as he took in the arrangement before politely holding Laura's chair for her, then sitting beside her. He'd heard enough of her stories about Mama.

Mama grilled him as the serving dishes made the rounds, and then moved on to Laura, asking about her job and the wedding.

"And then there will be more grandchildren!" she declared.

The corner of Ethan's mouth turned upward. He was watching Jake, who now looked hideously embarrassed. Not like he didn't know Ethan and his mom shared a bed and probably did "stuff," but the idea of his mother swelling with pregnancy still horrified him.

A reaction he was going to have to get over, because she and Ethan had agreed to work on the getting pregnant thing as soon as the wedding was over. She didn't want to be changing diapers when she sent her oldest off to college.

"Maybe," she said now, realizing Mama's commanding stare was turned her way.

After that, dinner passed pleasantly enough. Laura began to think they might get away without her having any kind of confrontation with Mama.

But, no.

With dessert over, Laura stood automatically with Renata to start clearing the table, but Mama rose, too, and seized her arm. "Laura, you and I need to talk. Renata has her girls for this."

No surprise, the boys weren't expected to help in the kitchen any more than the girls would be asked to mow the lawn or rake the leaves that had fallen from the big maple in the back yard.

Ethan grimaced with sympathy, but stayed behind when Laura let herself be steered into the living room.

"Your Jacob, he seems to be a fine boy," Mama said, sitting and gesturing Laura to do the same.

*No thanks to you.* More words Laura choked back.

"Yes."

"And he likes Ethan?"

"Very much. Ethan has been good for him."

Mama inclined her head, crowned with dark braids streaked with gray. "A boy needs a father."

"He's…struggled without Matt."

"It was wrong of us, what we did." Brown eyes darkened with unmistakable pain met Laura's. And then she said something Laura had never expected. "I understand if you can't forgive us for what we did. I know what I said to you, but I have not forgiven myself. I'm grateful you let us see our grandson. Our Matteo's boy." Her face contorted.

In that moment, Laura found in her heart the ability to take the first step to letting go of her bitterness.

"I can." She had to swallow. "I was angry at Matt, too. So angry. Now I wish… I wish…" And suddenly tears blurred her vision.

"That Matteo knew you had let the anger go?" Mama's voice was unwontedly soft. "I believe he does. I believe God forgives, too."

Laura wiped her cheeks. "I hope you're right."

A silence while they studied each other felt almost comfortable. It was Mama who broke it.

"The two boys, they look like brothers."

"Yes." Laura managed a smile. "Jake takes after his father."

"He is a Vennetti."

"Yes." Laura had a sudden, vivid picture of Matt, hoisting his young son into the air, grinning with joy and pride, and she said again, "Yes. He's definitely a Vennetti."

Ethan came looking for her shortly thereafter, his expression questioning, and then relaxing as he seemed to find what he sought in her face.

"Time to go?" he murmured, and she nodded.

But when she called Jake, he appeared with Nick at his side.

"Can I stay here tonight?" he begged. "Aunt Renata says you can pick me up after work tomorrow. So I don't have to go to Aunt Jenn's."

Tino smiled and nodded.

What could she say? "Well…I suppose so. Do you need me to come back with your toothbrush and pajamas? Oh, and clean clothes for tomorrow?"

"I can throw what he's wearing in the washer," Renata offered, appearing beside her husband. "And we have extra toothbrushes."

So she and Ethan left alone.

"And so it begins," she mumbled just as he unlocked the Yukon with his remote.

He glanced at her. "What begins?"

"The Vennettis."

He laughed at her. "This time around, they'll have to compete with the Winters."

Reassured by the reminder that his parents had definitely claimed Jake as their grandchild, Laura smiled. "Just think, a night alone."

"Want to go dancing?" he teased, opening the passenger door for him.

Intentionally provocative, she brushed against his big body as she went to get in. "Nope. I just want to go home."

His eyes had darkened. "You and me both, sweetheart. I can't think of anything better."

"Me, either," she whispered, even though he'd slammed her door and wouldn't hear. Her heart felt light. It was the most astonishing feeling. And no, it wouldn't always be this easy, but thanks to Ethan she'd been able to let go of so much anger and pain. And because she had, so had Jake.

"I love you," she told him when he got in behind the wheel.

He gave her a quick, understanding look. "Ditto," he said, and started the engine.

\* \* \* \* \*

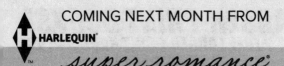

# LARGER-PRINT BOOKS!
## GET 2 FREE LARGER-PRINT NOVELS PLUS
## 2 FREE GIFTS!

**HARLEQUIN**

*super romance*

## More Story...More Romance

HSRLP13RR